T0157421

Rob Sissons

A Coach Load of Chaos

Order this book online at www.trafford.com
or email orders@trafford.com

Most Trafford titles are also available at major online book retailers.

© Copyright 2009 Rob Sissons.

Note for Librarians: A cataloguing record for this book is available from Library and Archives Canada at www.collectionscanada.ca/amicus/index-e.html

Printed in Victoria, BC, Canada.

ISBN: 978-1-4251-6209-2 (Soft)

We at Trafford believe that it is the responsibility of us all, as both individuals and corporations, to make choices that are environmentally and socially sound. You, in turn, are supporting this responsible conduct each time you purchase a Trafford book, or make use of our publishing services. To find out how you are helping, please visit www.trafford.com/responsiblepublishing.html

Our mission is to efficiently provide the world's finest, most comprehensive book publishing service, enabling every author to experience success. To find out how to publish your book, your way, and have it available worldwide, visit us online at www.trafford.com

Trafford rev. 8/12/2009

 www.trafford.com

North America & international
toll-free: 1 888 232 4444 (USA & Canada)
phone: 250 383 6864 ♦ fax: 812 355 4082 ♦ email: info@trafford.com

Chapter One

All I Have To Do Is Dream

WILLIAM Simpson was sitting by himself in a corner of Wallis Junior Common Room. The room was large enough to accommodate about twenty-five young boys and their paraphernalia: around the walls were arranged a number of desks, with bookshelves and small cupboards above each desk to hold each boy's belongings. The walls were painted in bright lemon yellow, obscured in places by posters of pop stars, and all the woodwork was a horrible turquoise gloss colour, which was flaking off in places to reveal a paler blue below. In the centre of the room a large table stood empty save for some half-eaten jam sandwiches on an enamel tray and a somewhat crumpled 'Daily Telegraph'. In one corner was an old upright piano; no-one ever played it, however, for its chief purpose in life was to act as support for Steve Vicks' stereo record-player, which habitually churned out Led Zeppelin or Deep Purple, but from which Suzi Quatro's *Devil Gate Drive* was booming today at full volume.

Leaning against the piano was a tall fair-haired youth, who was polishing the badges on his Junior Corps uniform while singing along with the music.

"You've nicked my bloody Duraglit!" shouted a fat swarthy boy as he snatched the round tin from the fair-haired one.

"It's mine, you stinking Dago!" John Bridger shouted as he ran out of the room, down the corridor and towards the changing-rooms, in pursuit of Mario Rottoli. Mario, however, was faster: he rushed back into the J.C.R. and threw the tin into the air. It landed fortuitously on William's desk.

"Give it to me, you four-eyed git!" yelled John.

"Let the little creep keep it, he needs to clean himself up! Look at all those blackheads!" This contribution came from third-former Jonathan Atkinson, a tousle-headed dark child whose angelic appearance belied his genuinely bad nature.

"Come on, stop ragging Little Willy!" This somewhat facetious remark was made by Mike Turner, so-called captain of the J.C.R. and the most senior boy in the room.

The conversation, if it could so be called, was interrupted by the entrance of a tall bespectacled boy in muddy sports gear who had evidently just come in from the games field.

"Crushed them this time! 32 - 3! They were pathetic! What's that there, Little Willy? Duraglit? Mustn't drink that, you know? Here, done old Bummer's French prep yet? Let me have a look if you have."

"Here, Hugh." William handed both the troublesome Duraglit and the requisite French Prep over to Hugh Bartlett-Nicholson. He didn't really dislike Hugh. Hugh was a frightful snob, he was far too good at sports and he fancied himself with the girls, but he didn't tease William too much. The main problem with Hugh was that he was just too popular - captain of the Junior Rugger team, cross-country run champion and a fine cricketer, he'd even been seen going around with a Lower Sixth girl, Miranda Morrison, and the rumour had spread around the school in record time. To William, Hugh represented everything he ever wanted to be. Small for his age, his face disfigured with acne and half-hidden by a pair of thick glasses, William was a most unprepossessing teenager who had never even spoken to one of the School's girls, except when Bailey-Filmer had entertained a girl in his study and he'd had to take a coffee in to them.

Near the door Mike Turner was remonstrating with Steve Vicks. Steve was an electronics wizard who had wired up a system of loudspeakers around the room. He had also once brought back to school a small portable television set, and had watched it clandestinely for some days, but in the end was found out and asked to take it home. Steve was pretty nasty. He treated William with the general contempt with which he viewed anyone whose taste in modern music differed from his own. Having had the batteries mysteriously disappear from his transistor radio, and found his LP's smeared with jam, William knew it was better not to meddle with Steve. Perhaps he was his worst enemy in the school; but, on second thoughts, no, that title went to Nick Patterson, a vicious IVth former from Eliot House who had once poured half a bottle of turpentine substitute over one of William's paintings during an Extra Art period.

A loud voice rang out through the room - "BOY!" The call came from the prefects' study. William knew instantly who it was - the Head of House, Ian Bailey-Filmer, asking someone to make him a cup of coffee. He looked around and saw that Atkinson had disappeared, leaving him as the most junior boy in the room and obliged to run the errand. As he got up to go to the tiny kitchen with its single gas burner a loud bell began to ring. Oh no! Not Prep time already, and that awful double French lesson with 'Bummer' Eveleigh coming up tomorrow …

The Prep bell rang on, becoming even louder and clearer as William fought with the bedclothes, stretched out a weary arm and stopped the alarm clock. Faintly the voice of Terry Wogan could be heard, wishing Mr and Mrs Bronson of Cleethorpes a happy Wedding Anniversary and hoping that they had enjoyed Suzi Quatro.

Half-past eight on a Friday morning. William always set both his alarm clock and his little portable clock-radio when he had to wake up early, and they had both accompanied him on journeys all over Europe for the past ten years. Today he was only going to London, and he didn't have to be in the office until eleven-thirty. But why did he have to dream about Chestfield? The events in the J.C.R. had happened half a lifetime ago: he hadn't set foot in the place for over fifteen years!

He got up, had a shower and dressed. He looked at himself in the bathroom mirror as he combed his hair. The adolescent from Wallis J.C.R., Chestfield School, had changed beyond recognition. The hair was longer, but just beginning to recede at the temples; the face was free of acne and had a healthy suntan. A neatly trimmed beard and moustache gave him quite a distinguished appearance: you might suspect him of being a research student writing a PHD at some provincial university. He was still small, but at five foot seven no longer small enough to be embarrassed about his height. The thick, dark-rimmed spectacles were a thing of the past: after several years of wearing contact lenses, which had only been a partial success, he had visited a London eye surgeon's and spent a fair proportion of one year's wages on corneal surgery. The operation had been a complete success, and he could now see perfectly. If you saw William Simpson walking in the street or standing by the bus-stop, you might not think he was especially good-looking, but on the other hand you could never call him ugly. As he walked to the station with his sports jacket and neat leather briefcase, he looked every inch a modern male, the archetypical young executive.

Indeed, William had come a long way since Wallis J.C.R. in the mid-seventies. Leaving Chestfield with three A-levels four years later, he had taken a degree in Modern Languages. Speaking French and Spanish fluently, he had seen an advertisement for a job as a Tour Manager with Orbit Tours in London and had applied. He had gone to the interview on a Friday, was given a brief test of his proficiency in his two foreign languages, handed a sheaf of papers and told to report to the West London Coach Station at 7 a.m. on Monday morning. He had been confronted with a group of forty-eight senior citizens bound for Spain and a coach-driver who spoke only German and had been expecting a trip to the Black Forest. But he had survived. That was over ten years ago and he was now into his eleventh season with Orbit. If you lasted as a travel courier for more than two seasons you must be good.

William had taken hundreds of happy holidaymakers the length and breadth of Europe. He had made Orbit's 'Scenic Delights of France' tour practically his own and always received excellent marks from his passengers on their little yellow pre-addressed comment forms which they sent back to the office after every tour. The elderly couples who made up the backbone of Orbit's clientele loved him; he was appreciated by the management, and it was generally accepted that he would eventually be found a position in Head Office. In fact, William was successful, and his University chums who had become schoolteachers or accountants were insanely jealous of what they saw as an idyllic lifestyle.

In one respect only could William's life still be described as a total failure: his relationships with women had hardly changed since the age of thirteen. No female had ever adopted the title of 'William Simpson's Girlfriend'. Not only was he still a virgin in his early thirties, but he had never even kissed a girl on the lips - or held a girl's hand for any length of time. except possibly at Primary School. William talked to women, of course, and he'd had several very-good-friends-who-happened-to-be-members-of-the-opposite-sex, but somehow things never got beyond that. A peck on the cheek of a Spanish teenager on a holiday beach many years ago, and the occasional slow dance in a Benidorm discotheque with a fat middle-aged client of Orbit's were the most erotic experiences of his life.

William had long since stopped worrying very much about not having a girlfriend. What had kept him awake all night at seventeen no longer troubled him much. If sometimes he saw a pretty girl in the street, or (most infrequently) had an attractive young female passenger on one of his coach tours, he was able to repress any natural feelings. It would never work out, he said to himself. Just like the sixth-form girls at Chestfield, women were a mystery to him. His adult knowledge of sex came mainly from a couple of films called *Le Professeur de Natation* and *Tendres Passions* which he'd seen a few years ago during an unexpectedly free afternoon in Paris. He wasn't really quite sure what he would do if he found himself naked in bed with a beautiful woman, but on the other hand he just couldn't ever imagine himself in that position.

Such thoughts were far from William's mind as he crossed the footbridge and walked along the up platform of North Malling station. The little wooden platform shelter was unkempt and dilapidated, patches of cream paint showing below the peeling white, and teeth missing from the rotting Victorian saw-tooth canopy. It was a hot day and bees were buzzing around the platform, investigating the straggling blooms which survived from some long-dead stationmaster's carefully-tended flowerbeds. The signal in the distance along the line to London changed to green, and almost silently the eight-coach electric train glided into the tiny station. William opened a door of the leading carriage and stepped into an empty standard-class compartment. Further down the train, an elderly couple with a large suitcase got out. There were never very large crowds at North Malling station.

William always used the hour-long journey to London to finish his paperwork. He opened his briefcase on his knees, took out a large blue plastic folder and a blue paper file, and began checking through pieces of paper. The blue folder was labelled 'F443 - Scenic Delights of France'. William didn't have much work to do - F443/06 had been a perfect tour. Everything had gone like clockwork.

He picked up a discarded newspaper from the seat opposite and glanced at the headlines. The main story was about Yasser Arafat returning to the West Bank. There seemed to be real hope of stability in the Middle East: William wondered whether Orbit would start operating holidays to Israel again. The second news item was of more immediate interest: there was yet another delay to the opening date of the Channel Tunnel. The Queen and President Mitterand had officially inaugurated the tunnel nearly two months ago, but it looked as if regular passengers would have to wait until the autumn. William was in two minds about the tunnel: as a confirmed Francophile he welcomed anything that would make it easier to travel to France, but as a true Man of Kent he was concerned about the effects the extra traffic and new road and rail links would have on his beloved county.

From Victoria Station William had to get the Tube to Embankment. The vast terminus was swarming with foreign tourists, wondering where to go, and he felt rather sorry for them that this dirty and decayed specimen of nineteenth-century engineering was their first impression of London. He showed two French students how to operate the ticket machines as he bought his own ticket and headed for the underground world of the Circle and District lines.

Orbit Tours and Travel, Ltd. had their headquarters in Charing Cross Road, opposite a second-hand bookshop and occupying most of a neat six-storey block sandwiched between a snack bar-cum-takeaway restaurant and a branch of the International Development Bank of Panama. The concrete and glass of Orbit House contrasted with the weathered Victorian brick of the buildings on either side. It had been built on a bomb site during the boom of the sixties that gave London so much undistinguished architecture. On the ground floor was a travel agency selling Orbit's holidays, and upstairs were the offices. A blue sign projecting from the first storey showed a coach superimposed on a globe with the words 'Orbit Tours' in flamboyant lettering. William swung open the glass door and stepped behind the counter - it was the one thing in his work which made him feel really important - and through a door marked 'Staff Only'. This was the secret inside of the travel industry which the holidaymaker never saw, which was perhaps just as well, for the dimly-lit narrow staircase with peeling paint on its walls and stacks of brochures piled up on the landings would hardly have inspired confidence in Orbit's operations. Whenever he walked up those stairs, often struggling with a heavy suitcase en route to the coach station, he always thought of the first time he'd ever come to Orbit, as a graduate just out of University, for his interview. Nothing had changed since then: it was a reassuring sense of security William felt as he ran up the concrete stairs two at a time, something he could never resist doing, and into the large, untidy office of Orbit Coach Operations.

"Hi, William! You've come in for debriefing? I'll be with you in a minute. Have a coffee." This was Margot, an attractive short-haired young woman of about thirty whose job went under the imposing title of Tour Operations Controller. It was her duty to brief the Tour Managers before they left on tour and debrief them when they returned, an important task as it was she who had the responsibility of issuing them with their foreign currency floats before the tours and collecting the remaining money afterwards. Most couriers were quite honest about returning the company's money, but Margot had to be sharp to spot exorbitant claims for phone calls and the like. A few years previously a new Tour Manager who had been taken on at short notice for a three-week tour of Europe had quite simply disappeared with his £2000 float and never been seen again, and Margot had to be quick-witted to make sure such a thing would never happen again.

William sat down in the plastic chair opposite Margot's desk and took the polystyrene cup she offered him. The stodgy brown liquid was typical machine coffee. Idly thinking back to his dream, he wondered what Bailey-Filmer would have thought of it. How many cups of coffee must he have made for that man, and what was Bailey-Filmer doing now? It was funny that the artificial divisions between people like schoolboys, prefects and masters just vanished once you were in the outside world. It was like leaving the Army and no longer having to worry about the distinctions between the ranks. If he were to meet Bailey-Filmer tomorrow, he would be able to speak with him on even terms, and certainly wouldn't be expected to make him a cup of coffee!

He finished the coffee with a grimace as he drained the last quarter-inch. Margot had told him quite sharply two years previously that he should not take any more sugar in his tea or coffee, and he never had since. Somehow, when Margot told you to do something, you obeyed her.

"Right. F443 dash 06?"

"Yes."

"Hotel vouchers?"

"Here." William handed her the pink slips, neatly stapled together. When you handed in work for Margot, it had to be tidy. When Mr Papadopoulos's secretary, Helena Rogers, was debriefing, which she did from time to time at the height of the season, you could hand in incompletely-filled forms and it didn't matter if you claimed an extra pound or two expenses without a receipt. But Margot Dalby was a perfectionist and nothing got past her eagle eyes.

"Is this a 1 or a 7?" she asked crossly, eyeing a photocopied accounts sheet.

"That's a 7. 7 francs 50 for a phone call to the Caves de la Côte D'Or."

"You should always cross your sevens," she said, bossily. "By the way, Mr Papadopoulos wants to see you".

Being summoned to see the boss wasn't something that happened that often at Orbit. Mr Papadopoulos always addressed all the tour managers together at the Annual Meeting at the start of every season, and from time to time would ask to see a courier personally if his work was giving cause for concern. But this summons to William was probably something very mundane; he probably wanted to ask William to bring back some of his favourite cigars or whisky from the ferry on his next trip.

Orbit Coach Operations office was open-plan, but Mr Papadopoulos had the luxury of a small private office separated by a glass-and-plywood partition from the rest of the floor. Outside the office sat his secretary, Helena Rogers, at a tiny cluttered desk dominated by a large word-processor. Helena was a small woman in her late twenties, who wore her blonde hair tied back and had half of her face hidden behind enormous thick-rimmed spectacles. She wore a drab blue skirt and a huge shapeless polo-neck sweater, in contrast to Margot's smart trouser suit. Helena raised her head from the keyboard towards William, but she didn't smile: William couldn't remember ever having seen her smile in the five or six years he had known her. She was a very ordinary dull London office girl, thought William; there must be hundreds of Helena Rogerses in London.

"I'll just see if he's busy," said Helena, tapping gently on the thin partition wall and opening the door a few inches. "Sorry, he's on the phone at the moment. Do you want to wait for him?"

"I'll wait. Margot's just doing my accounts." William perched himself on a corner of her desk. He noticed with surprise the colour of her skin. She had a really good sun-tan, quite unlike the pasty complexions of most London office-workers.

"Where did you get your tan from?" he asked.

"Crete. I got a special ticket from Mr Papadopoulos." Helena almost managed a smile. William noticed how white her teeth looked. Of course, he'd forgotten that all Orbit employees, like him, were entitled to free or reduced-rate holidays from the Company.

"Very nice".

"I wish I could come on one of your coach tours though," added Helena. "It must be wonderful going down the autoroute in one of those new Van Hools".

"We never have Van Hools on the 'Scenic Delights of France'. Usually just one of those boring old Mercedes 0303's".

"Don't be so mean about them!" Helena retorted. "They're probably still the finest touring coaches in Europe. They're outstandingly reliable as well. I could travel ANYWHERE on a Merc 303. They're better than a Plaxton-bodied Scania any day." Helena spoke with a passion which revealed the true love in her life. She spent much of her working day typing out letters about coach hire and she knew the chassis types and registration numbers of Orbit's hire fleet by heart. They were not just numbers but were individuals with their own personalities. She longed to be travelling on them instead of just writing correspondence about them, but, even so, the normally desk-bound Helena probably knew more about coaches than anyone else working at Orbit. She selected her complimentary Company holidays by choosing the ones with the most interesting coach to travel on, or the ones visiting places where unusual local buses were to be found. But in the height of summer, as now, Helena could never manage more than just a short break away, and could only look at the typewritten memoranda with the exotic registration numbers, and dream.

William found himself looking closely at Helena. As far as he could tell, she had no make-up or lipstick on, and her small ears were not pierced. No, there was nothing in the least glamorous or romantic about Helena Rogers.

"Okay, you can go in. Mr Papadopoulos is ready," she said, feeding a new sheet of 'Orbit' headed paper into her printer.

"Thanks." William pushed open the flimsy plywood door into the inner sanctum. The walls were decorated with large reproductions of travel posters. A huge Chapel Bridge from Lucerne covered one wall; another had a fine portrayal of some rugged Alpine scenery with a portly gentleman in the foreground blowing an Alpine horn.

A slightly older and somewhat more bloated version of the portly figure blowing the horn sat crouched behind a long and expensive-looking desk. On the desk was a blue and white model of a coach with the 'Orbit' fleetname and the globe emblem on its side, and next to it one of those irritating executive toys with the five steel balls on a piece of string. Mr Papadopoulos himself was on the telephone, remonstrating in fluent Spanish with a Costa Brava hotel manager about an overbooking. He motioned to William to sit down. Helena hadn't been quite right about him being ready, but then, he never was. A short, swarthy man, Marcus Popodopolous WAS Orbit Tours and Travel. When his wealthy father had been thrown out of Greece by the government for alleged illegal activities of some kind in the 1950s, the family had settled in Barcelona, and young Marcus had become rapidly fluent in French, Spanish and Catalan. In 1964 he launched his first holiday company, and forty-one British tourists in an elderly Bedford bus had travelled happily down to Calella for two weeks. It had rained every day, but that hadn't worried the holidaymakers or Orbit's bank balance. From that modest start, Orbit had become the fourth-biggest coach tour company in Britain with a turnover in millions. Still only in his fifties, Mr Papadopoulos was looked on as a father figure by most of the staff at Orbit, and in a company where use of Christian names was almost universal, very few people called him Marcus. Despite his apparent flair for languages, he had never really quite got to grips with the intricacies of the English tongue and its idioms. He had once wanted to have car stickers printed, with the words 'Orbit takes you for a Ride', until someone had fortunately persuaded him otherwise. He sometimes talked to William in Spanish, as he was able to express himself much better in that language than in English.

"Hallo, Peter!" started Mr Papadopoulos.

"William," corrected William.

"Quite, William. Well, William, how are you enjoying your season?"

"Oh, yes, thank you. You know I've always enjoyed 'Scenic Delights'…"

"Ah, the Delights scenic of France. Yes, this is where we have a problem. How do you enjoy the tour, Pete-er-William?"

"I like it very much."

"Do you think there are any ways in which it could be er-improved?"

"Well, yes. Perhaps we could do with an extra day in Beaune. Two nights there and we could have an included tour around the vineyards. There are always a lot of wine-lovers on that trip. And perhaps we could have a better choice of optional excursions. I mean, not everyone wants to go to the 'Grenouille Bondissante'."

"Why, you like not the 'Grenouille Bondissante'?"

"Well, you know, it's always the same. The clients pay a lot of money for a second-rate show with some long-forgotten artistes, they have a very indifferent three-course meal with cheap plonk and one complimentary glass of champagne. Why can't we go to somewhere really good like the Moulin Rouge or the Lido?"

"It would be too expensive. We always go to the 'Grenouille Bondissante'. If you not like the show, you not sell him. You have no commission."

'La Grenouille Bondissante' was one of the little-known night spots of Paris, where Orbit had special rates. The passengers paid William about three hundred francs from which he received a commission of 25%. For their money the clients got a three-course meal, usually rather overdone Boeuf Bourgignonne, and could go downstairs to the disco if they had any energy before the show started. This invariably consisted of a few acrobatic acts, an ageing French songstress who sang her own versions of Piaf, and a magician whose *pièce de résistance* was tearing up and burning a hundred-franc note and then retrieving it intact from inside a cigarette. For the English visitor who had never seen the show, perhaps it was exciting, but for William, who had seen it scores of times, it was the most boring way of spending an evening in Paris.

"I'm sorry, William, but you not sell Le Moulin Rouge. We have to remember Mireille. She is in charge of Paris bookings. You have to talk to her".

Of course, Mireille Darsac was Orbit's representative in Paris. She'd be bound to get a rake off from the Grenouille Bondissante. William could never change the Paris tours without her permission, which was unlikely to be forthcoming.

"I understand" said William.

"Well, William, what I was going to say. Tour F443 is not so well booked this season. On your next departure you have only fourteen passengers."

This was bad. William had sometimes taken out small groups before, but never as small as this. Small groups meant fewer excursions, fewer tips and therefore less money. When your basic salary was quite low you worried about such things. The coach drivers didn't like small parties much either, for the same reasons.

"Why is it such a small group? Are bookings down on last year?"

"Yes, they are down 'un poquito'. But that's not all. We had a party of ten South Africans booked for your next tour. And they've just cancelled."

"I see," said William, surprised that his boss was volunteering this information.

"So I have ten places booked which are not taken. Here is where I like to help you, I think?"

What was the man talking about, wondered William.

"You have been with us a long time. About eight years, it is not, Peter?"

"Ten years," corrected William.

"You have friends or family who want holiday. The ten places are for you. If you can find people to go they get free holiday. The South Africans, they pay us cancellation fees. The hotels, they not refund cancellation at short notice. Surely you have somebody who wants to come?"

This was quite an offer. But how did Mr Papadopoulos seriously think that he, William, could possibly find ten people to go on a week's holiday to France at a week's notice? His parents certainly wouldn't want to, and he had no relations living nearby whom it would be worth asking. His old friends from

15

University were nearly all married now, having children and paying off mortgages and definitely wouldn't be able to cast aside their cares and worries and come over to France just like that. But a glimmer of an idea was forming in William's mind. Once he was in that coach with that microphone HE was boss. How about it if he had Bailey-Filmer or Rottoli on one of his tours? He could give them the worst rooms, put things in their food, and really make life unpleasant for them. Of course, it was only a pipe-dream... but it was a very tempting one!

"I'll have a go, Mr Papadopoulos. But are you sure it really won't cost any money?"

"I explain. All cancellation fees paid by South African party. Your friends they cost company no money. Also twenty-four people on coach look better than fourteen, maybe you sell more excursions. You are a very good Tour Manager. I like to say thank-you."

"Can I have some brochures then, please? And use the photocopier?"

"Of course." Mr Papadopoulos took a stack of brochures down from a cupboard. "Take anything you need."

William took the brochures and left Mr Papadopoulos's office. The plan in his head was beginning to form into something concrete. He was starting to imagine sending the brochures to a selection of his old enemies from Chestfield, and telling them they had won a free holiday. They'd be crazy not to go. Human nature being what it is, no-one can resist the thought of getting something for nothing.

Outside the partition door Helena was eating a Mars Bar. "Have you got any 'Orbit' headed A4 paper?" he asked her.

"How many sheets?" Helena was biting all the chocolate off the outside of her Mars Bar, leaving the nougat and caramel inside till last. It was not a pretty sight.

"Oh, about a dozen."

Helena gave him at least twenty sheets. The top sheet had her sticky finger-marks from the Mars Bar on it. William headed over to an empty desk in a corner of the office by a window which looked down on the busy London traffic. It was very hot and the window had been jammed open with an out-of-date Italian phone directory. Orbit House did not run to air-conditioning. Jarring traffic noises filtered through into the office.

William put a blank sheet of A4 into the electric typewriter, normally used by Ms. Davina Prestcott (Special Parties), who was away attending a Travel

Trade conference in Vienna. William was fortunately quite a proficient self-taught typist. He began the letter "Dear ..., Congratulations! Your name has been selected by our computer to give you a unique opportunity to join our special Scenic France tour which has been tailor-made to suit your particular requirements..." William knew just how holiday brochures were worded. When he had written his standard letter, he went over to the photocopying machine and made ten copies of it on the headed paper. He also made ten copies of the page in the 'Orbit' brochure which featured the 'Scenic Delights of France' tour. He was pleased that the headed paper bore the signature of Mr Papadopoulos: it wouldn't do to send them out signed 'William Simpson'!

By now, several other couriers had come in for briefing and debriefing, and clerks from the Accounts department were busy sticking receipts in little brown envelopes. He noticed Helena Rogers getting up from her desk, walking around to several people in turn and showing them a small piece of paper. It couldn't be anything important - it was too small to be a memorandum.

Next William returned to Margot. His duplicated expenses sheet had come back from Accounts and he paid her back the remaining French francs. He noticed some nice A4 size envelopes with the 'Orbit' logo on them on top of her desk.

"Oh, haven't you seen these? They're the new ones. Would you like a few?" she asked.

"Yes please. They'll certainly brighten up my correspondence," replied William, putting at least two dozen into his briefcase. From the half-dozen fair-sized cardboard boxes of the things he could see under Margot's desk, he knew they wouldn't be missed.

William left the office for a meat pie and Coke in the small café next door. When he returned he continued with his tour preparation. He went to the filing cabinet where all the information on hotels and resorts in France was stored, and pulled out the file on Tour F443. Inside were brochures, postcards and price-lists from hotels and restaurants, most of which he himself had brought back on previous tours. He selected one or two items that he thought might help persuade his prospective customers to take the tour. These he photocopied and stapled to the letters and brochure extracts he'd already prepared, so as to form a mini-brochure on Tour F443. It looked a very professional piece of work, he thought to himself.

Another idea came to his mind. If he was going to put this crazy scheme into operation, he would need some help. He reached for the phone and dialled 0 for an outside line. Soon he was speaking to Monsieur Mercier, the head of the English department in the lycée where he had spent a year as part of his University course. The school was not far from Calais and William always passed near it on his coach trips. Did M Mercier remember the school play they'd done in which he and M. Renaud had dressed as gendarmes? Yes, he did, and they even still had the uniforms. Perhaps they could do him a little favour? He'd ring them back. He knew that Jacques Mercier would do almost anything for duty-free Gold Block tobacco.

He also phoned the Bar de l'Hôtel de Ville in Neuville s/Charente and spoke to Valérie. Yes, she still liked Morrissey. No, his latest CD wasn't out in France yet. Yes, she'd be prepared to do a small favour for him if he brought her a copy of it. He sent his regards to her father and told her he'd be seeing her in just over a week.

"You joining the firm or something?" William turned around and saw that the question was being addressed by Danny Bourget, one of Orbit's longest-serving Tour Managers and a great favourite with the customers. His brash, self-confident style was quite different from William's quiet efficiency, and he was most successful on the runs to the Munich Beer Festival or the cheap 'Sun, booze and sex' tours to the Spanish Costas. Danny knew every trick in the book. He got commission from practically every restaurant and every coffee-stop where his coach halted, he had an amazing ability to sell excursions to every passenger on the coach, and on one of his regular tours he even sold 'guided tours to the Palace of Versailles' for 100 francs a head. This was supposed to cover the mileage and the driver's time, but in any case the routing required a halt at Versailles, and it was no more difficult to park the coach at the palace than anywhere else in the town. Danny paid 30 francs a head for the admission charge and tipped the guide another fifty for the whole group, pocketing the remainder. It was rumoured that in one season he had earned £20,000 above his salary. But William could understand why Danny was anxious to make so much money. He was balding, fat and well into his fifties. The strain of the years of travelling, the duty-free cigarettes and the motorway lunches were beginning to show. Youth was one of the most important qualities of the 'Orbit' Tour Manager. Danny must be approaching his last season, even if news of his latest fiddles didn't find its way some day to Mr Papadopoulos.

"Hi there! What have you been doing with yourself lately?"

"Weekends in Paris, old man. It's a diddle! Fifty for the 'Grenouille', then lunch at the 'Elite' self-service, and then Charly's wine and perfume shop on the way back. I made over five hundred quid on the last trip. How are you doing?"

"Quite nicely, thanks," William admitted. "Seventeen for the 'Grenouille' and a bit of commission at the perfume shop."

"Seventeen only! You don't know how to do it! You've got to make the punters feel they'll be missing something really good if they don't go to the 'Grenouille'. Of course, you and I know it's really crap, but we needn't tell them that! And, another thing, don't stop at hypermarkets for shopping. You'll get no commission at the hypermarkets. And by the time you get to Charly's, all your punters have already bought so much they can't take any more. And don't waste time doing all that paper work; the fools here won't know the difference, they never do. Well, best of luck old man, I'm off on a mid-week special! Group of Canadian businessmen for two nights in Paris. Wow!"

"See you around." For William, Danny represented the unacceptable side of being a Tour Manager. He wondered how he'd been able to get away with it for so long.

It was past five-thirty. William was amazed at how quickly the time had gone by. He did a last few photocopies and gathered up all the documents in his briefcase. Saying goodbye to Margot, who reminded him that he'd be coming in on Saturday for briefing, he hastened down the concrete stairs towards the travel sales office. A figure was standing ahead of him by the outside door.

"Oh, you're leaving work the same time as I am," said William, in an effort to make conversation with Helena Rogers.

"Yes. Oh I do hate being stuck up in there in this weather," said Helena. The July evening was still warm and fine.

"Do you fancy a cup of tea?" asked William. It was a simple friendly request: he had often been with Margot to the café opposite.

"Ooh-yes, let's!" Helena strode into the road purposefully and William followed her. A taxi screeched to a halt. It was amazing the way Londoners coped with the traffic: he would have waited half-an-hour before crossing the road. They entered the café and sat at a formica-topped table. A waitress served them a pot of tea.

"Are you doing anything tomorrow?" Helena asked suddenly.

"No, er - I don't think so." William had forgotten that tomorrow was Saturday and that he had a whole week off before his next tour. He'd have to go to Chestfield one day, to put Phase 2 of his plan into operation, but there was no reason why he had to do it tomorrow.

"You see," Helena was getting two small pieces of paper out of her handbag, "I've got these two tickets for the Weald Bus Rally, and I can't find anyone else to come along. Would you like to come?"

William thought for a moment. He saw too much of buses in his work to want to give them a second thought on his days off, but on the other hand he really wasn't doing anything tomorrow. A day out would even take his mind off Chestfield and his plans for revenge.

"Yes. I'll come. Where do I have to go?"

"Headcorn Station car park at ten o'clock. Look, it says so on the ticket." She sounded as if she was briefing him for a tour. Helena got out a bag of crisps and tore it open. "I'm famished," she said.

"Well, alright, I'll see you there," said William, accepting a few of the proffered crisps.

"It should be very good. I'll be coming down from London in an RT".

"Well, I should find you." William wasn't quite sure what an RT was, but he knew where Headcorn station was and he thought he would be able to find her easily enough.

They chatted about work for a while. Two couriers about to leave on an evening departure joined them. William glanced at his watch and decided it was about time to go for his train. He said goodbye and received an uncharacteristic toothy grin from Helena. He'd taken more notice of her today than in all the half-dozen or so years since she had started at the office. He wondered if she shared a flat with someone. Did she have a boyfriend? It was amazing how little he really knew about her. Even in the office she was generally referred to as 'H.R.', which was her economical way of signing her memos and telex messages. Everyone knew who H.R. was.

He reached the end of Charing Cross Road and crossed Trafalgar Square. It was such a pleasant evening he would walk all the way to Victoria Station. The ducks and geese in St James's Park were happily munching the discarded packed lunches of foreign students who had eaten at McDonalds, and somewhere in the distance a band was playing. He was reminded of those long summer days in the school holidays when he had gone up to London with his parents on the train - and what a treat it had been then! London seemed altogether dustier, noisier and more crowded these days. Soon he was in Victoria Street, walking in the shadow of the giant concrete and steel blocks which had grown since his boyhood.

Meanwhile, in a small side-street off the east side of Tottenham Court Road, Helena Rogers unlocked the heavy door of a large red brick Victorian terraced house with a Yale key. It was one of the last residential streets left in Bloomsbury, and consisted of formerly elegant houses now split up into student bedsits and flats. She ascended the wide staircase to her own flat on the third floor and opened the door. She kicked off her shoes and removed her glasses, then untied her hair in a defiant gesture and flung the ribbon on the floor. She hunted for a record in her rack of LP's and put it on the stereo. Then she collapsed onto the bed and went into a kind of trance, her face buried in the pillow. It was a routine she'd been through many times. When the side finished playing she got up, turned the record over, carefully picked up the discarded ribbon, then wandered through to the tiny kitchenette and started devouring a packet of digestive biscuits while preparing her instant noodle supper. From the bedroom came the sound of the Bay City Rollers singing *Give A Little Love*.

Chapter Two

Helena

IT was one of those glorious Saturdays in July when the Kent countryside was at its prettiest. The hop gardens were full and green and the roses were blooming in the carefully-tended gardens of fifteenth-century listed cottages. Motor mowers roared across neat lawns and around pools with ornamental statues, and the sound of 'Breakaway' on Radio 4 wafted gently through the air from thousands of middle-class kitchen windows. In the neat brick semis the normally nine-to-five men were just rising. William closed the blue door with its imitation Georgian knocker behind him and strode to the drive. He unlocked his seventeen-year old Mini and put the key in the ignition, hoping and praying that the car would start. It purred into life. He manoeuvred carefully around his father's Vauxhall Cavalier and headed out into a country lane which led to the A274. It seemed that the roads of Kent were suddenly full of elderly cars: Hillman Hunters, Morris Travellers and Austin 1100s all heading for the seaside with their usual weekend-only drivers at the wheel.

The traffic was moving slowly as he entered Headcorn, owing to some road-works controlled by traffic lights. William wondered why it was that the highway authorities always waited until the busiest time of the year before doing any road works. He passed the old Parish Church with its ancient yews and turned left into the wide and picturesque High Street. A small red sign with a double-arrow symbol indicated where he had to turn for the station. The car park was full of activity: single and double-decker buses of all ages and colours were parked in a row along one side, and enthusiasts were milling about, taking photographs and noting down particulars in little books. William had seen nothing like it since he had once taken a party of train-spotters for a trip on a steam railway in Austria.

"Here!"

From the platform of a red London bus which was turning to park just ahead of him, he saw a teenage girl waving wildly. Then she jumped off the platform and came running up to the door of the Mini.

"Lucky I saw you. Come on, open up! I'll show you where you can park."

"Helena!" He reached across and opened the passenger door. Could it really be Helena? The girl had long fair hair which was loose over her shoulders. She wasn't wearing glasses. Her dress consisted of a pair of black corduroy trousers, trainers and a white T-shirt with 'RT Preservation Group' emblazoned on it in red under the silhouette of a double-deck bus. She looked even smaller than she did back at the office, and she definitely didn't look a day older than fifteen.

"Round here," she said, directing him to a part of the car park which had temporarily been designated 'Members Only.' "We'll be quite okay here," she observed. William locked the car and they strolled towards the buses.

"What's this? It looks like quite an ordinary London bus to me," asked William.

"Oh, you fool! That's an RT. That's the one I came down on. The preservation society runs it. It's one of the entries for the competition."

"Which competition?"

"The Best Preserved Vehicle Award."

"Claude ought to go in for that in his Mercedes 0303. He'd probably win!"

"Don't be silly! Would you like to have a look inside?"

"Why not?" William found himself following Helena up the stairs into the upper deck of the London bus. It was immaculately clean. The advertisements above the windows were all reproductions of old ones with prices in shillings and pence. The restoration work had certainly been done well.

"It's beautiful, isn't it?" asked Helena, and William was suddenly aware of her eyes. He'd always assumed her to have blue eyes, but these were deep brown eyes, very large and round.

"It's certainly impressive," said William, whose idea of beauty was more the soaring Gothic vaults of Chartres Cathedral. "But what's so special about an RT anyway?"

"Oh, don't you see, they're only the most famous buses ever used in London. They introduced them in 1939, and the last ones ran in service in 1979. It's the only class of bus that's been in service for forty years."

"Except Orbit coaches," William was tempted to add, but didn't. "And do we actually get to go for a ride on it?"

"Yes, of course. We're going to Tenterden. We should be leaving in a few minutes, but I think we've got time to look at the other buses first."

She grabbed him by the arm and William found himself taken on a guided tour of two more RT's, a Bristol Lodekka FLF, a Bedford OB and a Dennis Lancet. Helena seemed quite well known among the predominantly male enthusiasts, and William was introduced to several people as 'a colleague from Orbit'. Then he became aware of a general movement of the enthusiasts towards the buses. An official in orange day-glo clothing waved the first bus off. Helena led William back to the RT and they took the front seat at the top. 'Like a couple of schoolkids' thought William. Other enthusiasts soon filled the remaining seats, women and children too, out for the day. There were squeals of delight from some of the younger members of the party as the bus bumped over the hump-backed bridge over the railway line, and then the convoy headed south into the Weald.

Helena was even more of a mystery character than he had thought previously, William decided. Here she was, getting a largish bar of milk chocolate out of her handbag and putting a chunk of it into her mouth. She broke off a small piece and gave it to him. She was always eating, William thought, but it didn't seem to make her fat. Beneath the T-shirt her body looked quite slim, and he could almost distinguish the outline of her breasts, small, firm and round. Her neck, always hidden by those floppy sweaters she wore at the office, was rather shapely, and she had a jangling medallion or some other kind of ornament on a chain around it.

"Oh, you're looking at this?" Helena took the medallion thing in her fingers and showed in to William. "It's an old ship halfpenny. The year of my birth. We got it in change at a sweet shop, and then they got rid of the old money so I got Daddy to drill a hole in it and he gave me the silver chain for it. It's a kind of lucky charm."

William fingered the coin. It had been burnished to a soft golden colour and its ship design struck a chord in his memory, back to a pre-Chestfield time when everything had seemed safe and constant, and, no doubt, when RT buses roamed the streets of London freely. Other girls might wear gold sovereigns or silver St Christophers, but somehow an old halfpenny seemed awfully in character with Helena.

After driving through the picture-book village of Biddenden, and up the steep grade to St Michael's, the buses came into Tenterden High Street, a long and wide street flanked by pretty weatherboarded houses and shops. William was nearly unseated when, suddenly, the bus took a sharp right turn, bounced over a level-crossing and came to rest apparently in the middle of a field.

"Where on earth are we?" asked William.

"This is the Tenterden Vintage Transport Weekend. We'll see far more buses here! Come on!" Again he felt Helena's hand tugging at his sleeve. The chocolate bar had completely disappeared and Helena threw the screwed-up silver paper into the 'Used Tickets' box. The field was full of vehicles of all kinds, not just buses, but ancient delivery vans, traction engines and even vintage motorcycles and sidecars. Tents and makeshift stalls had been set up all around the edges of the field, selling model railway items, old bus tickets, a variety of ticket machines, uniforms, badges and other transport memorabilia.

Helena rushed off into the swirling holiday crowds and for a time William completely lost sight of her. He found himself staring at an open-top double-decker which gave its destination as 'Southend Pier'. It was almost the same colour as an Orbit coach. Perhaps Mr Papadopoulos ought to hire it as a publicity vehicle.

Helena was back, beaming with a terrific smile and her long hair flowing behind her.

"Oh, there you are! I've been looking for you! Come and have a look at this!"

William found himself dragged at breakneck pace through the crowd and over to another part of the field. They came to a halt in front of a large, elderly, double-decker bus. It was painted a deep maroon colour between the decks and below the lower-deck windows, while the rest of the vehicle was cream. A rosette was prominently displayed in the windscreen.

"Isn't it gorgeous?"

William would never have described a rather old bus as gorgeous.

"It's an AEC Regent V. This is one of the first ones made. See the door - it's the sliding type and not that concertina sort they have nowadays. Oh, it's beautiful!"

And with that she planted a kiss on the centre of its radiator grille.

William was wondering if Helena was quite sane. However, that was nothing compared to his surprise at what happened next. An enormous man with a shock of red hair and a luxuriant red beard came round from the back of the bus. Seeing Helena, he seized her around the waist and lifted her clean off the ground. He kissed her full on the lips before putting her down. "And how's my Number Two girl, then?" he asked, in a surprisingly cultivated voice.

"Fine, Don, this is William from Orbit. William, this is Don. We were at University together."

William shook hands with Don and wondered exactly what his relationship with Helena was. Don was a great hulk of a man, at least six foot four, with the sort of belly William associated with beer drinkers. His hands were hairy and rough and his handshake like an iron grip. He wasn't quite the sort of boyfriend he'd imagined for Helena: she had a remarkable capacity to fade into the background, but it would be impossible for Don to do that.

Don patted the mudguard of his pride and joy with affection. "What do you know, Helena? We got the award for the best pre-1960 double-decker at the Spalding rally last weekend. All the way to Lincolnshire and back and nothing went wrong! You did very well, old girl!"

This last remark was directed not to Helena, but to the bus.

"Hi there, Helena!" A small dark woman with long straggly hair came up to Helena and kissed her on the cheek. She was carrying two pint glasses of beer and gave one to Don. She encircled her slim arm around Don's enormous waist. They looked a most odd couple. The woman was hardly five feet tall. She was wearing a long gypsy-style frock and had silver bangles on her wrists, giving her the appearance of a hippy left over from the sixties.

"This is William" said Don to the woman. "Friend of Helena's."

"Pleased to meet you. I'm Maddy, Don's wife. We own this bus."

"You own it?" William thought this was taking a hobby too far.

"They're professionals," said Helena to William, "You tell him about it," she asked Don.

"We run our own business. Restoring and selling old vehicles. I trained as an accountant, and I met Maddy at University, but I'd always been interested in buses, and, you know, the hobby just kind of took over. We set up in business five years ago and we're doing very well now. We also supply old vehicles for films and TV series."

"You mean any TV programme?"

"Yes. If you see an old car or bus in a television programme, it may well have come from us. It's our most lucrative source of income, and it helps pay for the rallying. We're even taking the old girl over to France next week, aren't we, Maddy?"

"Oh yeah. Language school job, isn't it?"

"Yes. Britannia Language Schools in Paris. They're supposed to teach English the way it's spoken in England, so they want a TV ad showing a double-decker bus as something typically British. Should be great fun. They're paying very generous expenses."

"I go to Paris quite a lot myself. If you want a free night out, try this place. It's just off the Place Pigalle. Just mention my name and they won't charge you." And William handed Don one of the cards from the 'Grenouille Bondissante', which he always carried in his wallet.

"It means the Jumping Frog," Helena explained.

"Well, come upstairs!" Maddy had slipped into the driver's seat and operated the door, which slid back slowly. William followed Helena and Don inside. Like the RT, it had been splendidly restored.

"Where do you get all the old posters and adverts from?" asked William.

"Oh, here and there. Sometimes we write to the companies and they send them. It gives them a bit of free advertising after all. Or we go to one of the collectors' markets. There are quite a few dealers specialising in these things."

"When's the voting?" asked Helena.

"I don't think they announce the results until five o'clock." Maddy replied.

"Why don't we all go to the pub then?" suggested Don.

"You lead the way," said Helena.

They set off across the field, pausing to look at some of the stalls. William bought a number of stickers inscribed 'No Smoking In These Two Seats' for 5p each; you never knew when they might come in useful.

They strolled up Station Road and went into the White Hart in the High Street. They settled into a corner and ordered scampi all round. Maddy and Don finished theirs first and left apologetically. They didn't like leaving the bus unattended for too long, just in case vital bits disappeared into the collections of amateur souvenir-hunters.

"Do you want another drink?" Helena asked William.

"Ooh, yes please. I'd love another half of cider."

"I'll get it, then." And she picked up the two empty half-pint glasses and walked to the bar.

William didn't hear her order the drinks, but he did turn around in time to hear the contretemps at the bar.

"I'm sorry, young lady, but I'm not allowed to sell alcohol to anyone under eighteen." The barman had a kindly voice. "Now, if your young man was to come up here, I'd let him …"

"But I'm not under eighteen," Helena protested.

"Can you prove that?"

"Well, as it happens, yes I can. " Now William had got close enough to see Helena remove a small rolled-up scroll of paper from the depths of her handbag and thrust it under the barman's nose. It was a copy of a birth certificate.

"Goodness me!" He was clearly taken aback. "Well, I'm most sorry, young lady. Two halves of cider it is".

And Helena paid for the drinks and sat down again.

"Very useful precaution," she said to William. "Never leave home without it. Saves a lot of trouble in situations like this."

"What if you're going somewhere that charges less for under-eighteens?"

"Oh, I keep it hidden then, of course. Cheers!"

And with that they drank their ciders. Could this Helena, the girl-woman, really be the same person he knew at the office? Perhaps other people had double lives. Did Margot suddenly become a motorcycle mechanic or a bank robber in her spare time? Had anyone else at Orbit ever seen the other side of H.R.? He rather doubted it.

They finished their drinks and had a walk around the town. They looked at the church of St Mildred and the Old Grammar School, and browsed in the Antiques Centre. They looked at the collection of old enamel signs in the Colonel Stephens Railway Museum. Then the sound of a steam whistle caught their attention.

"Oh, shall we go for a train ride?" asked Helena.

"Why not?" said William. They strolled back down Station Road to the small brick station building and bought two return tickets. Trains were more interesting than buses, thought William; they had more history. They walked through to the platform and watched the little green tank engine couple up to a rake of brown and cream coaches. The carriage door was opened by a uniformed porter, they got in, heard the guard blow his whistle and the train gently chugged off for its short journey down the Rother Valley. The whole thing had an unreal quality about it, like an Agatha Christie novel. It was so different from the impersonal electric trains he got from North Malling to London. William felt himself transported back to some indeterminate period between the wars when English summers were always glorious and when he could have swept the fair maiden by his side off her feet in some chintz ballroom... How could he be thinking such thoughts about Helena? He looked again at the slim figure in her T-shirt and slacks, her hair blowing in the breeze from the open window. There was really nothing romantic about her.

Two enthusiasts were sitting opposite them. One had a large Pentax with a zoom lens on his lap; the other some papers held together with an elastic band. William could hear them talking, and he recognised the language as French. It wasn't unusual to see French visitors in South-East England nowadays. "Bonjour! Vous êtes français? D'où venez-vous?" Helena was starting a conversation with them. Like many apparently shy people, she was not worried by the prospect of starting a conversation in a foreign language, thought William. Like him, she spoke fluent French.

Pierre and Henri Rigaud were soon introduced to William. They were brothers who were setting up their own tourist railway in France, and were on a fact-finding mission to England to see how the thing was done.

"We have how-do-you-say-it leased a ligne secondaire from the SNCF. They run goods trains in the week, we have passager trains le weekend! We have a 141-R!"

Henri handed William a brochure from the packet on his knee. It was headed 'Chemin de Fer Touristique de la Charente' and had a picture of the 141-R, which, as Pierre explained, was a large steam locomotive from a batch sent over by the United States to help rebuild the French railway network after the war. The leaflet had a text in French and a brief summary in English and German. The English translation began by explaining that 'the organisation of the Chemin de Fer Touristique de la Charente is composed of voluntary persons which devote their spare time to the restoration of ancient materials and to the exploitation of steam trains', and continued with an enchanting description of the line, containing gems such as 'the engine lets off its steam with a vehement exhaust sound to the joy of the passagers curiously bending at the windows'…

"We are based at Mansle-la-Jolie, in Charente," said Pierre.

"Goodness!" exclaimed William. "I know Mansle-la-Jolie. I go through it nearly once a fortnight. It's on the road from Neuville to Limoges. I'll be going through there on Thursday week."

"Thursday week!" repeated Henri. "Formidable! That's when we're sending our Mikado to Vierzon."

"What?" asked William, a vague picture of Gilbert and Sullivan operas going through his head.

"Le Mikado. It is another name for the 141-R. They are doing a special exhibition at Vierzon station and we are loaning it. Come to Mansle-la-Jolie on Thursday and you might see it."

William had just had another idea. Mike Turner, the awful JCR captain from Chestfield, had been a fanatical railway enthusiast. He used to cycle along the disused railway line which ran not far from Chestfield, and unscrew rusty signs saying things like 'Persons trespassing on the Railway are Liable to a Penalty of Forty Shillings', with which he used to decorate the walls of his study-bedroom after he became a prefect. When he looked at the photo of the enormous locomotive belching smoke and fire, on the C.F. de Charente's brochure, he was sure that Mike Turner would love to be riding on it. He begged two leaflets from Pierre and Henri and folded them carefully into his wallet. He also promised to telephone them if he was ever able to make a stop at the railway on one of his tours.

The little train puffed into Northiam, its rural terminus just over the Sussex border, and Pierre and Henri were off across the fields, taking photos of the train before returning on a later one. William and Helena had a short stroll along the platform before reboarding and returning to Tenterden.

"I'm famished!" said Helena. They repaired to the station buffet. William had a cup of tea. Helena spooned three sugars into hers and drank it while tucking into a chocolate roll.

"How on earth do you manage to eat so much and stay so slim?" William could no longer resist asking her.

"I don't know. I must just have a very fast metabolism," she said.

They wandered back to the field behind the railway embankment. Helena took William to see a 1937 Leyland Tiger coach and explained to him the advantages of the AEC Reliance chassis over the AEC Regal. William bought a postcard of a 'Mikado' from another stall: it would look more impressive on the brochure he sent to Mike Turner than would Orbit's glossy prints of scenery and old cathedrals. They waited by the Tannoy system and heard the Award for Best Preserved Vehicle go to 'the 1959 AEC Regent V with Park Royal bodywork owned by Don and Maddy Taylor from Edenhurst'.

They went over to congratulate the winners. Helena kissed Maddy and Don affixed the new rosette inside the windscreen. William said he hoped he'd see them in Paris and reminded them about the 'Grenouille Bondissante'.

It was time to go, although there was still plenty of light left in the long summer evening. Another steam train whistled as it climbed up the gradient behind them, and a skylark twittered overhead. Helena grabbed William's arm again and led him back to the RT bus. A bus waits for no man, even if it is a preserved one. Soon the convoy of buses was on the road once again, the red livery of the RT's lending a temporarily metropolitan air to the quaint Wealden villages.

"When are you coming up to London for briefing?" Helena asked William.

"Saturday."

"Are you going back home afterwards?"

"No. I've got the F443 tour. I have to be at the West London coach station at six o'clock. It's too awkward trying to get to London for that early in the morning."

"Where do you stay in London?"

"Usually one of those cheap hotels near the coach station where they put our passengers who book a night in London before the tour leaves."

"Why don't you stay in my flat next Saturday night? That would save you a bit of money. It's quite convenient for the buses."

Helena's flat just would be, thought William. But an offer of somewhere to stay in London was not to be sneezed at. He used to have some University friends living in London, but they'd moved out of the city eighteen months previously.

"I'd be delighted. I'll come to the office in the afternoon, then. What time do you finish work?"

"Oh, you know. Depends on Mr Papadopoulos. Should be five-thirty but I might get out earlier. We can go for a drink after work if you like."

"Good idea." William wondered what sort of an evening he would spend at Helena's flat. Whatever happened, it would surely be more interesting than an evening in the smoky TV lounge of a cheap hotel in west London.

With a churning of gears the RT bus turned onto the gravelly surface of the car park at Headcorn station. William said goodbye to Helena and alighted. Helena waved him goodbye from the open platform at the back of the bus as he walked back to his car. Her hair was still blowing in the wind and she looked more like a teenager than ever.

Half-an-hour later William parked the Mini in his own drive. He had at one time hoped that he would earn enough as a Tour Manager to buy a modest house outright, but the huge increases in property prices in the eighties had made this impossible. Instead, when his parents had retired and decided to move house, he had joined forces with them and helped them select and buy a house which suited the three of them. It was a modern red-brick two-storey house, with what the estate agent had described as a 'granny annexe' on one side. This was where William lived: he had his own bathroom, kitchenette and bed-sitting room, but was free to come and go into his parents' house as and when he wished. The drawback was that the same arrangement applied to his parents, and William was forever returning from tours to find that some of his possessions had been displaced by his mother doing a little well-intentioned housework.

His mother was pruning a rose bush by the front door.

"Been out with a nice girl, dear?" she asked. His mother was always saying that he ought to get a girlfriend, but neither she nor his father had ever been able to offer him any really useful practical advice.

"No - er, just a colleague from the office." William wasn't quite sure whether Helena would come into his mother's category of 'a nice girl'. He added "A rather ordinary girl, actually." (How could he tell such a big lie? No-one in their right mind could ever describe Helena Rogers as ordinary.)

"Those sort are often the nicest ones, dear," said his mother. "You must bring her back to tea sometime. It would be nice to see you married. You're just the right age. There must be thousands of girls who would want a nice young man like you."

Everything was 'nice' in Mrs Simpson's world. William could not imagine himself married to Helena Rogers. He told his mother that he would join them for tea, and then opened his own front door. He made straight for his AA Road Atlas of Britain and turned to a map of East Anglia. Tomorrow he would have to put Phase Two of his scheme into operation.

Chapter Three

Back To School

SUNDAY morning dawned with a weak sun attempting to shine between gaps in the clouds. A few rays made their way through the chinks in the Venetian blinds into William's bedroom. He stirred and raised a hand to switch on the radio. No news about road works in Essex or Suffolk was good news. A gentle tapping at the window made him get out of bed and open it a few inches. There was a polite "Mieu" and Pepper, the old tortoiseshell cat, gracefully jumped onto the bed with an agility that belied her nineteen years and snuggled under the blankets.

Pepper had been William's confidante and friend since he had been in his teens. He well remembered the day he'd chosen her from a litter of kittens in the window of a pet shop in Maidstone and they'd brought her home in a cardboard box. He'd grown up with her, and the close relationship had been renewed with increasing affection every school holiday. She had never been an outstandingly beautiful cat. As a youngster, she'd always looked skinny and bedraggled; then they'd had her spayed, and she had grown fatter and lazier. Her eyes were a pale yellow and her fur a speckled black pepper colour which had given her her name.

William would often spend long hours with Pepper on his lap talking to her. She was a most attentive listener and didn't try to argue with him, although she did have a tendency to fall asleep. William wondered whether she ever regretted not having had kittens, and not having had the experience of free love and courting which alley-cats had, but he was rather glad that she hadn't. It somehow put her on the same level as him. Every time he went away on tour he used to phone home and put that most dreaded question to his mother or father - "How's Pepper?" - and breathe an audible sigh of relief at the reply.

One day, he knew, the end would come, and it would be goodbye to part of his childhood and to the only female who had ever been in love with him.

After getting dressed and having a quick breakfast, William returned to his room and took a ball-point pen and a small ring-bound notebook from a drawer. He got through hundreds of these little notebooks - they were invaluable when he was on tour for writing down such crucial details as coach mileages, telephone messages, notes for his commentary and the like. Tucking these items into his trouser pocket, he reached into the depths of his bed and pulled out the sleeping Pepper. He opened the door into his parents' part of the house and placed her carefully in her basket in the kitchen. Then he picked up his car keys, grabbed a light plastic anorak - you never knew when it might rain - and walked outside to the car.

The antiquated starter-motor whirred, spluttered and finally the car came into life, and soon William was heading up the A229 for the M2 which would take him to the Dartford Crossing. The car ought to know the way all by itself: when it had been his mother's, he'd sometimes been given lifts back to school in it after a weekend at home. They'd given him the Mini much later, after he'd passed his driving test. The little red car had scraped through its MOT test year after year, having a few vital components replaced in the process, but it was essentially the same vehicle that had taken him to Chestfield all those years ago.

After he joined the motorway the sun went behind the clouds. As usual, there was a contraflow system in operation and he had to dodge the orange plastic cones. He got his toll money ready and slid open the window to give it to the man in the little booth. There was hardly any traffic on the roads at this time in the morning. As he drove through the tunnel, William felt the same sense of foreboding which he always felt on entering East Anglia. He had never really liked East Anglia, and Chestfield must largely have the blame for this. His last visit to this part of the world had been about two years previously, to attend the funeral of an aged but much-loved aunt in Ipswich. It had been a cold November day with a thin drizzle falling on the mourners as they awaited the arrival of the hearse outside the cemetery chapel. Today, as he reached the end of the tunnel, he was greeted by a raindrop falling squarely on the centre of the windscreen, and it was followed by others. It always seemed to rain in East Anglia. How appropriate it was, thought William, that to reach Essex from Kent one has to drive through a dark tunnel, the portal of Hell, whereas to travel back into the Garden of England one now crossed a magnificent high suspension bridge, a most heavenly experience.

Driving past Chelmsford and Witham on the A12, William recognised old landmarks that used to help him calculate the number of minutes until he arrived at school - or home. He turned north of Colchester on the A134 and passed the barber's shop which had always made his heart sink as he realised how near he was to school. Then he crossed the Suffolk border. The countryside was predominantly agricultural, flat and uninteresting, looking quite as unlike a Constable landscape as possible. He slowed down to negotiate a sharp bend as the road passed under a disused railway bridge, and there on the right-hand side was the round tower of Chestfield parish church. It had a fine example of a Norman doorway, and every year on Founder's Day the whole school would troop to the church for a special service to honour the obscure illegitimate son of King Charles II who had founded 'Ye Charytye Schoole for Twelve Poore Scholars' in 1699 and whose immense alabaster memorial occupied most of the chancel of the small village church.

Chestfield was actually quite an attractive village, thought William, seeing the place as through new eyes. There was the same red telephone box from which he had made so many transfer-charge calls home, the same Village Stores and Post Office and the tuck shop which was run by the School. Passing on the left the red-brick Georgian pile of Eliot House, he entered the school grounds. As he would have expected for the last Sunday of term, there were not many people around. The sound of organ music drifted across from the mock-Gothic Victorian chapel: the morning service was in progress. Outside the Chapel a fine array of motor vehicles were lined up: Range Rovers, Jaguars and a Bentley or two, wealthy parents waiting to take their offspring out for Sunday lunch.

William drove past the Chapel and the duck pond, noticing the saplings which had been planted to replace the diseased elms, and glanced towards the brand new Sports Hall, built with money raised from Old Boys. He hadn't contributed towards its construction himself, and he wondered whether any of his contemporaries had. He still had unpleasant memories of compulsory sports at Chestfield, and his own lack of ability in any kind of sporting activities, and in his day they had still been using the old wooden gymnasium, with its primitive changing-rooms, dreaded communal showers and lack of modern facilities.

He had the same feeling as always in the pit of his stomach as he pulled into the car park in front of Wallis House. Wallis was a large, sprawling building dating from the nineteen-thirties, and the peeling paintwork on the sills of the sash windows didn't look as if it had been touched since he'd last seen it nearly sixteen years ago. Like the other school buildings, Wallis was deserted, though a glance at his watch told him that the boys would soon be coming out of Chapel.

He locked the car and walked the back way past the sanatorium towards the main school buildings. He didn't bother to go into Wallis, though he knew the Junior Common Room would be just the same as ever, with its rows of turquoise-painted desks and its pop posters presumably now featuring the latest generation of heavy-metal idols. He had a certain feeling of nostalgia walking past the sanatorium, which had always been an oasis of peace in the school, as there you got a bedroom to yourself, orange squash and the undivided attentions of Matron. It would be nice to pay her a visit if she was still there. But now he had more urgent work to do.

The main building of Chestfield School was a huge three-storey construction of late Victorian red brick. When approached from the First XI cricket pitch, it looked quite grand, with its clocktower and sweeping gravel drive, like an Oxford or Cambridge college transported to the wilds of Suffolk. But few visitors ever saw the school from the rear. Here were a block of lavatories whose glass roof had earned them the nickname of 'Crystal Palace', the school kitchens with smells that took William back sixteen years, and an immense archway which led to a short covered walk, rather grandiosely known as 'the Cloisters'. This gave access to the classrooms proper. William walked down the corridor with its instantly recognisable smell of school floor-polish, and the familiar names in letters of gold upon the polished wooden doors - Townley, Pritchard, Scott-Alderson ... Like the boarding houses, the classrooms were named after distinguished Old Boys or masters.

At Bartley classroom, opposite the curving stairway going up to the school library, he paused. The door was slightly ajar and he could not resist having a peep inside. The rows of dark wooden desks, the master's desk and chair on their raised dais, and the dog-eared map of France hanging on the wall had not changed in sixteen years. The only concession to modern technology was the florescent strip lighting, which had replaced the dim old light bulbs he had known. On the bottom right-hand corner of the blackboard was a notice on a piece of card about a foot square. William knew exactly what it said:

'I MAY BE A COMPLETE IDIOT, BUT SURELY I CAN COPY CORRECTLY'.

This was part of the indispensable teaching equipment of Mr B.A. Eveleigh, B.A., and over two years of ploughing through Shortman's Audio-Visual French course William had been reminded of that notice many times whenever he deigned to make a spelling mistake in his prep. The Shortman course, as used in the third and fourth forms, was based on the adventures of a ridiculous fictional French family called the Auberts who went to circuses, spent an inordinate amount of time shopping at outdoor markets and gave extremely boring dinner-parties. Monsieur and Madame Aubert had a very tedious son called René, who was 'insupportable', and a seventeen-year old daughter called Marie-France who had an incredibly dull boyfriend called Robert. You never saw Marie-France snogging Robert or even going to a disco and drinking too much *vin rosé* or having an abortion or anything interesting like that: usually she was portrayed just talking with her parents or going to see a *film sensationnel* at the Cinema Ritz. William could see now the first chapter of Shortman's Book One with the picture of the insipid-looking girl with the round face and the long fair hair, and the sentence: *Je m'appelle Marie-France Aubert. Je travaille dans une épicerie.*

And that had been school French. Looking back, it seemed remarkable that William had ever got to be fluent in the language. But the real French, which you could hear in the street in Paris or Geneva or Lyons bore little resemblance to the strange language in Shortman's Book One. The French he had learned from Mr Eveleigh belonged to some far-off imaginary world where young boys could buy big bags of sweets for a single franc, where Italian ice-cream vendors with long flowing moustaches roamed the streets of Paris, where boys in awful long shorts travelled to school in funny old buses while their fathers drove to the bureau in big black Citroëns straight out of Maigret. How he had hated listening to tapes and having to write a resumé of some wonderful story such as 'M. et Mme. Aubert vont au Cirque!' Mr Eveleigh's pupils left the Fourth Form frequently unable to string two words of French together, should they ever accidentally happen to be stranded in Calais, but quite capable of relating the entire life history of the awful Aubert family. William had always been around the bottom of the set in Mr Eveleigh's French classes, but he had gone on to obtain an A-level and degree and long ceased to worry about René's antics or M. Aubert cutting himself while shaving.

The glass-fronted cupboard by the master's desk was locked as usual, but inside through the chalk dust William could discern the four red-bound volumes of the hateful Shortman's course and the matching reels of tape. And there, too, was Cicero. Cicero was a drumstick with which Mr Eveleigh used to beat his pupils when they made especially silly mistakes. It didn't hurt much, the whole thing was done in jest and was far preferable to being kept in detention on Wednesday afternoons, but it was a kind of humiliation to be asked to go to the cupboard and get Cicero out. William wondered whether Cicero was still administered regularly.

Leaving Bartley classroom, William walked up the stairs to the Library. It was an open-metal type staircase and he remembered how as a thirteen-year-old he had liked to stand underneath if any of the school girls were coming down, and get an otherwise unavailable view of female legs. There were only girls in the Sixth Form at Chestfield, and, when he had been there, there had only been twenty to thirty girls in a school with over four hundred boys.

In the Library a couple of serious-looking A-level candidates were poring over their set texts, but, apart from that, the long room with its grim mahogany tables and battered armchairs was empty. Few boys would be coming here straight after Chapel on the last Sunday of term unless they had particularly urgent exams in the last week.

William headed for the bookshelf under the portrait of F.W. Strachan, Headmaster 1860-1874, and pulled out a large volume bound in maroon leather. On its cover it bore gold block lettering with the School coat-of-arms, the name *Chestfield* and *Alumni 1871-1880*. This book evidently contained fascinating details about the late Mr Strachan's pupils, some of whom had no doubt been eaten by cannibals in primitive nations or killed fighting for Queen and Empire in obscure Colonial wars. But this was not the book he required. He bent down and sorted through the other tomes on the inconveniently sited shelf, which was half-hidden by an armchair and obviously little used.

He replaced *Alumni 1871-1880* and extracted a similar volume lettered *Alumni 1971-1980*. It was almost identical to the earlier book, but its leather binding was a brighter, plum colour, and it was not quite so thick. In this precious book he could find details of all the boys who had left the school during the decade in question.

On the first page of his notebook he had written down a list of ten names:

Mr Eveleigh
Mario Rottoli
Mike Turner
Jonathan Atkinson
Hugh Bartlett-Nicholson

Miranda Morisson
Ian Bailey-Filmer
Nick Patterson
John Bridger
Steve Vicks

The first name obviously needed no further research; he just had to hope that Mr Eveleigh wasn't around this weekend. There was little likelihood of him coming into the library; he usually spent Sundays at the comfortable house down in the village where he lived with his elderly sister. It was funny, considered William, how he had always thought of Mr Eveleigh as being very old, and yet he couldn't have been more than about fifty when he'd been at Chestfield, and had possibly been even younger.

William turned to the letter A:

'Atkinson, Jonathan P., mi. (W) b. 14.10.61. Entered school '74(3) Left '79(2). Univ. of Cheshire '79-'82. Joined Atkinson Furnishings, Hitchin, 8/82. Address: 14 Terminus Road, Hitchin, Herts.'

So Atkinson had joined the family firm. It was only to be expected. For many of Chestfield's pupils there was no uncertainty about finding a job, no need to worry about interviews or application forms. After school and a three-year holiday at University, they stepped into a management position in their parents' firm or farm. It was interesting that Atkinson's degree result was not given. Either it had been so bad they hadn't wanted to communicate it, or he'd been thrown out of University before he'd finished the course. Knowing Atkinson, perhaps he'd just got bored and walked out a week before Finals. Anyway, here was the address of the boy who had borrowed his bicycle without permission and wrecked it seventeen years ago. William wrote it down.

Next he turned to B. He was certain John Bridger had gone into the armed forces - there had been something about it in the Old Boys' section of the school magazine which he was still mailed three times a year. His vague recollection proved correct.

'Bridger, John F.N. (W) b. 20.3.60. Entered school '73(3) Left '78(2)...' A description of a career in the RAF followed, with a BFPO number in Germany.

Bailey-Filmer's career history was more obscure. After leaving Chestfield in 1975 he had taken a degree in Archaeology at Cambridge, but his most recent employment appeared to be at a bookshop in Oxford. William reckoned he ought to have got a job as chief taster for Nescafé Gold Blend.

It was Bartlett-Nicholson's entry which produced the greatest surprise. After detailing his various academic and considerably greater sporting achievements (Captain of 1st XI cricket, Rugby 1st XV ...), came the entry 'married Miranda Morrisson (G '75 -'77) October 1985.' So it had been more than just a school romance. Bartlett-Nicholson was now working on the family estate.

Nick Patterson (E), despite his artistic talents, had left Hull University with a Third and apparently joined an insurance company in Southend. William wondered if he was selling insurance: he certainly wouldn't want to buy any from him. As with all the entries, he made a note of the home address. Then he turned to the letter R. Rottoli had left Chestfield after his disastrous O-Level results, and there had been some kind of scandal about him and one of the Lower VI girls - William still remembered the graffiti that had appeared on some of the classroom desks at the time. The address given was Ristorante Loredana in Colchester. Mario's father had owned an Italian restaurant. It looked as if Rottoli junior was still working there. It seemed a strangely unexciting career for someone who had regaled the dormitory with his tales of under-age sex and once claimed to have driven a lorry filled with drugs across the Franco-Italian border.

Mike Turner had at any rate made a success of his life. He had got a 2.2 at Cambridge, gone on to train as a quantity surveyor, and was now married and living in North London. William wondered if he were still a railway enthusiast. There was nothing in the book to say that he was, but William expected he still would be: teenage fashions come and go, but if you were a fanatic at the age of eighteen you tended to remain one.

The final name on his list was that of Steve Vicks. He had studied electronics at London University and was now running his own business, Vicks Sound Systems Ltd. William well remembered his old enemy's love of hi-fi. It was natural that he should now be making it.

Before closing the book altogether, William turned to the letter S and looked for his own entry:

'Simpson, William A. (W) b. 8.12.60. Entrance Scholar. Entered school '73(3) Left '78(2). Univ. of Berkshire '79-'83: BA French 2.1. Joined Orbit Tours & Travel, Charing Cross Road, London W1 6/84.' This was what any of his contemporaries who had bothered to fork out the £21.50 for the book would know about him, if they had ever troubled to look.

With the addresses safely in his notebook, William replaced *Alumni 1971-80* on the low shelf and left the library. The corridor downstairs was still deathly silent. He hesitated, then opened the door of Mr Eveleigh's classroom once more and walked up to the blackboard. The dreaded notice stared him in the face: 'I MAY BE A COMPLETE IDIOT BUT...' William tugged at the card and wrenched it off the board. He turned it over to its blank side, and, selecting a fibre tip pen of a virulent shade of red from the top of the master's desk, he wrote as elegantly as he could, in the same flowing letters he produced for tour posters:

'I AM NOT A COMPLETE IDIOT, BUT OCCASIONALLY I MAKE THE UNFORTUNATE MISTAKE OF NOT COPYING CORRECTLY'.

He dug the drawing pins out of the blackboard, replaced the card the other way around, and closed the door of Bartley behind him as he ran up the corridor towards the Cloisters. Just now he really felt as if he were fifteen again.

Rain was falling thick and fast. William ran out of the brick arch and back along the track towards Wallis. He had left his plastic mac in the car. Pulling up his collar as protection against the driving rain, he made it to the car and unlocked the door. He turned the key in the ignition. It refused to start. He waited a few moments and tried again. The engine turned over a couple of times, but the Mini wouldn't move an inch. What was he to do, stuck in a part of Suffolk he utterly disliked with a broken-down car?

There was movement inside Wallis House. William glanced around to the side door and saw a tall young man in games clothes leave the house. He was probably a new assistant master. He was followed by a troupe of boys in tracksuits and running shoes. They must be practising for the cross-country run; sports at Chestfield never stopped for bad weather, as William well remembered.

As the figures left the doorway and ran out into the rain it brought back to William painful memories of afternoons on the games field. But then he had an idea. Sliding open the window of the Mini, he called to the games master:

"Excuse me, I can't start my car. Can you give me a push?"

The challenge was accepted as if it were a compulsory extra part of the daily exercise. William found the car being pushed by half a dozen burly sixteen-year-olds as he steered it round the drive towards the Chapel. After twenty yards or so the engine roared into life. William waved grateful thanks to his miraculous saviours and kept his foot down. He didn't want to stop until he got back into Kent.

Not so very far away from Chestfield, in the leafy surroundings of the Epping Forest, Helena Rogers had just finished having Sunday lunch with her parents. She visited her parents most weekends, and today her father had dropped her off at the bus stop on his way to a round of golf. A plump, cheerful-looking man in his mid-sixties, he could have been mistaken for a minor member of the aristocracy with his greying moustache and tweed jacket. In fact, he owned a chain of butcher's shops in a small area of south-west Essex.

Driving back later from the Golf Club, Mrs Rogers remarked to her husband:

"I thought Helena seemed a bit funny today."

"That girl! It would be amazing if she didn't seem funny!"

"Oh, Henry, what did I do that was wrong? Why have I been such a rotten mother?"

"Now, Jane, do stop worrying. You can't be blamed for Claire … And Helena, now, she's doing all right for herself, really."

"But she never seems to have FUN. I mean, when I was young, I always seemed to be going out to parties and dances and things … and look at her. Twenty-seven and she's never even had a boyfriend! She never wears any make-up, never has her hair done …"

"She's doing what she wants to, dear."

"But what sort of life is it for a girl of twenty-seven? When's she going to meet some nice young man? I do blame myself. I let Claire do whatever she wanted, and look what happened… and now Helena. I was over-protective towards her and now she might just as well be a nun!"

"Do stop worrying about her. She's a grown woman, you know. She's not a little girl any more." Henry Rogers was very proud of his clever daughter who had gone to University and was working in London, but secretly he shared many of the same fears as his wife. Yes, the girl didn't have much of a social life, and if she was going to get married and start a family then she'd better hurry up and meet someone quickly. Perhaps he was old-fashioned, but he still thought that at her age you were getting on: soon she'd be on the shelf. Perhaps it had been a mistake for him to have asked his brother, the London university lecturer, to let her use his spare flat all these years. If she had been sharing a flat with other career girls she would have enjoyed much more of a social life.

The large Rover purred smoothly into the semi-circular drive of the long white bungalow, and crunched to a halt on the gravel beside the ornamental pond with its concrete cupids. A blackbird was singing his head off in one of the big trees in the garden behind the house. Henry and Jane Rogers opened the dark wooden door with its imitation leaded glass and entered the hall. In the half-light of the dying summer evening Mrs Rogers's steel grey hair could have been Helena's, and her profile, with a slightly snub nose and a still firm chin, resembled her daughter's.

On either side of the mirror in the hall in its heavy gilt frame hung two photographs. One was of Helena, taken when she was nineteen. Eight years later she was still instantly recognisable. The other picture showed a serious-looking girl with long dark hair and an attractively mischievous glint in her eyes. Claire Rogers had died of a drugs overdose at the age of twenty-two.

****

On Monday morning, William had one final task to do. He needed to receive the replies from his 'clients', but obviously he couldn't give Orbit's address. His home address was likewise out of the question. What could he do? His gaze fell on the *Mid-Kent Reporter* lying on his hall table, one of those free papers which were regularly pushed through the letter box. Box - that was it - a Box number! He called the paper and explained that he had a car for sale, but that because he spent most of his time working overseas he would prefer the replies to go to a box number. Was that alright? It was. He dictated a hastily-written ad for his Mini, and put the phone down. The phone? Here was another problem. Many people preferred phoning to writing, and if, say, his letter to John Bridger in Germany took some time to be delivered, there might not be time for him to reply in writing. The answer to the problem was staring him in the face: his telephone answering-machine. Why not put an announcement on the tape saying it was Orbit Tours and asking callers to leave a message? He could then put his own number in the letters. He received very few phone calls at home anyway, and any personal caller who received the strange message would just assume they had dialled a wrong number.

Now William wrote an individual letter on his word-processor to each of his intended victims, using the Orbit headed paper, but requesting them to reply to Box No. 7225, Mid-Kent Reporter, or to leave a message on North Malling 227315.

The pillar box outside North Malling sub-post office had a collection at 12.45. By 12.00 the letters were all in the box. Phase 2 was complete.

Chapter Four

Return To Sender

ABIGAIL Bartlett-Nicholson heard the sound of the postman push something through the letter-box, and rushed to the hall. Already, at the age of seven, she was showing signs of the beauty which had made her mother the main topic of conversation in the dormitories of Chestfield many years previously. She came rushing in to the spacious, stone-flagged kitchen, where her mother and father were at breakfast.

"Mummy! Daddy! A letter! Look!"

Mummy and Daddy turned to Abigail. The child was starting to get bored at home, Miranda thought. It was only the beginning of the school holidays. She knew that her mother in Somerset would love to have Abigail for part of the holidays, but she felt guilty wanting to send the child away so soon. It was a pity there were no children of Abigail's age in the neighbourhood. She would have to talk it over with Hugh.

Hugh meanwhile was slitting open the envelope with his breakfast knife. He was a large, handsome if slightly balding man in his early thirties. He pushed his spectacles onto the bridge of his nose and began to read.

"I say, my dear. We've just won a holiday in France!"

"What's that? How can we have won it? You know we never go in for any of those silly competitions".

"It says here that our names have been selected by their computer. It's Orbit Tours. They're a well-known firm - I've seen some of their brochures. It's a coach tour - seven nights in France".

"Do you think it's some kind of joke? I mean, you hear all about people being told they've won something expensive, and then turning up and finding it was only a cut glass ashtray worth 50p or something."

"No, dear, it looks quite genuine to me. Shall we go?"

"But - a coach tour! They're terribly common, aren't they? I mean, it's not like driving down to the Dordogne and staying in a Gîte. We'd be sitting on a bus for hours with heaven knows who, eating awful food and staying in second-rate hotels that serve lager to fat oiks singing The Birdie Song!"

"No, darling, it doesn't look a bit like that. There's a letter enclosed… Visit some of France's finest wine-producing areas and learn all about the best vintages. Sample excellent food and drink in our specially-selected hotels and restaurants. This is an exclusive tour and the group will not number more than 25. It sounds quite an upmarket affair. It should be good. The Price-Worthingtons went away with Abercrombie and Kent a couple of years ago. This is the same sort of thing."

"Here! Let me have a look!" Miranda took the sheets of paper from her husband. She was still an extremely attractive woman. She glanced through the itinerary and exclaimed:

"But, Hugh! We MUST go! It visits the Loire Valley, Cognac and Burgundy - three of the really top wine areas! And Paris as well! It's years since I went to Paris!"

"So do you really think we ought to go? It leaves on Sunday. That doesn't give us much time. And what do we do - about Abigail?" His daughter had abandoned her cornflakes again and was playing in the hall.

"Abbey can stay with Mummy. You know she's been screaming at me to let her have her. We can drive her down in the middle of the week. She'll be ever so happy there, with the ponies. And her little cousins can come and visit, so she'll have someone to play with."

"You're right there, of course!" Hugh was suddenly looking forward to the prospect of spending a week in France. And they had now changed the Customs Allowances so you could bring back almost as much wine as you liked. He would ask the expert guide who accompanied the tour which would be the best vintages to lay down for a few years. As for the farm, he knew he had no worries there. Jim Cooper was the best farm manager any landowner could wish for - what did he pay him for, in any case?

Abigail ran back into the room, brandishing a half-eaten piece of toast. There was marmalade smeared around the sides of her mouth. Her father playfully grabbed her by the pony-tails as she came to a halt before her mother.

"Abbey, darling! Mummy and I are going to go away for a little holiday. How would you like to go to stay with Granny for a week or two?"

"Wow! Can I?"

"Of course, love!" Miranda bent down towards her daughter and wiped her face with a napkin, and then kissed her on the cheek.

"And can I ride on the ponies?"

"Of course, love. Now run along and play!" She salvaged the fragment of toast from Abigail's fist and deposited it on a plate. Miranda refilled her cup with coffee and raised it to her lips. She closed her eyes and imagined herself on the terrace of a luxurious hotel, with a huge open-air swimming pool surrounded by marble statuary. A warm Mediterranean sun bathed the pool in light. Beyond the pool, vineyards stretched as far as the eye could see, golden brown with ripening fruit and dotted with a few cypress trees. Cicadas were singing. Her train of thought moved on to Paris, where she and Hugh were enjoying a gourmet dinner in a luxury restaurant, washed down with fine wine, while romantic music floated from an accordion somewhere in the distance.

****

Ian Bailey-Filmer was stacking shelves at the large academic bookshop in Oxford where he worked. The letter he had just received from Orbit Tours was in his jacket pocket. He hadn't asked his boss yet about having time off, but he supposed it would be alright. They were never that busy during the long university vacation.

After all, it wasn't that he had that much to look forward to at the moment. He had been born at just the wrong time. When he had realised he was gay, the word had still meant 'cheerful' and 'happy' to most people; to his horrified contemporaries and family he had been a 'raving poofter' and a 'queer'. Had he been born twenty years later, he could have flaunted his homosexuality openly and no-one would have cared: it was now quite fashionable to be gay; scarcely a day went by without some successful film star, novelist or pop singer declaring that they were. Had he been born twenty years earlier, whilst he might still have suffered the stigma of being different from the majority, he could possibly have kept it hidden more easily. He briefly imagined himself as Head of House beating the bare bottoms of trembling thirteen-year-olds. But Chestfield, despite its compulsory P.T., endless rules and military regime, had been in one way a very progressive public school; corporal punishment, with the sole exception of Cicero, had been abolished by a liberal headmaster in the 1960s. At least he *had* enjoyed the power of being able to call on young boys to serve him endless cups of coffee.

He thought back to the events which had led to his own downfall. As a lecturer in Cambridge, he had been flattered by the attentions paid to him by a certain innocent first-year undergraduate, who had been in the habit of knocking on the door of his rooms night after night and then chatting with him for hours over coffee. It was just unfortunate that he had mistaken an interest in his intellectual gifts by an anxious young student determined to learn the most about his subject, for an interest in his physical body. He had got so far as putting his hand on his visitor's knee and stroking his thigh, without apparent trouble. But when, after one particularly long evening discussing the Dark Ages in Provence, he had asked the boy to come to bed with him, that had been it. "You're nothing but a bloody poofter!" he could remember the child screaming, as he had wrenched open the door and torn away up the corridor. The following day it had been too late to do anything about it: the only consequences were disgrace and his resignation.

Bailey-Filmer remembered the good times he had enjoyed during his Cambridge days. The archaeological digs he had led in France, where he had located no less than five previously unknown sites which had shown continuous occupation from the fourth to the ninth centuries. He thought of Marvin, the lean, bronzed American youth, who had shared his life until his car had suddenly and tragically spun out of control on one of those spiralling clifftop roads in the Côte D'Azur… And here at least was a chance to get back to France, to be with people who didn't know about his sordid past, and to enjoy relative luxury for a week. He'd be an idiot not to take it. He got down from the ladder and went off in search of the manager.

****

The unpredictable German rain was beating down on the windows of the concrete RAF barracks building in the Black Forest. Squadron-Leader Bridger strode through the door, glancing back over his shoulder at the trim Harrier on the runway. He was proud of the little air base near Lahr. Here he was respected, he was looked up to. He had been serving his country for the last fifteen years, but he hadn't had any real work to do. Thank God that he hadn't.

And now it was all coming to an end. The Berlin Wall had come tumbling down. The Cold War was over. At the end of the week he was due to return on indefinite leave to the U.K. and some inevitable desk job. He would have to tell Angelika, of course, the beautiful, empty-headed Bavarian who had shared his bed for the last five years. She would talk again about marriage, about coming over to England with him, about starting a family. But John Bridger knew it was all over. It was time to make a break.

He walked purposefully over to his desk and examined his mail. A couple of circulars, a letter from his sister, and what was this? He slit open the long brown envelope and examined the contents. A holiday brochure - someone was always trying to sell him something he didn't want. Something fell out. He read the accompanying letter. A FREE holiday? And starting on Sunday? It seemed a pleasant way of spending the first part of his leave. If he caught the overnight sleeper from Karlsruhe to Paris he could pick up a connection to Calais and join the tour there. It would make more sense than flying back to London, staying one night, and then going out again. He dialled the number for Orbit Tours and left a message on the answering machine. He spoke slowly and clearly, stating his desire to join in Calais and leaving his personal fax number. When there was so little time to go before the start of the tour, speed was a matter of priority, and Squadron-Leader Bridger had been trained to make quick decisions and to get it right first time.

He thought once again about Angelika's soft thighs and full red lips. Here he had made a decision too, and a final one.

****

"But you'd PROMISED to come with me to Mummy's at the weekend!" wailed Lucinda at the foot of the loft-ladder. From upstairs a vague grunt of acknowledgement could be heard.

"Alright then, I'm coming up!" Lucinda made her way up the aluminium ladder, taking care not to soil her dress. She hardly ever went into the attic, but drastic action was needed in drastic cases.

Mike Turner sat on a swivel chair at the centre of an enormous model railway layout which ran around virtually the entire loft at waist level. The layout represented a section of the Great Western main line near Dawlish Warren, with a fictional branch-line running to an inland terminus. The model was complete to the smallest detail: sunbathers on the beach at Dawlish, vintage cars on the road, tiny trees, quaint Devon cottages and little red telephone boxes. A main-line passenger train with a sleek dark green engine hauling chocolate and cream carriages was moving along the main line, whilst a goods train of miniature cattle trucks stood in the branch terminus awaiting a locomotive. The model was not only painstakingly accurate: it was also ingenious, as the baseboards were hinged in various places to allow removal for display at exhibitions.

"Why - hallo dear!" Mike turned to his wife. She didn't usually come up to the loft as she didn't share his enthusiasm for model railways, and it was a little early for her to be telling him lunch was ready. Perhaps she'd just made him a coffee.

"Don't Hallo Dear me! You know perfectly well we were going down to Mummy's on Saturday. It is her seventieth birthday, after all. All her side of the family will be there."

Mike reflected with horror: the thought of meeting ALL Lucinda's mother's family was almost too awful to contemplate.

"And NOW," continued Lucinda, "I find this man on the phone asking for you and talking about a model railway exhibition".

"But, dear, you must realise I've taken a week off work to prepare the exhibit. It's the big one - the North London Railway Modellers' Association. I've got to be there in the Town Hall all day Friday, Saturday and Sunday. You go to your Mother's without me".

"It's always the same with you, isn't it?" shrieked Lucinda. "Every evening, you get back from the office, bolt down your dinner, and rush up to the attic to play with your bloody train set! Every Saturday, every Sunday, up in the loft playing trains. When did you last lend a hand with the housework? When did you last do anything in the garden? We never even have a holiday together; you're always off on some Steam Special with a load of old buffers! And when was the last time we had sex?"

Mike Turner did not reply. He couldn't remember, except that it had probably occurred sometime since the electrification of the Hastings line and before the withdrawal of the Class 50's.

"What sort of marriage do we have? What other wife waits alone in bed every night while her husband fondles a bloody Black Five?"

"I never fondle Black Fives! The Black Fives were L.M.S. locomotives. You know I only model Great Western ..."

"I've put up with this for too long. You'll just have to choose between your blessed train set and me!"

"I - er."

"It's beautiful, isn't it? If only the care that went into this could have gone into our marriage!" Lucinda had lifted up his plasticard model of Dawlish North signal box, which had taken him weeks to make, and was admiring it. Suddenly, to his horror, she was crushing it between her hands.

"Darling, stop! This is madness!"

"And as for this, is this Henry the Green Engine?" Horror turned to dismay as he realised she was holding *County of Merioneth*, a scratchbuilt model of a 4-6-0 which he'd spent months over.

"Don't!" shouted Mike Turner, somehow frozen with shock in his swivel chair as Lucinda dashed the engine to the floor and stamped on it with her high-heel shoes.

"I said you would have to choose between this bloody railway and me!" she stormed. Now fury had turned to a raging hurricane, as she swept along the nearest side of the model, uprooting the tiny trees, scattering cars and pedestrians and throwing locomotives and carriages to the floor.

By now Mike had at last managed to come over to his wife and grab her to prevent any more destruction.

"We've got to talk this over, dear. Perhaps I have been unreasonable in the past..."

"No. It's too late for talking now," replied Lucinda. "I'm calling a taxi. I'm going straight to Mummy's. Don't bother to phone. You will be hearing shortly from my solicitor".

And with that she stormed down the loft ladder. Mike heard from downstairs the sound of drawers being opened as she did some hurried packing. He meanwhile surveyed the wreckage of his layout and of his beloved *County of Merioneth*.

Some time later he heard the front door slam. He made his way downstairs in time to see the taxi disappear from sight at the end of the Close.

On the table by the phone he noticed a letter. Lucinda must have put it there when the postman delivered it. He opened it and saw a holiday brochure. Looking more closely, he saw a magnificent photograph of a steam locomotive crossing a magnificent curved viaduct in majestic scenery. He remembered the 141-R's. When he'd been on a day trip to Calais from Prep School he'd seen them shunting at the docks. But he'd never had the chance to travel on one. Now, as he read the letter which had enclosed the brochure, he was invited to come on a free coach holiday to France which would include a unique trip on a steam train hauled by a 141-R locomotive between Mansle-la-Jolie and Vierzon.

The tour started on Sunday. He stared again at the photograph of the Mikado. He could almost hear the roar of the iron monster as the steam flowed through its veins. It was telling him to travel on it. He would never be able to make good the damage to his layout in time for the exhibition in any case, and if he was going to have to get used to doing his own washing and cooking his own food again, then a week away from home would at least cut down on the housework.

****

"And can you tell me the model and year of manufacture of the vehicle, madam?" Nick Patterson entered the details on his VDU, thanked the client, and pushed the button on his headset. He was now free to take another call. Working in the Tele-Sales department of a major insurance company was not his real career, he knew that. He was still going to be a successful artist, some day. He had resisted any chances of promotion to enable himself to keep as much time as possible free for painting. He would leave work at five on the dot and head home to his studio, or, if he needed time off to attend an exhibition, he would work overtime for a couple of weeks and then take the extra hours off in lieu. He was glad his company had a flexible working time policy.

Nick Patterson's main problem was that he had never quite decided what sort of painter he wanted to be. At Chestfield he had made quite a name for himself with his big, bold abstracts, which had contrasted quite vividly with William Simpson's neat little sketches of Chestfield parish church at the school Art Exhibitions on Speech Day. As a student he had visited Florence, and afterwards dreamed of becoming a great painter in the Classical tradition. Later he had tried to set himself up as a portrait painter, but found that the East Anglian public of the 1980s did not seem to require a new Gainsborough or Reynolds. At present he was experimenting with pop-art and collage in an Andy Warhol-esque manner.

There were no more callers coming through for the moment. He took the letter out of his pocket and read through it again. Yes, he really had been offered, no catches, a free week's holiday in France, a tour, so the letter told him, taking in the landscapes which inspired so many great painters and with 'ample opportunity to visit museums and galleries in your spare time.' He thought of Van Gogh and Gauguin in Provence, of Matisse and Picasso on the Côte d'Azur, of Cézanne's landscapes and Monet's water-lilies. From this heritage would come his next inspiration. Checking that his supervisor was nowhere to be seen, he dialled 9 for an outside line and then called North Malling 227315.

****

"But OF COURSE you must go!" Phyllis Eveleigh poured her brother a second cup of tea from the delicate bone-china teapot. He had been talking about France ever since the brochure had come through the post that morning. Of course, schoolteachers did receive special offers like this from time to time, but a free week's holiday in France was something which had never happened before.

"But I couldn't possibly go without you!" Bryan Arthur Eveleigh and his sister had spent their holidays together in a little guest house in Budleigh Salterton for almost as far back as he could remember.

"You know how I detest foreign food. And how would I manage getting on and off the coach all the time with my hip? No, Bryan, you must go on your own. You might even meet some interesting people!"

Phyllis was right. The letter accompanying the brochure had spoken of small numbers, luxury hotels and first-class food and wines. It was an opportunity too good to be missed. And he would be able to speak French again, the way it should be spoken, not the way IIIC spoke it. He had accompanied the occasional day-trip to Calais with the third form, and once had gone to Chamonix with the Lower VI on a ski-ing trip, but those places were both too full of foreign visitors to be really French. Now here was a trip which would take him right to the French heartlands - the Loire Valley, the Charente, Burgundy and Paris.

"If you're sure you'll be alright, then I'll go."

"I'll be alright." Phyllis Eveleigh was secretly quite looking forward to not having her brother under her feet for a whole week. She would be able to get on with her housework and listen to *Women's Hour* and *The Archers* uninterrupted. And it would also give her the chance to spring-clean his bedroom properly, something she had been longing to do for years.

And, thought Phyllis, the best thing about it was that it had also given Bryan something to look forward to. He always went into a kind of sullen depression at the start of the long summer holidays, moping about and trying to do the *Daily Telegraph* crossword. Now he would be dancing around the house singing *Auprès de ma Blonde* for the next few days. With a bit of luck she would probably even persuade him to take her out to dinner that evening.

****

Steve Vicks was eating his takeaway lunchtime pizza in the Portakabin which served as main office of Vicks Sound Systems Ltd. All around him were the carcasses of cassette decks, tuners and amplifiers awaiting repair or cannibalisation for spare parts. He had started his business as a small repair shop, but his skill had soon won him large contracts, and in the mid-1980s he had been custom-building and supplying sound equipment to several major

TV and film companies. Then had come the recession. He had turned to drink, his wife had left him, and the company had all but disintegrated. Now things were on the upturn at last; he had just been asked to design a new audio system for a West End theatre, and the repair shop was doing well, as members of the public were tending to hang on to their hi-fi equipment longer and were therefore more likely to need to bring it in for repair.

Heavy rock music was blasting from an enormous ghetto-blaster on his desk. Steve Vicks pulled out from his anorak pocket the folded envelope which he had picked up from his doormat as he had left for the office. Tearing it open, the words FREE OFFER leapt to his eyes. He read through the brochure and its accompanying letter carefully. A week away would do him no harm. He had old Albert working in the shop, he was always handy with a soldering iron. And there was Andy, the YT trainee. Steve liked Andy: they were into the same kind of music, and with his blue hair, nose ring and Doc Marten boots Andy was just the sort of rebel he had not been allowed to be at Chestfield.

"Andy!" Steve shouted above the roar of the music.

"Yeah?"

"Andy, would you and Albert mind looking after the shop for a week or so?"

"Uh - yeah".

Steve returned to his last slice of pizza. He looked at the photographs of France. True, their pop music was awful, but the French had style. He thought of the slim, long-legged French girls he would meet at the discos, and of the cheap booze and sex. The letter with the brochure made it plain that the tour was designed for the young and lively, and that there would be plenty of nightlife. He would have to bring his ghetto-blaster to play on the coach. As he savoured the last of the pizza he considered which cassettes he would bring.

****

"M-A-R-I-O!" Mrs Rottoli's voice rang out through the corridor which ran above the restaurant, "Are you still in bed?"

Mario pulled open his bedroom door to let his mother in. At his age, it was humiliating the way she could still order him about.

"Letter for you!" she said, as she dropped it on the bed in front of him. "And you were late last night. It was Tracey again, wasn't it? You think I don't have enough trouble getting waitresses for this place without you getting them into trouble!"

"I was very careful. You know me, Mama - always careful."

"And what about Maureen, then?" Maureen had been a delightful sixteen-year old Irish girl who had come to Colchester for a job and returned home seven months gone.

"I offered to pay for the abortion, didn't I?"

"Mario, if your Papa could hear you talk like this!" Sometimes Doreen Rottoli, née Carter, wondered what she and her husband had created, this lazy good-for-nothing son who had hardly done a day's honest work in his life. Mario was far more Italian than she ever would be, and when he'd been staying with his little cousins in Naples as a boy he'd soon become just like them, the streetwise kids who stayed out late, grew up early and yet remained profoundly attached to their family.

Mario had by now opened the envelope and was looking at its contents without too much enthusiasm.

"What's that you've got there, Mario?"

"Some brochure from a tour company. They say I've won a week's holiday to France."

"To France? But that is splendid! When does it start?"

"Next Sunday. But I can't go."

"Why not, Mario? Of course you can go."

"But Mama, you and Papa... the restaurant..."

"Now, Mario, you know we can manage perfectly well without you for a week. You go on the trip. I know why you want to stay here. It's Tracey, isn't it? Well, you go off to France and meet some nice girls there, and meanwhile I'll send Tracey back to her parents in Lancashire where she belongs. You understand?"

"I understand." Mama had an uncanny way of always being right.

Reading through the brochure again, Mario decided he might be onto quite a good thing after all. He would probably meet some decent bits of skirt either on the coach or once he got over there. When he got up he would send the quick-reply coupon back to Orbit Tours.

****

"Luxury stereo car radio-cassettes! Luxury stereo car radio-cassettes! What do you think I'm asking for these? £50? £40? £30? No! Just £20! Yes, £20! All brand new and guaranteed. Auto-reverse and everything..." Jonathan Atkinson continued his familiar patter in the market. Since leaving University in 1982, his career moves had been down, down, down.

Not that he had been a brilliant success at University. Sent down for dealing in cannabis in industrial quantities, with other students, in his third year, he had subsequently spent several months wandering around Europe, in and out of work, before returning like the prodigal son to Hitchin and joining the family firm. At first things had gone well: he had helped Yuppies fill their flats and weekend retreats with designer furniture, and he had even driven a second-hand Porsche with a private number-plate. Then had come the recession, coupled with the growth of the big out-of-town discount stores, and, after 125 years, Atkinson Furnishings Ltd. had ceased trading. The Porsche and the Yuppies had gone. From then on, one venture after another had collapsed, and now Jonathan Atkinson was selling South Korean car radios of doubtful provenance and dubious quality on an outdoor market stall in East London.

Bruiser Baxter was selling satellite TV receivers at the other end of the stall. He worked part-time as a night-club bouncer, and was an ex-boxer with a large broken nose. Atkinson helped him shift some of the gear at the street markets, much of it originating from ram-raids on premises in other parts of London.

Atkinson turned his head to look at the van. It was a nondescript old red Ford Transit, and at this moment two policemen were engaged in making a close examination of the windscreen.

"Pigs! Christ - I forgot to renew the bloody tax disc! Baxter will kill me!"

Atkinson abandoned the car radios and crawled under the stall. Baxter was still doing his mock-auction act with the crowd. Trying to look like a customer rather than a stallholder, Atkinson stared in horror as he saw the police walk around to the back of the Transit and peep inside with the help of a flashlight. From where he was standing he could even hear one of them speaking into a walkie-talkie radio:

"Golf Alpha One to Tango Two-One-Four, Golf Alpha One to Tango Two-One-Four. Tango Two-One-Four, do you read me?"

Whether Tango Two-One-Four could read him or not, Atkinson did not wait to find out. Diving behind a stall selling ladies' underwear, he nipped under the perimeter fence of the market and out into the street. Across the road a bus was just pulling up at its stop. He ran across and leapt onto the platform, continuing upstairs where he collapsed with relief on an empty seat.

He'd got away. But they'd probably get Baxter. In any case, the van would be traced back to him soon enough. He couldn't risk going back to the flat in the Old Kent Road. He'd have to lie low somewhere until it all blew over.

Lie low somewhere? He pulled out of the pocket of his jeans the crumpled brown envelope which he'd been carrying around for three days. ENJOY A FREE TRIP TO FRANCE, the letter had said. He'd assumed that it was just a shabby con-trick, an attempt to get him to buy a time-share or double-glazing or something else he didn't want.

He took out the letter and re-read it. What if it were genuine? A coach tour would be the perfect way to disappear for a few days. He'd been over to Calais with his mates from the boozer just before Christmas to stock up on wine and beer, and he'd been amazed at how the whole coachload had just been waved straight through Customs, both on the way there and back.

Yes, that was it! He'd have to give these Orbit people a ring. As for the next couple of nights, he would stay with his girlfriend, Shirley, at her place in Shepherd's Bush. It would be handy there for the West London coach station, and he had a feeling he'd left his passport there too. Shirley wouldn't squeal, and she didn't have much idea of his business activities in any case. By the time he got back from France it would all have blown over.

Chapter Five

London Town

ON Thursday William drove to the Head Office of the Mid-Kent Reporter in Tonbridge. He collected six replies to Orbit Tours accepting the free offer of a holiday in France, from the Bartlett-Nicholsons, Mr Eveleigh, Mike Turner, Steve Vicks, Ian Bailey-Filmer and Mario Rottoli. He had already received two telephone messages, from Nick Patterson and John Bridger. Only Jonathan Atkinson remained unaccounted for.

Nine out of ten was pretty good going, anyway, thought William as he drove back home in his old Mini. In addition to the 'Orbit' letters, he had also received two 'bona fide' offers for the car, one from a dealer offering him little more than the scrap value, and an equally derisory one from a seventeen-year old who wanted to use it for banger racing.

William was back home, with Pepper on his lap, when the phone rang.

"Hello!" William was careful not to give his name or number.

"Hello. Is that Orbit Tours?" The voice sounded anxious, almost desperate. There was a lot of background noise on the line, as if the call was being made from a payphone, perhaps in a house split into several bedsits.

"Yes."

"You sent me a letter saying I've won a free trip to France. Sorry I've been so late getting back to you, but it was forwarded on from my old address in Hitchin. What I want to know is, is the offer still on?"

"Yes, sir. You are referring, of course, to the 'Scenic Delights of France' departing on Sunday?" William kept it as formal as possible.

"Yeah, that's the one. Well, I want to go. Is everything O.K.?"

"Yes, everything is quite in order. Can I have your name please, sir?"

"Atkinson. J.P. Atkinson. You're quite sure the trip's still on?" Jonathan Atkinson was worried. William could picture him looking around all the time to make sure no-one was overhearing him on that public phone. It didn't sound like the school bully of sixteen years ago.

"Yes, Mr Atkinson, your booking on the tour is confirmed. Please report at the West London coach station at 7 a.m. on Sunday. Do you know where that is, the West London coach station?"

"Yeah, I know. But can you tell me something about this tour?"

"Certainly. What is it you want to know?"

"At Dover, when we go through to catch the ferry. Do we have to go through passport control or anything?"

"Are you an E.C. passport holder?"

"Ur - British, yeah."

"Then you've nothing to worry about. You will just stay on the coach while it drives through Passport Control."

"And on the way back, is it the same?"

"Yes, normally - if you've got a British passport."

"Good!" Atkinson seemed relieved. "I'll be there on Sunday, then" he said. After he had rung off, William wondered exactly what was the matter with him. United Kingdom passport holders didn't usually have problems with Passport Control, and he couldn't remember Atkinson having had a foreign mother or father or anything which might have given him a strange passport. Perhaps, like some people, he was just scared of certain officials even when he hadn't done anything wrong. If so, it was funny how he, William, the little boy who had always been picked on, had become so full of self-confidence, while Atkinson, the bully, had turned into a wimp.

William afterwards printed out a neat list of his ten travellers and drove back to Tonbridge, where he called at a small stationery and office equipment shop that he used frequently. Here he faxed the list to Orbit, thinking as he sent it that in all probability it would be Helena who would retrieve the fax from the machine and take it to Mr Papadopoulos. He felt a strange desire to see her again. He also sent a fax to John Bridger in Germany, giving him precise instructions on where to join the tour in Calais.

****

Saturday afternoon saw William once more on the platform of North Malling station. He had just had an excellent lunch with his parents, which reminded him of the lovely meals his mother had always made him just before he was about to go back to Chestfield. He had said goodbye to Pepper and walked to the station, with his briefcase, Orbit shoulder bag and bulging suitcase. His suitcase seemed to be bulging even more than usually, but then he was taking more bits and pieces with him for Tour F443/07 than he did for a normal coach tour.

One hour and twenty minutes later, William stowed his suitcase and shoulder bag under the counter of the travel agents' and pushed open the door that led to the staircase. As with many tour operators, Orbit's offices did not shut down on Saturday, and a kernel of staff kept at work during the operations period.

William could see Margot at her desk. Sitting opposite her was Danny Bourget, sorting out his receipts. Further up the office, Helena's chair was empty. William sat down in the empty chair next to Danny.

"Good afternoon, William. You'll just wait until I've finished with Danny, won't you?" Margot looked as smart and efficient as usual.

"Yes, of course," replied William. He turned to Danny: "And how did your mid-week special go?"

"Great! Another few hundred quid in the bank! And, boy, you should have seen the crumpet on that tour. There were these two Canadian birds, mother and daughter, and when we got back from the 'Grenouille' I had both of them in bed with me at the same time. The mother, she must have been about thirty-seven, and the daughter, about nineteen. What a pair of ..."

"That'll do, Danny!" Margot sounded stern but not shocked. She had heard the tales of Danny Bourget's conquests many times before, and, like William, she was not inclined to believe them.

"But I thought your group was just Canadian businessmen" said William.

"Businessmen *and* women. And some of them had brought their families with them. Here, Margot, have you finished with my expense sheet yet? I want to be getting back home to Wandsworth".

"I won't be a minute." Margot was scrutinising the duplicated expenses sheet.

"And have you been doing anything exciting this last week, then, Will?" asked Danny.

"Well - yes. Last Saturday I went to the Weald Bus Rally at Tenterden."

Both Danny and Margot looked at William.

"You didn't go with H.R., did you? The ice-cold virgin of Bloomsbury? She came up to me with these tickets when I was in the office and asked me if I wanted to go. I said I wasn't going to drive all the way down to Kent for a ride on a bloody bus!"

"It was quite interesting, actually." said William.

"She's a strange girl, our Helena, isn't she?" said Margot.

"I suppose so."

"Have you ever been to her flat?"

"No," said William, not liking to say that he would be going there very shortly.

"I doubt if any man ever has been allowed in there!" added Danny.

"Probably not even to read the meter."

"I went there once last year," said Margot. "Helena went down with the 'flu and I had to go over and collect some files she'd been working on at home. You should see the place - it's ghastly! All full of photos of seventies pop stars, you know, like the Osmonds and the New Seekers!"

"Where is Helena now?" William asked.

"Oh, she had to go over to the Coach Station with a new supply of coach signs for tomorrow. I expect she'll be back soon."

William hoped she would, but he didn't really want to talk to her with both Danny and Margot there.

After ten or fifteen minutes Danny was off to his flat in Wandsworth. "See you at the 'Grenouille' on Saturday!" he yelled to William as he left. Danny would be taking out another Paris trip, and would be visiting the night club on the same night. They would not, however, be using the same hotel: Danny's *Paris A La Carte* weekends stayed in a three-star hotel in the centre of Paris; 'Scenic Delights of France' used the two-star Hotel Royale on the outskirts of the city.

"Right, William!" Margot said. "I've got your papers ready. You've got twenty-four passengers. Here's your Rooming List."

William took the Rooming List. There was nothing on it to identify the Chestfield passengers; he suspected that Mr Papadopoulos had kept to himself the knowledge that William would be bringing some friends on the trip: at any rate, Margot didn't seem to know anything about it.

When William had started working for Orbit, the Rooming Lists had been straightforward sheets of A4 paper, typed out, photocopied, and then sent to the hotels. Then, a few years ago, a new computer system had been installed, and theoretically it now became possible to produce a Rooming List at the touch of a button. Unfortunately, what the computer actually produced was a smudged and illegible document on green and white stripy paper about six feet long and impossible to photocopy. Because the computer printer would advance the paper automatically at the end of every sheet, husbands and wives would sometimes get 'separated' on the list and occasionally would even be allocated separate rooms by hotels. Worst still, passengers who had any kind of special request which made their holiday slightly different from the usual - a request for vegetarian food, or an overnight in London before or after the tour, often got ignored altogether by the computer and excluded from the Rooming List. Faced with riots from angry passengers, Tour Managers, and hotels not quite sure what sort of accommodation to allocate to their guests, Orbit had abandoned the computerised rooming lists, and now once again the lists were neatly typed by Margot, H.R. or another competent typist on ordinary A4 paper using a conventional electric typewriter.

"Ferry tickets" said Margot.

William put the tickets carefully in his briefcase. They looked like long, thin credit cards, with a magnetic strip down one side.

"You've got a coach from Cars Châtillon. The driver will be Claude Chasseur."

This was very good news. One of the most important aspects of a successful tour was being able to get on with the driver, and Claude was someone with whom William had worked on many occasions. He also knew that he would be able to count on his help with his little scheme.

"Here's your float. Two thousand French francs and two hundred pounds in Traveller's Cheques."

William signed for his float, and then signed each of the cheques once in Margot's presence. The float was meant to cover all his expenses whilst on tour, including his own meals, telephone calls, road tolls, and any entrance charges to places of interest visited on the itinerary.

"Here's the rest of your paperwork." William was very familiar with the various sheets of paper which he required, some of which he had to complete for every tour, and some of which he hoped he never would have to complete. There was a daily log, a form to fill in with the coach details, a wad of vouchers to give to the hotels, some excursion sales tickets, spare luggage labels and a variety of forms including the 'Lost/Damaged Luggage Report' and the 'Details of a Passenger detached from a tour through Accident/Illness/Death' report.

"Have you got one of those forms I have to fill in if there is a change of coach?" asked William.

"I hope you won't be needing one of those."

"No, but better be safe than sorry!" Margot found the form and handed it to William. William also helped himself to a few more of the 'Details of a Passenger Detached ...' reports than he would have for any other tour.

"Well, I think you're ready. Don't forget! Tomorrow morning at 6 o'clock at the West London Coach Station. Are you spending the night in London?" she asked.

"Yes," said William, not wishing to say where he would be spending the night.

At that moment the door from the stairs swung open and H.R. drifted in. Her blonde hair was slightly out of place and the baggy trousers and large floppy sweater were the same as normal. She smiled at William behind her enormous glasses.

"Hi! Sorry I've been away. I had to deliver some coach signs to the coach station, and you know how awkward it is to reach that place by public transport!"

William knew only too well. "That's alright. Margot told me. She's just finished briefing me."

"Oh, good. I've just got some filing to do. I should be finished in an hour or so."

"That's okay. Do you mind if I make one or two phone calls?"

"Not at all. Go ahead!"

"I'm off for the weekend!" said Margot, taking her jacket from the back of her chair. "Have fun, you two!"

"Bye, Margot!" said William. Did Margot really suspect that there was something going on between himself and Helena?

William moved around to the other side of Margot's desk and reached for the phone. His first call was to the Hotel de France where he would be staying tomorrow night. It was a matter of precaution to call each hotel before you got there, to make sure they had the right room allocation and to be aware of any potential problems. There were none on this occasion. At the Hotel de France everything was in order.

Next William called his old friend Jacques Mercier. Yes, everything was okay for tomorrow. M. Mercier thought it seemed rather odd that William should want to play a trick on an old friend, but, then, he'd heard of kiss-o-grams and the like and didn't suppose it was all that different. And he'd watched Jeremy Beadle on television when he'd been on holiday in Yorkshire: he knew the English had a rather zany sense of humour.

William's third call was to Henri Rigaud at the Chemin de Fer de la Charente. He had an old friend who would love to come for a ride on the steam train on Thursday. Could he bring him along? Well, it was highly irregular, said Henri; the train was just an empty stock movement and wasn't supposed to be carrying passengers, but, yes, as it was a friend of William's, he was sure there would be no problem in him riding on the train for a few kilometres.

"Are you ready?" Helena asked William.

"Yes. Where are we going?"

"Why don't we go out for a drink first? You can leave your bags here if you like. Then you can collect them before we go to my flat. I've got a key."

That sounded a good idea. William locked all his papers in the briefcase and left it under the counter of the now-closed travel agents' as they left Orbit House and walked into Charing Cross Road.

"Where are we going?" he asked, as they walked down towards Leicester Square.

"Just come with me." Helena led him across St Martin's Lane, along New Row and King Street and into Covent Garden Market.

"Oh, there are quite a few nice places around here," said William.

"I always like going to the Museum."

"Museum?"

"The London Transport Museum." They were now standing in front of it. "It costs a bit to get in, but it's worth it, and it's really such fun!"

William went into so many museums free of charge as a Tour Manager in Europe that he rather resented having to fork out good money to get into one. Nevertheless, he paid the admission charge and followed Helena through the turnstile, which resembled the entrance to a London Underground station.

"Here we are!" shouted Helena. "This is the Museum's RT. It's a little different from the one we travelled on last weekend: they're not from the same batch."

William examined the RT, and went on to inspect a "B" type, a "Q" type single decker, a "T" type motor coach and various trams, tube trains and trolleybuses.

"What about that drink, then?" he asked her at last.

"Right. We'll go to the coffee shop!"

Over their pot of tea, they chatted about the previous weekend. Helena took off her glasses and put them on the table, and untied her hair to let it hang loose. Now she looked more like the adolescent from the Weald Bus Rally. But here, in London, on her home territory, she seemed altogether more sophisticated. William hadn't realised quite how much he had been thinking of Helena over the past seven days.

Helena mentioned that she had been to visit her parents last Sunday.

"I still live with my parents, well, in a sense." William told Helena about his unusual accommodation arrangements.

"That sounds very nice. I wouldn't mind something like that with my parents, but I wouldn't want to commute every day from Upper Nazeing."

"Do you have any brothers or sisters?" William asked. As soon as he saw the expression on her face he wished he hadn't asked her.

"I had a sister, ten years older than me. She was called Claire. She died of a drug overdose during her final year at university."

"Oh - I am so sorry," said William. "Was it su - I mean, did she want to kill herself?"

"No, I don't think so. I think she was just larking about with a lot of other students after the end of finals and she didn't realise what she was doing. She was a brilliant girl - she had a lot to look forward to."

So there was one of the events which must have helped shape the character of the enigmatic H.R. To lose an elder sister when you are about twelve must be an unimaginable catastrophe. Not that William could really imagine what it was like to have a sister…

"And you, do you have any brothers or sisters?"

"No, I'm an only child." William finished his tea.

"Shall we go?" asked Helena.

"Yes." William and Helena left the museum, paused briefly in the piazza to admire a juggler, and then walked back to Orbit House. The last of the Saturday staff had now left. Helena unlocked the door of the ground-floor travel agency. William picked up his suitcase, briefcase and shoulder bag and struggled out to the pavement.

"My! You carry a lot of luggage, don't you?"

"I have to in this job," said William. "How far is it to your flat?"

"Oh, not very far. About ten minutes walk if you're not carrying any luggage."

"We'll get a taxi."

"Oh, no, we won't. There's a direct bus service. Come on, the stop's only just down the road."

They walked down to the stop. A bus was just approaching.

"Shall we get that one?" asked William.

"No. Let's not. It would take us there, but it's a modern bus. I prefer going on the old Routemasters."

They let the modern double-decker pass. A few minutes later the familiar shape of a traditional open-platform bus pulled up at the stop. Helena helped William stow his luggage as the Routemaster headed up Charing Cross Road.

"This is the best way to travel!" said Helena.

The bus reached their stop before the conductor had even had time to come around to William and take his fare. As they got down from the bus, William was inclined to agree with Helena about the advantages of Routemasters.

"Here we are," announced Helena, "Home Sweet Home!"

She led William across the road to the small side-street and took him to the Victorian terraced house. She unlocked the front door and William found himself in a dilapidated entrance hall, with letter-boxes for the various residents affixed to one wall, and an antiquated lift in a wire cage.

"Does that thing work?" William asked doubtfully.

"Yes, of course. I don't use it much myself, but it's useful if you've got any luggage."

They closed the open ironwork door behind them and pushed the button for the third floor. With a fearful grating of metal on metal, the lift slowly ascended.

"It reminds me of the one they've got in the Hotel du Duc de Guise in Blois," said William.

They reached the third floor with a bump, and Helena opened the door to her flat. William put down his suitcase just inside the door and followed Helena into what appeared to be the living-room.

"Take a seat," urged Helena. "Can I get you a drink?"

"Do you have anything cold?"

"Coke, mineral water, orange juice…"

"Orange juice would be fine." While Helena went off into the kitchen to get the drinks, William looked around him. The walls of the room had at some stage in the past been painted in an unattractive turquoise gloss colour. Now, where had he seen that colour before? Of course, the old J.C.R. at Chestfield.

Just like the J.C.R. in Wallis House, the walls of Helena's sitting-room were covered with posters, although the subject matter was rather different. Many of them were glossy travel posters of the sort that were sent free of charge to Orbit Tours by foreign tourist offices and the like - there was a superb one showing Cologne Cathedral by night, and a reproduction of the photograph of Mr Papadopoulos blowing the Alpine Horn that he had seen at Orbit Head Office. Another poster had evidently come from the London Transport Museum, and showed London buses of various vintages. But dominating them all was a series of huge posters depicting pop groups from the mid-Seventies. Abba, in their weird and wonderful clothes, stared down from one wall; Donny Osmond and David Cassidy looked across from another towards Sweet and the Bay City Rollers on the wall opposite.

"I like Seventies music." Helena handed William his orange juice and sat down on the settee opposite him. She was drinking a Coke with a straw in the can. She had removed her glasses again and her hair was loose around her shoulders.

"Wow! It's hot!" Helena pulled off her large baggy sweater. Underneath, William noticed, she was wearing a T-shirt showing a double-decker London bus, with the words 'I'VE BEEN ON TOP' emblazoned across it.

William started looking through the collection of LP's beside his chair. They reflected much the same taste of music shown in the posters which adorned the walls. Helena reached across to the rack, withdrew a record and put it on the auto-change of her stereo record player. The pickup arm lowered itself gently onto the record:

'IT'S A TEENAGE DREAM TO BE SEVENTEEN
AND TO FIND YOU'RE ALL WRAPPED UP IN LOVE ...'

"The Rollers' songs have wonderful lyrics, don't they? Not like the sort of music that's around nowadays."

"I suppose you're right," said William. At school he had been teased for preferring such teeny-bop type records to the unintelligible rock which had thump, thump, thumped through Steve Vicks' stereo system day after day, and afterwards he had come to think of Seventies pop as cheap and tawdry. Now, in a world where pop lyrics had ceased to have any meaning, with one short-lived fad succeeding another, the simple optimism of the Bay City Rollers was a refreshing change. But what relevance could these words have for a man in his thirties in the 1990's? 'You've got to Give a Little Love?' What on earth did that mean?

"Where do you want to go for dinner tonight? There's a Chinese around the corner and there's a Tandoori just up Tottenham Court Road. And there's

Pedro's Pizza Parlour - that's the nearest place."

"Let's go there," said William. "I like Italian food".

"We'll go to Pedro's then." Helena felt the evening was going well. William was the first man she had ever invited up to her flat, and she hoped she was being a satisfactory hostess.

"Before we go, please can you show me the ..." William, like many middle-class people, was unsure what familiar word was used for the smallest room in the house where he happened to be a guest.

"Oh, of course - just down the corridor! The light switch is on the right before you go in."

William entered the bathroom with some trepidation. A notice on the door proclaimed 'SEATING CAPACITY: UPPER SALOON 40 PERSONS, LOWER SALOON 32 PERSONS'. After he had finished his business, he noticed on the other side of the door two more signs, saying 'THANK YOU FOR TRAVELLING WITH US' and 'HAVE YOU LEFT ANYTHING?' Below them hung a 1975 calendar with photos of pop idols of the period.

Helena flicked the lever of her auto-change and the Rollers stopped in mid-verse. They left the flat and walked downstairs. As Helena had said, the restaurant was not far away. They took a table for two in a little alcove at the back, away from the street.

"I fancy the Spicy Hot Seafood Special" said William. "How about you?"

"I'll have a Vegetarian one," Helena replied. "With an extra topping of Italian Sausage," she added.

"Shall we share a bottle of House Red?"

"Ooh, good idea." Helena seldom drank any alcohol unless she was at home with her parents for Sunday lunch, or at a bus rally with Don and Maddy.

Soft, romantic music was playing in the background. The pizzas were excellent and the wine was refreshing. Helena was talking about Europe, of the places she wanted to travel to. William thought of a distant Mediterranean shore, with the warmth of a July night in London and the taste of Italian wine on his lips. He thought of the beautiful woman with the deep brown eyes who was sitting opposite him. Could this be the same dull office girl he had known for years, and the same adolescent who had led him by the hand around Tenterden? He thought of Helena's firm round breasts under the T-shirt, and of her thighs under the table. As the wine flowed, so did their conversation.

They finished their coffees and paid. Helena and William returned to the flat.

"Will you be quite alright here on the settee?"

"Yes, I'll be fine. That's one of the advantages of having spent ten years as a Tour Manager - you can go to sleep anywhere!"

"I'll leave you to it, then! See you in the morning."

"Yes. Goodnight!"

"Goodnight!"

Helena closed her bedroom door behind her. William undressed and slipped into the sleeping bag which she had laid out for him on the settee. He hadn't been entirely truthful when he had told Helena he could go to sleep anywhere. The truth was that even after so many years he always had difficulty going to sleep the night before a tour. And before a tour for which he had planned so much, but been unable, for obvious reasons, to discuss with Helena, he knew he would have even more difficulty in going to sleep than usual. The thought of Helena in her bed just a few feet away made matters worse still. He hadn't even kissed her. He had thought about giving her a chaste little goodnight kiss, but hadn't been quite sure how she would have reacted. He wouldn't have wanted to throw away his free night in London either.

In her bed, surrounded by her childhood toys and under her Beatrix Potter duvet cover, Helena too was having difficulty getting to sleep. Did William really like her? Why hadn't he kissed her good-night? And if he had kissed her, how would she have reacted? She thought back over the evening, over their conversation, and reflected on this gentle and pleasant man who was quite unlike any other she had met. Why, he had never even uttered a single swear word! She was even beginning to find him quite attractive, she thought, as she at last drifted off into unconsciousness.

Meanwhile, on the settee, William was at last asleep. He was having the most vivid dream since the one about Chestfield. This time, he was working as a Tour Manager, and was giving his commentary through a microphone, but the passengers behind him were just empty faces, holograms rather than real flesh-and-blood characters. And the coach wasn't an ordinary coach. It was an old-fashioned double-decker bus with one of those cut-away driver's cabs at the front. And the driver? It was a woman with long flowing hair, wearing a T-shirt and jeans. It was H.R.

She was driving fast. William turned to talk to her, but the cab was separated from the rest of the bus by a glass panel. He tried to attract her attention, but her gaze was on the road. William looked ahead. An enormous monster with great snapping teeth was in front of them. The bus ran straight into its jaws. William felt something slimy and wet engulf him as he woke up in a cold sweat.

There *was* something there, thought William, as he reached for the table lamp and turned it on. A huge crumpled face was staring at him: the poster of Donny Osmond had fallen onto his bed during the night.

Chapter Six

It is Better to Travel Hopefully

SUNDAY morning dawned bright and clear. William glanced at his travel alarm clock, on the floor by Helena's settee. Four-fifteen. It was hardly worth trying to grab another half-hour's sleep. He pulled on his dressing-gown and went to the bathroom.

By the time Helena came into the living-room, William was dressed, packed and listening to the news on BBC World Service on his small portable radio.

"Good morning! How did you sleep?"

"Very well, thank you," William lied.

"What would you like for breakfast? Tea or coffee?"

"I'll have a cup of tea, please. I'll be on coffee for the next week - they don't really know how to make tea south of Calais!"

"That's true," said Helena.

She reappeared five minutes later with a mug of tea and two slices of toast and peanut butter.

"Oh, thanks!"

"How are you getting to the coach station?"

"I'll get a taxi. It's too early for the Tube, and I've got a lot to carry."

"Do you want me to come with you?"

"No, it'll be alright." Helena might well have secret bus-spotting reasons to want to visit the West London coach station at 5.30 a.m., but he didn't want her to be around, especially if there were any immediate problems with the Chestfield passengers.

William finished his toast, paid a last visit to the bathroom to brush his teeth and run a comb through his hair, and then allowed Helena to help him down the three flights of stairs with his luggage. On such an important morning he wasn't going to trust that archaic lift!

He opened the door to the street. A taxi passing by on the other side of the road had its sign illuminated. William stepped out and raised his hand. The taxi did a complete turn and stopped outside the house.

"Well, goodbye, then! Best of luck with the tour!"

"Thanks ever so much for the bed and breakfast".

"Any time." William felt Helena meant it. The taxi-driver took his suitcase and loaded it in the front of the cab. Just now, William's face was inches away from Helena's.

"Goodbye!" William bestowed a gentle peck on Helena's cheek. She smiled at him and closed the door. William picked up his briefcase and shoulder bag, and the taxi sped through the empty streets to the West London Coach Station.

The West London Coach Station is unknown to almost everyone, apart from those people who have bought a package tour by coach to Europe. It is situated in that part of London bordered by Kensington High Street and Cromwell Road. Even if you *have* been there before, you always come upon it by surprise; a large, open space created either by the Luftwaffe in the forties or by an eager developer in the sixties, it is surrounded by advertising hoardings. There are bays with enough space to park twenty to thirty coaches, and the entire passenger facilities consist of a yellow-painted Portakabin containing a wc, some plastic stacking chairs, a broken drinks vending machine and a small office area, unattended except during peak departure periods. Behind the Portakabin is a vague area of weeds and rubbish where a superannuated Ford Cortina lies rusting.

On either side of the coach station are streets with elegant, white-painted Edwardian houses, now somewhat gone to seed and converted either to cheap hotels (if any London hotel can be described as cheap) or to embassies and consulates of Third-World countries too impoverished to be able to afford premises in fashionable Kensington or Bayswater.

All this William could now see as the taxi turned into the coach station and came to a halt before the Portakabin. He got out and paid the driver. The worst thing about the West London coach station, he thought, was its location: it was about half-way between Kensington and Earls Court tube stations, but too impossibly far from either for anyone to walk with their holiday luggage. Orbit Tours had been receiving complaints about the place for years.

William opened the door of the Portakabin with some trepidation. What if they were all there, the Chestfield crowd? What if they had got together already, and lynched him as soon as he came in. He longed for one moment for the security of Helena's flat and the sensation of her lips upon his cheek... The place smelt of stale cigarette smoke as usual. Most of his passengers would be there, thought William; only the 'Scenic Delights of France' left London at such an unearthly hour on Sunday morning.

The first person William recognised was Mr Eveleigh. Sitting in one corner of the room, looking rather uncomfortable on the plastic chair, 'Bummer' Eveleigh was smoking his pipe while reading through his tour itinerary. He looked exactly as he had in Bartley classroom all those years ago.

The well-dressed couple in their thirties, sitting near the front and chatting excitedly, just had to be the Bartlett-Nicholsons. Hugh looked older and plumper than William had expected; obviously no longer a top sportsman. Miranda's long auburn hair was shorter than before, and she too had put on weight, but she was still most attractive.

The lean, balding man in the obviously-new leather jacket and designer jeans was either trying to be trendy or attempting to recapture his lost youth. William noticed the luggage at his side - a long sausage-type bag and an enormous stereo radio-cassette player. He thought back to Wallis J.C.R. It was none other than his old enemy, Steve Vicks.

William instantly recognised Ian Bailey-Filmer. The slight, ascetic figure in the anorak and grey flannel trousers, reading a book on archaeology, he seemed smaller than William had remembered and it was hard to imagine how he had been so in awe of him many years before. He also looked much older than his age: Bailey-Filmer could only be in his late thirties. This man looked nearer fifty.

A few seats from Bailey-Filmer sat a pale young man with an earnest expression on his face. Among his luggage was an open carrier bag in which William could see some sketch-books. Could this clean-shaven orthodox-looking junior clerk really be the temperamental and artistic Nick Patterson?

The broad-shouldered, ruddy-faced man with a large camera around his neck and a bag of photographic equipment was not immediately recognisable to William. However, the copy of *Railway Magazine* he was reading gave the game away. Mike Turner had come on time.

A young man with dark curly hair was sitting right in the far corner. He had a Sunday paper open and almost seemed to be hiding behind it. Remembering the terrified character on the 'phone, William wondered whether this was Jonathan Atkinson. If so, then everyone he had expected had turned up, with the exception of Mario Rottoli.

A figure had appeared behing the desk in the office section of the Portakabin. It was old George, who worked part-time as Duty Officer for Orbit and took it in turns to see the tours out. He said hello to William, and raised a small section of the counter to let him pass through.

"Sit down here for a minute. Your coach will be in shortly".

William took a seat and opened his briefcase. He had been thinking so much about his old enemies from Chestfield that he had almost forgotten that there were fourteen other passengers on the tour, fourteen totally innocent holidaymakers who had paid for and who were going to get the best holiday possible. He looked at the names on the Rooming List. True, he would not be able to recognise these passengers, but it made sense to see what their names were. For the next eight days their destiny was going to be unavoidably linked with his own.

Disregarding the ten Chestfield passengers, the list read as follows:

Mr Maxwell	Mr Charlton
Mr Murray	Mrs Charlton
Mrs Murray	Miss R Charlton
Mr Tjeong	Miss J Charlton
Mrs Tjeong	Miss Crosbie
Master E Tjeong	Miss Mora
Master A Tjeong	Miss Garcia

William wasn't quite sure what nationality the Tjeongs were. He could see an Oriental-looking couple, with two young boys, sitting in the middle of the room. They looked Chinese, but they may even be English. It was so hard to tell. The Charltons were obviously the very English-looking family drinking their tea from a thermos flask, Mum and Dad and their two daughters, perhaps in their early teens. And he could not fail to notice the two beautiful Spanish-looking girls, one of them tall and slim with short hair, the other shorter, with a fuller figure and glorious long dark hair. He had found Miss Mora and Miss Garcia.

There was the toot of a horn from outside.

"Your coach is here!" George said.

William stopped contemplating the passengers and went outside. Parked outside the coach station building was a clean, comfortable coach. It bore the Orbit fleetname and the globe emblem. Its front bore the familiar Mercedes star and its flanks the raised metal figures 0303.

"Mais - c'est formidable! Salut Guillaume!"

"Bonjour Claude!" William exchanged greetings with Claude. A small, bald man in his forties, with quite a pot-belly, Claude had worked with William on many previous occasions. William knew him to be a good driver, whose chief concerns were the comfort and safety of his passengers and the immaculate condition of his coach.

"How is the coach?" William asked.

"Oh - it's running very well."

"That's a nasty crack you've got on your windscreen!" William remarked. It was indeed a long crack, starting at the bottom in the middle of the windscreen and extending up across the right-hand side of the screen. It was the only thing which marred the otherwise perfect appearance of the vehicle.

"Oh, yes. It was a caillou. I was hit by a pebble driving up here. But it is not so bad. The coach goes back to the depot after the tour. They put in a new windscreen then."

William understood very well. Modern coach windscreens were always laminated, and so the driver could go on using the coach if a crack appeared in the screen, provided that it did not obscure the driver's vision.

"And how is your wife? And little Virginie?" William had heard the story of Claude's marriage many times. He was forever falling in and out of love with his wife. Five years ago, to William's astonishment, they had produced a daughter, Virginie. Claude was very proud of his daughter, and the driving cab of his coach was always decorated with photos of her.

"Virginie is very well. But my wife - tu sais, mon ami, it does not get any easier. She keeps saying I must stop the coach driving, or she will divorce me. Oh - les femmes! Quelle chance that you do not have this problem."

William made no reply. It sounded as if Claude's marital relations were much the same as usual. He fetched his own luggage and stowed it on the coach. Now was the time to carry out his standard pre-tour check. He took one of the 'Orbit' forms and noted down the coach registration number, the mileage reading, and checked that the on-board w.c. and drinks machine were in working order. He then attached a copy of the Rooming List to his clipboard. It was time for loading to begin.

George gave the thumbs-up sign to William through the Portakabin window. William returned the gesture. George took the microphone on the desk and made a call through the P.A. system for all passengers on 'Scenic Delights of France' to join the 'Orbit' coach parked in front of the terminal building.

William waited outside the coach door while the passengers trooped out of the Portakabin, left their luggage with Claude at the side of the vehicle and got on board. He checked their names on his Rooming List as they boarded. "Maxwell's the name. Bob Maxwell. No, I know what you're going to say - no relation!" Mr Maxwell was a florid Australian of about fifty, dressed in a T-shirt and a pair of shorts. He carried an enormous camcorder. William knew the type. In all probability Mr Maxwell had taken several months leave, and the French tour was just a small part of a lengthy itinerary which would take him all around Europe.

"Excuse me, is this the right coach for 'Scenic Delights of France'? My name is Miss Crosbie." William ticked off the name on his list. Miss Crosbie was a well-spoken and well-groomed spinster, with something of a bewildered expression on her face, probably well into her seventies. He could imagine her forgetting the departure times or trying to join the wrong coach. He would have to keep a careful eye on Miss Crosbie.

After Miss Crosbie came Mr and Mrs Murray, an American couple in late middle age. They were casually dressed and greeted William in a low Texas drawl. William had sometimes encountered difficulties with Americans on these low-budget European tours: their expectations were not always fulfilled. He thought of the small family hotels and set meals to come, and fervently hoped that the Murrays weren't expecting uniformed bellhops, 24-hour room service and *à la carte* menus.

The two Spanish girls were the next to board, followed by the Tjeongs and the first of the Chestfield passengers, Mike Turner. One by one the remaining passengers mounted the steps to the coach. Not one showed any sign of recognition. They were, it was true, bleary-eyed and weary after an early start to get to the coach station. William was glad that his Orbit name badge showed his first name only. The name 'William Simpson' might have meant something to another former Chestfield pupil, but hardly anyone at the school had ever addressed him as William. To Mr Eveleigh he would have been merely 'Simpson', to the others 'Little Willy'.

As Mr Eveleigh boarded the coach, William requested him to extinguish his pipe, which he did. Giving his old schoolmaster this order gave him an incredible sense of superiority. Next, Steve Vicks then climbed on board with his immense stereo radio-cassette.

"I hope you understand that you won't be allowed to play that on board the coach," said William.

"Oh, yeah, sure, but I can't put it in the boot to get all knocked about with the luggage, can I? Do you realise how much this thing cost?"

William had a fairly good idea. Even at Chestfield, Steve Vicks' hi-fi equipment had always been of the highest quality.

The last of the passengers to leave the terminal building was Jonathan Atkinson. Still hiding his face with the newspaper, and with a Marks & Spencers carrier bag as his only luggage, he shuffled up to William and said:

"This is the coach to France - yes?"

"Yes," replied William. Behind the paper, William could distinguish the curly hair and baby face of the adolescent Atkinson, now transformed into early middle age. Atkinson made his way unobtrusively down the central aisle of the coach and sank out of view into one of the seats at the very back.

As Claude put the cases in the boot, William went back into the office to talk to George.

"Got all your people, then?"

"No, there's one missing. Mr Rottoli."

"Better wait a bit, then." If any passenger was missing, it was customary to wait until the last possible moment before leaving for Dover. William returned to the coach and walked down the central aisle. The vehicle was barely half-full and all of the single travellers had taken window-seats. None of the Chestfield passengers were talking, except the Bartlett-Nicholsons. William wondered how long it would be before they got to know one another. Probably a few hours at least; coaches didn't make for easy conversation, and British people were naturally reticent. He wondered whether any of them would recognise their old friends. Perhaps not. But surely all of the ex-Chestfield group would recognise Mr Eveleigh.

Mr Tjeong tapped William on the shoulder as he passed down the coach.

"Excuse me, we have this bus for the whole tour?"

"Yes" said William.

"Oh! My children are a little disappointed. They think that because we are travelling with English bus company we travel on English bus."

"No, I'm sorry. This bus is French. But I can assure you that it's just as comfortable …"

"That is not what I mean. We expect big English bus, you know, with two decks." He pulled out a crumpled Orbit brochure and showed William the page entitled 'Extend your holiday with a few days in London', which had a large photograph of a London bus outside St Paul's Cathedral.

"That is just for London. Here, I can show you the coaches we use on the tours." William took the brochure and leafed through it to find the 'Scenic Delights of France' page, where a coach identical to Claude's was shown at the foot of the Eiffel Tower.

Mr Tjeong did not seem to be convinced. "Is there any chance you change this bus? For a proper English one?"

"I can't promise anything. But I'll see what I can do." William turned to Mrs Tjeong and the children, and asked them if they were comfortable. He discovered that they were from Indonesia, and that the children were called Erwin and Abraham. Erwin was fourteen, but looked young for his age. Abraham was ten.

A squeal of brakes made William look outside. A mini-cab had just pulled up in front of the coach terminal. Getting out of it was a fat, swarthy man in a light jacket. His luggage consisted solely of a shoulder bag.

"Mr Rottoli?" William had walked up to meet the latecomer.

"Yes. Sorry I'm late. This bloody place is so hard to find. Have I got time to get a drink?"

"I'll serve coffee on the coach on the way down to Dover."

"Great." Mario Rottoli hurried on board the coach and took a seat towards the rear. William signed a copy of his Rooming List and handed it to George. Old George waved to Claude to go, and the coach pulled out into the road, then swung into Kensington High Street and headed east towards Knightsbridge. There was no turning back now. Tour F443/07 had begun.

****

It was customary for William to use the two-hour journey to Dover to prepare his passengers for the tour ahead and to make them feel at their ease. He introduced himself and Claude, and explained how to use the air-conditioning, the reclining seats and the on-board w.c. He didn't try to get too much information across too quickly. He knew how sleepy people could be at the beginning of the tour.

Once they were out of London and on the A2, he started walking down the coach checking all the passports. This he did at the start of every tour, in order to make sure every passenger had a valid passport, and to take a note of all the passport numbers. In some countries the hotels would ask for this information before they gave out the room keys. In France they did not, but William still preferred to have a separate note of all his passengers' passport numbers, so that, if anyone became separated from their passport, he would still have the details on file.

Checking the passport details was another chance to break the ice with his passengers. He talked first to Mr Maxwell, who was sitting at the front behind the driver's seat. Mr Maxwell, he learnt, was a widower who had just sold his own business, a small publishing house in Melbourne, and was now touring Europe on the proceeds. Even as he spoke to William, Bob Maxwell had one finger on the trigger of his camcorder, anxious to get some record of the Kent countryside as it sped by.

The Charltons were from the Bristol area. Their two daughters were younger than he had at first thought; Rebecca, the elder, was thirteen, and her sister, Josephine, was only ten. Both were anxious to try out their school French and were practising among themselves:

"Monsieur Aubert se rase avec un rasoir électrique" said Rebecca.

William's heart sank. So, even after all these years, the Shortman audio-visual French course was still being used in schools other than Chestfield.

When William inspected Steve Vicks' passport, he noticed that the photograph and details of Vicks' wife had been deleted from it. So had Steve Vicks been married and then divorced? He wondered what had caused the break-up. The photograph of a young woman with frizzy blonde hair was at least eight years out of date, and her expression, which was like that of most people when having a passport photo taken, did not give anything away.

William noticed that Mario Rottoli had moved a few rows along the coach and was now sitting opposite the two Spanish girls. That did not surprise him: they were both very beautiful. William's initial impression had been that the shorter, longer-haired Miss Garcia was the more attractive, but when he looked more closely at her companion, he found it hard to choose between the two. Although Miss Mora's hair was cut short in a boyish style, which William did not particularly like on girls, her features were delicate, her figure was perfect and her deep brown eyes were hauntingly beautiful. How different, thought William, were these Spanish eyes from the equally beautiful but paler brown English eyes to which he had bid goodbye that morning.

Maria Fernandez Garcia was eighteen and a University student in Costa Rica, in Central America. Her friend, Lucia Gonzalez Mora, was twenty and came from Paraguay. They both had family in Spain, and William concluded that their wealthy parents had forked out for a once-in-a-lifetime vacation for the two girls. After returning from the 'Scenic Delights of France' tour, they were both due to travel on Orbit's 'Swiss Lakes and Mountains'.

William had checked through all the passports, and exchanged pleasantries with all his passengers, when he reached Jonathan Atkinson at the back of the coach. The man was still crouched like a terrified puppy.

"Do you really have to take my passport details?"

"Don't worry. I won't pass them on to anyone else. I only take them for our own records, and I'll destroy them at the end of the tour."

"You promise you won't give them to anyone."

"I give you my word."

Jonathan Atkinson reluctantly handed over his passport and William copied down the number on his Rooming List. He then made his way back to the front of the coach.

After they had crossed the Medway Bridge, William passed along the coach again and took orders for hot drinks. He was amused that Ian Bailey-Filmer was one of those who ordered a coffee.

"With two sugars, please. And not heaped teaspoons, just level measures. And not too much milk."

How incredible that he should be making coffee again for Bailey-Filmer! But this time Bailey-Filmer was going to be disappointed. The coffee in Claude's machine came in only three varieties - black with sugar, white with sugar and white without sugar. All the ingredients were already mixed up in the plastic cups; you just added the hot water. He prepared a usual stodgy machine coffee and took it to his former Head of House. As he walked back to the courier's seat at the front of the coach, William fancied that, out of the corner of his eye, he could see Bailey-Filmer pulling a face as he took a sip.

William enjoyed giving a commentary as he travelled through his native county. They passed endless acres of hop gardens on the right and Canterbury Cathedral on the left. Before long they were in Dover. A passport official came on board the coach and asked those passengers with non-EC passports to pass through Passport Control. The others remained on the coach: even from the front of the vehicle, William fancied he could audibly hear Jonathan Atkinson's sigh of relief. Soon the coach was parked on the quayside waiting for the ferry. William gave the passengers half an hour to go shopping or get their money changed.

Once the coach was in the hold of the *Pride of Dover*, and all the passengers had gone up to the decks, William and Claude locked up and made their way to the Commercial Drivers' Restaurant. Here they could have a decent brunch

- for it would be almost lunch-time when they arrived in Calais - and talk in peace.

"Claude, do you know the village of Marles-en-Artois? Just after the Canadian War Memorial at Vimy?"

"Yes. Qu'est-ce-qu'il y a?"

"Do you mind if we make a little stop there?"

"Of course not, mon ami. You are le grand chef. I stop where you like."

"Well, Claude, it's just that I've arranged a kind of special surprise for one of our passengers there. He's an old friend of mine. You're not to worry about it." And William explained briefly to Claude what he had planned for Rottoli.

"But that is magnifique! You English and your sense of humour!"

William had expected he'd be able to depend on Claude. He pushed away his plate of sausages and beans untasted: he wasn't very hungry. He went down to the Duty Free Shop. He mustn't forget Jacques Mercier's Gold Block Tobacco.

All too soon the ferry docked in Calais. An announcement told all passengers to rejoin their vehicles. William made it down to the coach just as Mr Maxwell was boarding with his video-camera. He waited for a few more passengers to board, and then counted them. Twenty-two, so someone was missing. A quick check revealed it to be Miss Crosbie.

It was a real nuisance when someone got lost at Calais. You just had to hope that they would find their way off the ferry with the foot passengers and meet up with you at the terminal. But it was a worrying moment and it wasted precious time. William could see that the bow doors were open and that the final preparations were being made for the vehicles to leave the ferry. He took a gamble and walked back to the stairs that led to the upper car deck. Once there, he headed to the far end of the deck where he could see a few coaches.

"Oh! But thank heavens it's you! I don't know what they've done to our bus!" Miss Crosbie practically fell into William's arms.

"You didn't go down all the way - you got out at the wrong car deck! Here, come with me!" And William started leading her back down the stairs and towards the Orbit coach.

"You must think it's terribly silly of me!" said Miss Crosbie. My poor dear father always said I was not to be trusted anywhere."

"Here we are!" William let Miss Crosbie board. The cars in front of Claude's coach had already left the ferry, and a motorist behind it was hooting impatiently. William was relieved that he had all his passengers.

They passed through the Customs and Passport Control without any formalities. Just past the docks, William motioned to Claude to stop. A tall man with a rucksack was waiting. Even in civilian clothes, his military bearing was obvious.

"Orbit Tours?" demanded the military gentleman.

"Squadron-Leader Bridger?" asked William. He would never have recognised Bridger.

"That's me. I came on the train from the Black Forest. Seemed too good a chance to miss."

Bridger got on and the coach set off again. The 'Scenic Delights of France' tour was not designed with the autoroutes in mind, so Claude ignored the signs for the A26 and headed towards the town centre. Here William arranged a photo-stop at the statue of the Burghers of Calais in front of the Town Hall.

"But were they beefburgers or vegeburgers?" asked Josephine Charlton.

"Now, don't be silly," said her mother.

The journey continued south through the uneventful but pleasant pastoral countryside of the Pas de Calais. William interspersed his running commentary with helpful hints about currency, buying stamps, how to use the 'phones, not to forget the one hour time difference. So far, everything was going smoothly.

The first official stop on their itinerary was Arras. Claude parked the coach on one of the great arcaded squares, and the group wandered around the town. Although the shops were shut, a number of pavement cafes were open, and it gave the passengers a chance to stretch their legs. William noticed that Atkinson seemed to have perked up since they had arrived in France. He was out of the coach as soon as they stopped, and chatting amicably with other passengers.

William made a final phone call to Jacques Mercier, just to be on the safe side. As he walked back to the coach he saw Mario Rottoli drinking and chatting with Lucia and Maria on the terrace of a cafe. He even had his hand on Maria's leg. What a swine! He was sure that Rottoli was not the sort of young man that Maria and Lucia's parents would want them to meet. He had travelled with Latin American passengers before, and knew that among the upper classes the traditional family values of fidelity and no sex before marriage were still widely respected. How glad he was that Mario would soon be leaving the tour.

From Arras the group moved on to the Canadian Memorial at Vimy. A young Canadian guide took them for a tour through the trenches, with squeals of delight from the Charlton girls and bemused looks from the Tjeong family. William had seen it all many times before, but it could never fail to move him, that great waste of young life that had been the First World War. Whatever their schooldays had been like, his generation had been lucky.

Walking back from the concrete stelae of the Memorial towards the coach park, William noticed two figures just ahead of him who were deep in conversation. They were Mr Eveleigh and Ian Bailey-Filmer. As he walked pass them he overheard the word 'Chestfield'. So two of his victims at least had got together.

"Eh bien!" Claude remarked to William, as they approached a small village a few kilometres after Vimy, "this is Marles-en-Artois now. Are they here, tes amis?"

As the coach rounded the corner they found out. Two men in uniform signalled for it to stop.

"Police?" asked Mr Maxwell, from his seat behind Claude.

"I'll just find out," said William. He got down from the coach and said hello to Jacques Mercier and Henri Renaud.

"Is your friend ready?" asked Jacques Mercier.

"I'll just go and check." William went back into the coach and took hold of the microphone. He asked everyone to remain seated and to keep calm. Then he went looking for Rottoli. The fat little man was now seated next to Maria, and Lucia had now taken his former seat across the aisle.

"Mr Rottoli?" asked William discretely.

"Yes, what is it?"

"There seems to be a problem of some kind. Would you mind stepping out of the coach for a moment?"

A puzzled Rottoli followed William out of the coach. Mercier and Renaud were superb. As Rottoli stepped off the vehicle, one of them grabbed his arms and tied them behind his back. Rottoli just had a glimpse of the uniforms before the other tied a blindfold around his head.

"What the f...! Are you the police?"

"You are Mr Mario Rottoli."

"Yeah. What is it?"

"Mr Rottoli, we are Customs Officials. We understand that you drove a lorry loaded with heroin across the border from Ventimiglia to Nice in 1975."

"But that's impossible! I was just a kid then! Jesus, I didn't even have a driving licence!"

"We have a witness who says you told them about the crime."

"This is ridiculous! I demand to see the British Consul!"

"All in good time, Mr Rottoli. In the meantime we must take you to the station. The police are waiting to question you."

William followed Jacques Mercier and Henri Renaud down the track which led to the old farmhouse which Mercier was restoring. The house itself was almost completed, and was being used as the family home. It was surrounded by a low range of outbuildings, in varying stages of delapidation. William opened the door to a small lumber-room which was empty save for a few bales of straw, and helped Renaud and Mercier manhandle Rottoli in.

"Someone will be with you shortly," said Jacques Mercier.

"Mr Rottoli," said William. "I will talk to these men. I am going to try to get you released. In the meantime, I advise you to co-operate with them."

"Of all the f...ing..." Mario Rottoli's obscenities were silenced behind the stout wooden door which William shut and bolted behind him.

"Well, William," said Jacques, " all I can say is that if that's the way you treat your friends on their birthday, I no longer want to be counted as one of them!"

"Don't worry! I'll be along to release him shortly!" They walked back up the farm track to the main road. William got the carrier-bag with his duty-frees and handed it to the two teachers.

"Why, thank you, William! Gold Block and a litre of Johnny Walker Black Label! I don't know when I've been so well repaid for just a few minutes work!"

"I couldn't have managed without you!" said William, as he stepped back on board. The coach disappeared down the road at the end of the village.

"Bizarre! Absolument bizarre!" Henri Renaud was not quite as fluent in English as Jacques Mercier, but he had understood everything that had taken place.

"Ces Anglais!" Jacques Mercier still held a soft spot for William Simpson. After ten years or so, they still remembered him as an assistant teacher. It had been strange how this outwardly shy young man had been able to animate and interest his classes the way he had. William Simpson was evidently a great loss to the teaching profession. But he was obviously happy in his chosen one.

William took the microphone and briefly explained the 'official' reason for the disappearance of Mr Rottoli to the group. There was a horrified gasp from Maria, and stunned silence from the rest of the party. They were still somewhat subdued when they arrived at the Hotel de France at Bercy-en-Artois twenty minutes later.

The Hotel de France was an untypical example of a small French provincial hotel. It was a bold modern concrete building which occupied one side of the main square of the small village of Bercy. In front of the hotel was the square, with the statue of some distinguished nonentity on a plinth in its centre. To one side was the village post office, to the other the Mairie. Opposite the hotel the main road ran along the fourth side of the square, and, across the road in the distance, could be seen a clump of trees, an old church and a windmill. Black and white Fresian cows grazed in the fields beyond. Although the hotel itself was ugly, the view was most picturesque.

The hotel had a charming rear garden, with a pond and a collection of peacocks and other exotic birds. But, thought William, what made the Hotel de France so different from the others was the way it was organised. William knew that, as soon as he pulled up in the coach in front of the hotel, the owner, Thierry Delagrange, would jump on board the coach, distributing room keys and informing all his guests of the times for breakfast and dinner, while an army of porters would appear as if by magic and whisk all the luggage up to the rooms. There was really nothing left for the Tour Manager and driver to do but look on.

William had changed and was about to go down to dinner when Thierry called him from the reception desk.

"Excusez-moi. I have one of your passengers on the phone."

It was Miss Crosbie.

"Is that William?"

"Yes, it's me. Can I help you?"

"Well, I don't want to be a nuisance, but I seem to have lost the door to my room!"

"What do you mean, Miss Crosbie?"

"Well, dear, I know that I must have got in here somehow when we got off the coach, but now I can't find the door. There are only two doors in my room. One goes to the en-suite bathroom and the other has a notice hanging on it saying *Do Not Disturb*, so I can't open that one!"

William explained patiently to Miss Crosbie that the *Do Not Disturb* sign was for her to hang on the outside of the door if she did not want to be disturbed.

The Hotel de France seated William and Claude in a separate area from the main dining-room where the group were eating. William liked that. He could talk in French to Claude, and plan the itinerary for the next day, without being continually interrupted by the passengers. Two or three times during the course of the meal he did get up and wander across to their part of the restaurant, to make sure everything was in order, but the group were just eating calmly and had no queries or questions. Perhaps they were still stunned by the sudden departure of Mario Rottoli. More likely, they were simply exhausted after the long day.

After dinner, Monsieur Delagrange invited Claude and William to a coffee and cognac at the bar. That was another hallmark of the Hotel de France. William accepted the coffee but declined the cognac.

"Not drinking?" asked Thierry Delagrange.

"No, thank you," said William. "As a matter of fact I was just going to ask you if I could borrow your car and drive to Marles".

"Of course." Thierry Delagrange knew that William had friends living not far from Bercy, and he had lent him the car before. "It's parked on the main square in front of the hotel".

William found the old Renault without difficulty. As usual, the car had been left unlocked and the keys were in the ignition. William loaded Mario Rottoli's shoulder bag into the back of the car and headed back to Marles-en-Artois.

When he reached the old farm, he listened at the door. Not a sound. He drew back the bolt carefully. Mario Rottoli was fast asleep on a bale of straw.

William left the shoulder bag in the lumber-room and drove back to the Hotel de France. As he collected his key and went up to his room he noticed that the lobby lounge was almost empty. Almost all the guests had gone up to their rooms. Just Mr Eveleigh and Ian Bailey-Filmer were deep in conversation at the bar.

Chapter Seven

Val De Loire

MARIO Rottoli woke up and rubbed his eyes. It had been a strange and most unpleasant day. He'd got in around 3 a.m. after a night out in Southend with Tracey, the waitress, and then suddenly at five his mother had woken him and bundled him off in the taxi. He'd never really wanted to go to France anyway. He'd arrived late and almost missed the coach, and had been startled to recognise his old French teacher, Bummer Eveleigh, among the passengers. He'd managed to avoid talking to him, and had in fact struck up quite a relationship with a dishy Spanish bird, when suddenly he'd been bundled off and thrown in this smelly old room.

Were the men who had tied him up and blindfolded him really Customs officers? He'd certainly done nothing for which they could have arrested him. And they were quite an amateurish bunch, really. He'd been able to slip the rope off and remove his blindfold in a matter of seconds once he'd been locked in. Not that he'd been able to see very much once the blindfold was off - the door was bolted on the outside, and the walls and ceiling seemed to be quite solid. He'd seen so little of the two men who had arrested him - it had happened so quickly - that he'd never have been able to recognise them again. He kept thinking a man with a microphone would burst through the door any moment and say it had all been a joke, the sort of thing they show on telly.

He'd tried banging on the door for a while after they'd left him, protesting his innocence, but no-one had come. And then, he supposed, he must simply have fallen asleep. And why not? There was plenty of straw to lie on, and he'd only been in bed a couple of hours the night before. He'd needed the sleep.

Mario shivered in the draught which was coming through the door. Although it was July, there was quite a chilly breeze. Draught? He opened his eyes again and looked towards the door. It was open! And down at his feet he could see something. It was his shoulder-bag. So perhaps the Customs Officers had brought him his belongings from the coach but failed to secure the door.

Mario put the bag on his shoulder and ventured outside. The building where he had been held looked more like an old farm than a police station, but he didn't want to take any risks. They might have guard dogs. He tiptoed along the narrow track which led up to the main road. No, that was a mistake. If they discovered he was missing, the first place they'd search would be the main road - they'd assume he was trying to rejoin the coach tour. No, assuming they were going to follow him, it was best to take another route. He followed the farm track in the other direction, across fields of oilseed rape and into a muddy pasture. The sky was lightening in the east. Mario could just make out the digital figures on his watch. It was 4.30 a.m.

He paused to rest for a moment, and then noticed a line of telegraph poles running along the bottom of the next meadow. The line continued in both directions as far as he could see. This could mean only two things: a road or a railway line. He strode across the field until he came to the fence at the end, with the two shiny rails on their bed of ballast beyond.

The railway line ran roughly east-west. He started walking towards the west. He reckoned that this was the way towards Boulogne and Calais, and he must come to a station sometime.

****

William woke at about 6 a.m. after a sound sleep. He'd been dreaming about Helena again, but this time it had been a pleasant dream: he'd been with her in Paris, and they had ridden on the funicular up to the Sacré-Coeur, where he had bought her a red rose from a street vendor. The strange thing was that Helena had been stark naked - well, come to think of it, they had both been stark naked, but that hadn't seemed to worry the Parisians all around them in the dream.

It was not William's normal procedure to banish such carnal thoughts by means of a cold shower, but he did so unwittingly by misjudging the sensitivity of the amazingly complex bathroom fittings in the Hotel de France, where a tiny nudge of the shower tap could turn the water from near boiling point to freezing.

After dressing and packing his bags, William let himself out of the front door of the hotel and crossed over to the square. Claude was there already, sweeping out the inside of the coach. He said good-morning, and crossed the road. In the field across the road a solitary figure was seated.

As he got nearer, William realised that the figure was Nick Patterson, He had his sketch-book open, and was drawing a very accomplished sketch of the windmill and church with the little clump of trees on the knoll.

"That's beautiful!" exclaimed William, quite truthfully. It was nothing like the huge, ugly abstracts Patterson had produced at Chestfield.

"Thanks. I'm really grateful to Orbit for having given me this free trip. I'm going to do a sketch in every town we stay in. I'm also going to visit some of the museums in Paris so I can see some of the French Masters".

"Do you paint professionally, then?"

"Well, not really, strictly speaking. I get the odd commission now and again. But I'm hoping to do it full-time some day".

What a change, William thought, from the self-confident fifteen-year old who had derided his own artistic endeavours and described them as 'crap'. If Patterson had no doubts about his talent, he was certainly being realistic about its possible commercial success.

William returned to breakfast at the Hotel de France. Here the hotel was also refreshingly untypical. None of the dreaded hard rolls: the continental breakfast consisted of a well-stocked buffet with tea, coffee, fruit juice, a selection of fresh fruits, soft buns with sesame seeds, croissants and even ham, cheese and cereals. William was only too aware how it contrasted with some of the other hotel breakfasts, where absentee staff flung vacuum flasks of coffee on the tables, and guests had the allocation of one hard roll and one croissant per person, with a rap over the knuckles by the hotel proprietor if anyone should try to take more than one!

Whilst the group were finishing their breakfast, William went to see Thierry Delagrange. He handed over the voucher from Orbit for the night's accommodation, and asked if he could send a fax message.

"Desolé, mon ami. Le fax est en panne. But you can send a telex. I show you."

William had used telex machines at a number of hotels in the past, and once he had been shown the basic controls he knew just what to do. Five or six years ago virtually all his contact with Head Office whilst out on tour had been by telex, but now more and more hotels were replacing their telex machines with faxes, which were not only cheaper but also much easier to use.

His telex this morning was a short one:

'ATTN. H.R. PAX ROTTOLI X 1 LEFT TOUR YESTERDAY. BELIEVED ARRESTED FOR SMUGGLING. EVERYTHING ELSE OK. LOTS OF LOVE WILLIAM F443/07.'

William suddenly became a little worried about the 'lots of love', but as the machine clicked away, and Orbit's telex in London answered back, he realised that it was too late now to change it.

By 8.45 everyone was in the coach, and the jovial figure of Thierry Delagrange was waving them goodbye from the village square. Today they had a long journey south, to the Loire Valley. Claude took the dreaded autoroute for a short distance, allowing him to make a mid-morning stop at a service area where the clients could get a drink while he filled the coach with diesel.

Leaving the motorway and cutting across the country, William decided it was time to put on some music. Yesterday he had been giving a commentary almost all the time, but when you reach the great open spaces of central France you can go for miles without seeing anything of special interest.

William knew that some drivers could be tricky about music. Although, strictly speaking, the Tour Manager always had control over the radio/cassette player and microphone, in practice it was the driver who was in charge. William had known drivers who would cut off the sound of the microphone altogether so as not to interrupt their favourite pop track.

Claude was not a bit like that, but he did need to be handled tactfully. William knew that as soon as he mentioned music, Claude would take out one of his own cassettes and insist it was played first, and then leave it in most of the day so that it played over and over again. The main problem was that Claude had only three cassettes, all of which William had heard time and time again. One was a collection of piano music by Richard Clayderman; another was a recording of Dvorak's *New World Symphony*. The third cassette was filled with a recording of an entire 'hit-parade' taped from Radio Monte Carlo, vintage July 1975, complete with disc-jockey chat, advertisements and news flashes.

"Can we have some music?" suggested William.

"Eh bien oui - pourquoi pas une de mes cassettes?"

"I thought we'd have one of my tapes first."

"Oh, juste une cassette. Tiens voilà! Richard Clayderman."

Claude deftly removed the cassette from its box and inserted it into the player without for a second taking his eyes off the road. The coach became filled with the sound of a piano. *Ballade Pour Adeline* was playing. At least

Claude had chosen the one out of the three tapes that was most socially acceptable as background music. Nobody was likely to object to Richard Clayderman.

They reached Versailles in time for lunch. A visit to the famous palace was not officially included in the itinerary, and it was in any case closed on Mondays, but most of William's passengers seemed content with an exterior view. They parked in the large coach-park in front of the palace. William, as usual, helped the passengers down from the coach and didn't pay much attention to where they went. Mr Murray seemed very impressed. As he got down from the coach, he turned to William:

"Jeez, this Louis the Fourteenth must have been quite a guy. What was he - a movie star or something?"

"Something like that," said William, as the Murrays went off to join Mr Maxwell and his camcorder.

"Excuse me, William!" William turned and saw the Bartlett-Nicholsons.

"Yes. How can I help you?"

"It's just that… well, you've obviously spent a long time in France, you know a fair bit about the country."

"Yes."

"Well, the truth is," continued Hugh, "we want to build up a nice cellar of really top quality wines at home, but the truth is, neither I nor my wife know anything about wine. So I wondered whether you could help us choose some wines to take back home?"

"Do you want wines to lay down - to keep for a few years - or to drink fairly soon?"

"I think we'd like some of each. We're quite prepared to pay a bit more for the best quality wines. Is there any particular wine you think we should get?"

William reflected for a moment. "One of the best vintages ever was in 1968. If you can still find some Bordeaux from that year it will be well worth getting."

"But will it still be available in the shops?" asked Miranda.

"Probably not," replied William. "But wait until we get to the hotel in Blois tonight. They've got a very good cellar. I've no doubt they'll have some there."

"Oh, you're wonderful!" exclaimed Miranda. "Come on, Hugh, let's go and have a look at the palace!"

From Versailles they moved on towards Chartres. Claude's Richard Clayderman cassette came to an end while William was up at the far end of the coach serving coffee to Lucia and Maria. Maria seemed to have got over the loss of Mario. By the time William returned to the courier's seat, Claude had changed the tape. It was now the old Radio Monte Carlo hit-parade playing. The first song on the tape seemed strangely familiar. Of course, William had heard that cassette countless times, but he had heard this particular song very recently. Something about it being a teenage dream to be seventeen. He suddenly thought of Helena Rogers.

"You're thinking of something, mon ami?" asked Claude.

"Oui. Une fille."

"Oh, that is bad news. Les filles, that is la malheur!" Claude hummed along to the lyrics of *Give a Little Love*, which then ended abruptly on the tape and was followed by a jingle advertising pastis.

As they approached the outskirts of Chartres, William interrupted the music to give a brief introduction to the city. He told the passengers to look out for the two different styles of architecture in the Cathedral. He explained that, whilst the transepts and quire were in early Gothic style with pointed arches, the first two bays of the nave had round-headed arches and had been built by the Normans.

"Gee! We have them in the States, you know, at Salt Lake City," Mr Murray remarked to his wife.

"Honey, I think those are 'Mormons'. He said 'Normans'."

****

"I've longed to go to this cathedral all my life. For me, this is the highlight of the trip!" Everyone had a highlight to their holiday, and it usually turned out to be the part of the trip which had to be cancelled owing to bad weather or adverse local circumstances. It looked as if this might be the case with Miss Crosbie. For, when Claude had attempted to park the coach in the usual place not far from Chartres Cathedral, he had found the side of the road roped-off and workmen digging a large hole. He had eventually managed to find somewhere to pull in with the coach, but right over on the other side of the town. All the other passengers had wandered off quite happily, but William knew he couldn't trust Miss Crosbie to find her way back to the coach through the narrow maze of streets in the centre of the city.

"Don't worry, Miss Crosbie. You come along with me!" And he had led her across the busy main road, through the pedestrian streets with their elegant boutiques, and finally up to the façade of the Cathedral with its two spires of different styles.

"Here we are!" William led her into the Cathedral. It was cool and dark inside. "You look around and then wait for me here. I'll be back in three-quarters of an hour".

William needed to get to a telephone. The first one he tried turned out to be vandalised, but from the second he succeeded in getting through to the Hotel du Duc de Guise in Blois. He checked the room allocation and gave them his approximate time of arrival. Everything appeared to be in order.

On his way back towards the Cathedral, he heard laughter and loud English voices from a corner cafe. He looked across the street and saw Mike Turner, Steve Vicks, John Bridger and Jonathan Atkinson sitting at a table having drinks.

"Hi there!" shouted John Bridger. "Do you know, the most incredible thing has happened. All of us went to the same school together, and we haven't seen each other for years. And now we meet up on this tour!"

"That's amazing!" exclaimed William, adding innocently: "Did you book it as a kind of school reunion or something?"

"No, that's what's so unusual about it. We all received these letters in the post saying we'd won a free tour."

"You were lucky!"

"I still say it's just unbelievable that we could all be on this trip together. And with old Bummer Eveleigh and Bailey-Filmer as well, not to mention Hugh and Miranda. How come your company sent us all these offers?" This was Mike Turner speaking now.

"Well, I can't pretend I understand how our Marketing Department works," started William, "as I don't work in the Head Office, but I believe that they do buy mailing lists from other companies. Perhaps your school has an Old Boys' Magazine or something like that? I expect Orbit bought the mailing list."

"Yes, that seems logical," said Turner. It was the only possible solution. After all, there may have been lots of other Old Chestfieldians who were offered free trips, but they may not have been able to take them owing to other commitments, such as family, other holidays, or even - he sighed - model railway exhibitions.

William walked back to the Cathedral. Miss Crosbie was standing by the same pillar at the West End where he had left her.

"Well, did you enjoy the Cathedral?"

"Yes, it was magnificent. I could have spent the whole week there. Thank you ever so much for taking me here."

"That's quite alright." William started guiding Miss Crosbie back to the coach. He shared her enthusiasm for the great Gothic cathedrals: no matter how often he came to Chartres, Reims or Nôtre-Dame de Paris, they never failed to move him.

Back on the coach, they left the cathedral city behind and headed across the Beauce. The only objects of any interest visible were large grain silos on the horizon. Claude's tape played on, treating the passengers to an intriguing, and long-forgotten, ditty called *Pas Besoin D'Education Sexuelle*, and going through works by Michèle Torr and Sacha Distel before returning to the Rollers.

"I say, can't someone turn that bloody rubbish off?" It was Steve Vicks, sounding just as he had in the J.C.R. many years previously whenever William had the temerity to play one of his own records.

The question remained unanswered. William hinted to Claude that the cassette had indeed gone right round and started at the beginning again, whereupon he ejected it and substituted the *New World Symphony*. The tape had not been fully rewound, and it was the Third Movement, the *Molto Vivace*, which came booming from the P.A. system.

"I love this music!" exclaimed Miss Crosbie.

After a few minutes, however, William became aware that there was some noise emanating from the back of the coach which did not come from Claude's tape. He looked back, and saw that Steve Vicks had switched on his ghetto-blaster and was listening to it on the very back seat of the coach, together with Mike Turner and Jonathan Atkinson.

Claude responded to this threat to his musical supremacy by turning the coach P.A. system up louder, but this was just met by more volume from the rear of the vehicle. Mr Maxwell went down the coach to remonstrate with Steve Vicks. William knew he would have to take charge of the situation:

"Ladies and Gentlemen, please may I remind you that you are not permitted to play portable stereos on our coaches. We shall have no more music for the rest of the day." And he left the microphone switch on, thus cutting out Claude's cassette. Steve Vicks turned off his ghetto-blaster and stowed it away again on the overhead rack.

It was early evening when they pulled into Blois, on the silvery banks of the River Loire. It was one of William's favourite French towns; he had first visited it when, with Jacques Mercier and Henri Rigaud, he had escorted a school group there during his year as an assistant teacher.

The Hotel du Duc de Guise was in the heart of the city, near the Château.

93

From the outside it looked like a traditional city centre hotel, but inside all the bedrooms had been refurbished and fitted with every modern convenience. The refurbishment work seemed to have stopped with the lift, an ancient metal cage contraption which could take no more than two people at once. There were inner and outer doors at each landing that had to be closed manually after you got out; they did not shut automatically. If one door was left slightly ajar, the lift would not work.

William was soon out of the coach and obtaining the room keys from the Reception Desk. He distributed them in the coach, and told the group when to come to dinner. There was a general cheer when William announced that tomorrow morning would be free for everyone to do their own thing, and that they wouldn't be leaving for the included excursion to Chambord Castle and the wine-tasting until 2 p.m.

The Chestfield passengers all seemed to be getting to know one another, thought William. It had to come. But would any of them ever recognise him? He mounted the three flights of stairs to his room and opened the door. From the window he had a fine view over the slate roofs and stone walls of Blois to the cathedral perched on its hill. William was always happy in Blois: he felt now that he was in the 'real' France.

Mr Eveleigh sat down on his bed with a sigh. He had just been struggling with the complexities of the hi-tec shower cubicle in his room. How France had changed since he had known and loved it! All he had seen today were out-of-town shopping centres and self-service restaurants. The countryside seemed to be disappearing under a sea of tarmac. And this modern hotel room, like the one the previous night, was so different from the ones he remembered, with the tortuous wiring, the striped wallpaper and the bidet. It was, he reflected, not a bit like the France in the Shortman's Audio-Visual French books.

The coach party came down early for dinner. At the Hotel du Duc de Guise there was always a chronic shortage of staff. The owner, Monsieur Lejeune, also did the cooking, and the two waitresses, Sylvie and Catherine, doubled as chambermaids. William often went into the kitchen to help them.

"Can I take any drinks out to the guests?" he asked.

"Of course. Put a bottle of mineral water on each table. The girls will take orders for the wine in a minute."

William took out the water. He knew that the Tjeongs, at any rate, would be satisfied with just that.

"Monsieur Lejeune?"

"Oui, mon ami."

"Do you still have any 1968 Bordeaux left?"

"Yes, I believe I have a couple of bottles. I always used to joke that I was keeping them for my mother-in-law!"

"Could I buy one, please?"

"But I could not possibly ask for any money for that wine! It was a terrible summer in Bordeaux. Six weeks of rain and storms! And when they picked what grapes were left on the vines, it was a poor little watery wine. It will by now have turned to vinegar. It was, of course, Le Bon Dieu's punishment for the terrible happenings of mai soixante-huit!"

Monsieur Lejeune spoke with true feeling. But William really wanted to get his hands on that wine.

"I would be quite happy to buy a bottle, as a souvenir."

"Look, mon ami William, if you really want some Bordeaux '68 you can have it. The bottles are somewhere on the left-hand side as you go down to the cellar. I think you'll find two there. But please don't give me any money for them and please don't try to drink them!"

William made his way down to the cellar. Monsieur Lejeune had his cellar well-organised, with the wines arranged by regions and vintages. He soon found the two bottles of 1968 Bordeaux. They were covered with dust and cobwebs, which he did his best not to wipe off. They added to the authenticity.

William saw Hugh and Miranda Bartlett-Nicholson looking at the wine list, and decided it was time he went over to help them.

"Ah! Glad you're here, old chap! We've got the list, but there doesn't seem to be any 1968 Bordeaux on it."

"No. You won't find an old rare wine on that sort of list. But I do know they have some here. I can get you a bottle. But it'll be very expensive."

"That doesn't matter," said Miranda.

"And you must promise not to tell anyone else about it. You see, it could be a bit embarrassing for the hotel if other people saw what you were drinking and ordered more of the same, because they're down to their last two bottles."

"We understand," said Hugh. "Now bring us the bottle."

William reappeared with a cobweb-covered bottle of 1968 Bordeaux.

"I'm afraid it'll be 500 francs."

"That's a bit over fifty quid, isn't it? That's not so bad. Look, I'll give you the money now, so that'll avoid any embarrassment later." He handed William a 500-franc note. "Can you open it for me?"

William was speechless. "You want to drink it now?" Then he saw that this might actually work to his advantage. "Don't you realise that a wine of this age and quality needs to be opened well in advance, so it can be brought gradually to room temperature?"

"You may be right," said Hugh, "but I've heard so much about this 1968 Bordeaux that I've just got to have a drink of it now. Can you open it for me, please?"

William took a corkscrew from a little side-table and opened the bottle. In the manner of the professional wine-waiter he emptied a little of the wine into Hugh Bartlett-Nicholson's glass. Hugh sniffed it and drained it. He pulled a face.

"Well, darling, what was it like?"

"It was - well, it was a truly great wine. The trouble is, we drink all this supermarket stuff, we're just not used to it. Here, you try some!" Hugh poured her a large glassful.

"You're right, darling. It's like caviar, I suppose. Once we get used to the taste we'll really love it!"

Leaving the Bartlett-Nicholsons with their wine, William returned to the table he shared with Claude and started on his soup.

Towards the end of the meal, William decided he would offer to help again. In the kitchen Sylvie and Catherine were pouring out coffees. He took a tray of four and delivered them to the Charltons. Then he took another cup of coffee, and carried it over to the side of the kitchen. He poured a small amount of salt into it from a salt-cellar, and then found some crushed garlic and dropped some of that in too, for good measure. He then placed this coffee on a tray with an ordinary cup and took them out to the table where Mr Eveleigh and Bailey-Filmer were sitting.

"Thank you," said Bailey-Filmer, as William handed him the coffee. Mr Eveleigh had just been telling him about how France wasn't quite the same as it used to be.

It seemed as though Bryan Eveleigh was right, Bailey-Filmer reflected as he took his first sip. He had always thought that the French made excellent coffee. The substance in the cup in front of him at this moment was the most disgusting concoction he had ever tasted.

Chapter Eight

Trouble In Touraine

WILLIAM was down to breakfast early on Tuesday morning. The weather was perfect in the Garden of France. He sat down on his own in the dining-room and had his roll, croissant and coffee - breakfasts at the Hotel du Duc de Guise did not amount to anything more. Catherine and Sylvie wished him good morning. They were both quite attractive girls in their own way, Catherine a tall willowy blonde, and Sylvie a small redhead with mischievous green eyes. He had sometimes wondered if one of them would be prepared to go to bed with him, but he had never worked out how he would go about asking them, and, besides, he definitely wasn't in love with either of them. This morning, in any case, his thoughts were on one woman alone. It was unbelievable how H.R. seemed to be taking over his life. Now it would be amazing if he woke up one morning without having dreamed about her.

The Orbit passengers were drifting down to breakfast in twos and threes. William saw Nick Patterson go off early with his sketchbook, and Lucia and Maria, giggling, went off to change some travellers' cheques and look around the shops. At ten o'clock William left the hotel with Mr Eveleigh, Ian Bailey-Filmer, the Tjeongs, the Murrays, Miss Crosbie and Mr Maxwell, all of whom wanted to have a look at the Château. He shepherded them across the busy road, and then up the stone stairs beneath the Gaston D'Orléans wing to the broad terrace overlooking the Loire. Here he took them to the visitors' entrance beneath the equestrian statue of King Francois I, and arranged for a guided tour in English. He did not stay with them: surely even Miss Crosbie would have no problem finding her way back from there to the hotel.

Strolling back across the terrace, he admired the view across the Loire. It was one of his favourite views in France, looking towards the great river with its sunken gravelly shores which represented the psychological barrier between the north and the south. He was not the only one to admire the view. Perched on the stone ledge looking over to the river was Nick Patterson. William drew nearer and looked at the sketch. Patterson's bold lines showed the dark ribbon of the river, the silhouette of the Church of St Saturin on the opposite bank, and, in the foreground, the twin spires of the Church of St Nicolas.

"Very good," remarked William.

"Yes. I'm pleased with this one myself. It really seems to be flowing at the moment."

Not sure whether Patterson was referring to the River Loire or to his own inspiration, William left the Place du Château and walked back towards the hotel. Here he crossed the main road to the Post Office. Blois post office was one of William's regular pilgrimage centres, for it had a philatelic counter where one could buy all the latest new issues from France, Monaco and Andorra. Since he had been a Tour Manager, William had started building up a collection of stamps from the countries he visited, and, when he got a free afternoon in a big city, he would go around the dealers and buy some of the earlier issues that he was missing. He would devote quite a lot of his spare time during the quieter winter season to the laying-out and classification of his collection, which was now worth several thousand pounds.

After buying the latest issues from the post office, William went to the telephone box outside. He had to call the Hotel Beau-Séjour at Neuville-sur-Charente, where they would be staying tomorrow night.

"Allo! Ici Hotel Beau-Séjour."

"Ici Guillaume d'Orbit Tours. Le groupe de demain. Vous avez reçu le Rooming List?"

Once again, everything had been arranged perfectly by Head Office. The hotel had exactly the right number of rooms.

"Please could you tell me," continued William, "are all the rooms in the annexe or in the main hotel building?"

"All the rooms are in ze main hotel. You have only a small group. We don't use ze annexe now unless we have to. It is old-fashioned. I think we will soon have it demolished."

"Well, is there any chance - I mean could you, if I asked, put some of my group in the annexe?"

"Of course I could. But why do you want them to be in ze annexe? Usually Orbit tells me to put all zeir clients in ze main hotel."

William explained that some of his party were travelling together on a special trip - a reunion of old pupils from an English public school. They would be used to the lack of comfort in the annexe.

"Ah, je comprends. Ze public school - I know, ze cold showers, ze beatings, ze cricket. I understand. Of course zese people can have ze annexe."

"And, would there be any possibility of this group eating in the separate little dining room? And having a different meal from the rest of the party? You know, something French, like escargots and cuisses de grenouilles?"

"But of course. I think I have some frozen cuisses de grenouilles left over from a French party. The escargots, zey are no trouble. Yes, I will put ze persons you mention in ze annexe. But, it is not my fault if I get any complaints from Orbit!"

William assured him that he would get no complaints from Orbit.

He made a second phone call, this time to Henri Rigaud at the Chemin de Fer Touristique de la Charente. He just wanted to check that everything would be okay for Mike Turner on Thursday.

"Yes, Monsieur Simpson. Everything is fine. But you make sure you tell your friend that he must get out of the train at Montluçon. There you can pick him up in your coach. When the train goes to Vierzon, they will lock it in a shed. There is a very big manifestation at Vierzon - there will be big people - the Ministry of Transport, the head of the SNCF. Vierzon depot will be heavily guarded. They will not want strangers around."

Pleased with his morning's work, William went for a stroll down the Rue Denis Papin, the main thoroughfare of Blois. Some fruit from an épicerie and half of a nice fresh baguette would suit him fine for lunch. Walking along the street, he heard heavy metal music blaring a few feet away, and, looking ahead, he saw Steve Vicks with his abominable ghetto-blaster. Whilst William still enjoyed listening to his own favourite music, he had long since grown out of that adolescent phase when he needed to carry it with him 24 hours a day. Steve Vicks, it appeared, had not.

****

Back in London, Big Ben had just struck eleven. In Orbit House, Margot got two coffees from the machine and took one to H.R.

"Are those two men still in with Mr P?"

"Yes," replied Helena. "It's been forty-five minutes now."

"Have you any idea who they are?"

"No. I've never seen them before." Helena put down the little strip of paper from the telex machine which she had been re-reading. Lots of Love, it said. Did William really mean that?

"They looked like the police to me," Margot remarked.

"Police? But they weren't wearing uniforms or anything ..."

"No, I don't mean ordinary bobbies from the beat. I think they're plain-clothes detectives. If you ask me, something's up. I just hope it's nothing to do with Mr P. and his tax returns. I couldn't bear to be made redundant if they shut the firm down."

Helena pondered for a moment. There was no sense in worrying about it. She looked again at William's telex message. She was certain he hadn't ever signed a telex message that way before. She would have to go to the filing cabinet and check some of his old telexes just to check how he had worded them.

"Margot?"

"Yes."

"What do you think of William? William Simpson, I mean."

"William? Well, he's terribly shy, but he's quite a nice lad, I think. You're not thinking of ..."

Margot broke off as the door to Mr P.'s office swung open and the two visitors left. A few moments later, Mr Papadopoulos himself emerged. Margot was relieved to see that he was not in handcuffs.

"Would you two ladies mind coming into my office for a minute?"

They followed him in. Mr Papadopoulos shut the door behind them and sat on the swivel armchair behind his desk.

"You know the Scenic Best of France tour that's out at the moment?"

"Yes," said Margot, "Tour F443/07. William Simpson is on it."

"Did you know that I let him take ten of his old school chums on it?"

"Yes, I'd heard you say something about that. It was because that South African party pulled out".

"Well, these gentlemen come from the police. They say one of William's friends is a crook."

"Do they mean Mr Rottoli?" Helena asked excitedly. "William sent a telex to say he'd been arrested in France."

"No, not Mr Rottoli. It seems that there is a Mr Jonathan Atkinson on the tour. He is wanted by the police for the stealing of electric equipment - you know, car radios, CD players. He has been selling them on markets in the East End."

"This seems incredible," said Margot. "And with that other man who was arrested in France as well! I would never have expected someone like William to have friends like that. We're certainly seeing a new side of his personality."

Helena Rogers blushed.

"What are you going to do?" she asked. "Are you going to tell William?"

"No, I don't think that's a good idea. If William finds out his best buddy is wanted by the police, what do you expect he will do? I think he helps the buddy to escape. No, I tell the police the tour is coming back to Dover on Sunday, I give them the ferry time, they arrest Atkinson at Dover. You understand?"

The two girls nodded in assent.

"Right. You not mention this to anyone. At Orbit Tours we always co-operate with the authorities, yes!"

Margot and Helena returned to their desks and their lukewarm machine coffee. The exciting part of the morning was over. Only one horrible doubt haunted Helena: could her William really be associating with a bunch of criminals?

****

William returned to the hotel to get his briefcase in readiness for the afternoon trip. As he closed his bedroom door and started walking down the stairs, he glanced down through the balustrade and saw Jonathan Atkinson get into the lift on the floor below. Thinking it an opportunity too good to miss, he walked back up to the fourth-floor, waited until he could hear the lift start and then pulled the outer lift door open slightly. There was a shuddering noise as the lift came to a halt between floors.

Racing downstairs, William went to the coach park. Claude was not there yet but a few passengers were waiting, including the ever-eager Mr Maxwell. Steve Vicks arrived, carrying his ghetto-blaster and leather jacket.

"Oh, isn't the coach open yet? Can I leave these here for a minute. I'm just off to have a piss."

And Steve Vicks left the stereo and the jacket on the ground behind the coach.

"Salut, mon brave!" Claude was looking in high spirits today. Perhaps he had just received good news from his wife, or possibly the morning's lie-in had done him good. He unlocked the coach and got into the driver's seat. Pulling open the driver's window, he motioned to William outside:

"I have to reverse the coach to turn it so we can get back onto the main road. Can you tell me if it's okay to go back?"

"Certainly," said William. "You're fine to go straight back. There's nothing behind you."

Claude started the coach, and it moved back with a small cloud of black fumes and the rumbling of its diesel engine. Suddenly there was an ear-splitting crash.

"Oh, mon dieu!" Claude stopped the coach and leapt down from the cab. "Have I hit something?"

Underneath the offside rear wheel lay the shattered remains of Steve Vicks' radio-cassette player. Its plastic outer casing had been smashed to a thousand pieces. A solitary battery, broken free from its compartment, rolled pathetically away from the wreckage.

Steve Vicks arrived just too late. He saw the scene of the murder and headed straight for Claude:

"You bloody idiot! Didn't you see that I'd left it there? Are you blind?"

Claude failed to respond. Vicks turned to William:

"Why didn't you stop him?"

Mr Maxwell turned to Steve Vicks:

"I think Claude deserves a medal for this. All yesterday afternoon you were annoying us with that wretched contraption! You won't be able to do that now!"

"I was just trying to listen to some decent music rather than that rubbish the driver was playing."

"Some of us," said Mr Maxwell, "rather enjoy the sort of music the driver was playing yesterday. And you know the rules. No personal stereos to be played on the coach. You should have thought of that before you booked the tour!"

Steve Vicks was speechless. Claude had now completed his manoeuvre and he could at last examine the remains of his pride and joy, but even the most competent repairman would have been unable to do anything with it. He scooped up the pieces and deposited them in a large dustbin full of kitchen refuse behind the hotel, picked up his fortunately unharmed leather jacket, and went to sit on the coach.

William waited until everyone had boarded the coach before doing a count. Twenty-two. There was one passenger missing. Of course! He rushed back to the hotel, ran up the stairs to the fourth floor two at a time, and carefully pushed the outer lift door shut. The ancient machinery below creaked into action. William sprinted downstairs and reached the bottom just in time to see a shaking, pale-faced Jonathan Atkinson stagger out of the lift.

"It got stuck - between the floors... I thought I'd be there all afternoon." Atkinson had become once more the snivelling wimp he had picked up in London.

"These old lifts, they do break down sometimes," said William, as he hurried Atkinson off to the coach.

Their half day excursion took them over the old bridge across the Loire and along the south bank of the river before they turned off into the Forest of Chambord. Claude parked in the coach park and William led the passengers up to the castle. He explained that he was going to give them a brief guided tour.

The chief feature of the interior of Chambord castle is the magnificent spiral staircase which goes from the ground floor right up to the roof. It has two separate spirals, so that two people may climb the staircase at the same time but never meet, although they will see each other through the central stairwell with its decorative banisters. William divided his party into two groups as he handed out the entrance tickets, asking the Chestfield group to go up one of the ramps, whilst he followed, with the other passengers, on the second ramp.

"Look at them across there!" William shouted to Mr Maxwell. Through the openings in the side of the staircase they could see Steve Vicks, Mike Turner and Jonathan Atkinson walking up, with Mr Eveleigh and Ian Bailey-Filmer coming just behind. William sneered at them through one of the openings and shouted "Bet you can't catch us!" and started running up the stairs. He was followed by Mr Maxwell, by the two Tjeong boys and by the Charlton girls, who started taking the game very seriously, pausing at every landing and pulling faces at the Chestfield group and shouting "Tee-hee-hee! We'll get to the top first! We are the champions!"

William arrived almost breathless on the roof of the castle, with Rebecca and Josephine Charlton, Erwin and Abraham Tjeong and a red-faced Mr Maxwell. He walked around with them to the other exit of the staircase. Mike Turner and Jonathan Atkinson were just emerging.

"Tee-hee-hee! We got here first!" shouted Rebecca Charlton.

"How the hell did you do that? I never saw you walk past us!" gasped Mike Turner.

"It's because we're magic!" shouted Josephine.

William left it at that. Being accredited with magical powers was the very best thing that could happen to a tour manager.

After visiting Chambord, the group returned to the coach and headed back towards Blois. The excursion was also supposed to include a wine-tasting, so Claude took them to a wine-merchant's on the outskirts of Blois. Partly set in one of the natural limestone caves which are a feature of the region, Les Caves du Loir-et-Cher, S.A. specialised in quality local wines, but also kept a good stock of cheap table wines from all over France, to suit the less discriminating, usually British, passing trade.

William paid from his float for some bottles of the local sparkling wine, which were opened and passed to the group for tasting. Soon the conversation was all about wine. William chinked glasses with Lucia and Maria, and helped Miss Crosbie choose a very light red to take home to her sister. Then Hugh Bartlett-Nicholson came up to him:

"I say, William. Do you suppose they've got any of that 1968 Bordeaux here?"

"No, not here. It's a very rare wine, you know. You're lucky to find it anywhere these days."

"Well, do you think you could recommend something which would taste like it? Don't they have something which is nearly as good?"

Fortunately for William, Les Caves du Loir-et-Cher did not show the prices on their bottles, but displayed them in a list consisting of several sheets of A4 paper stapled together, and all in French. There was little likelihood that Hugh would check the price of the wine.

"I think they've got just the thing," said William, and darted off to the neighbouring part of the cellars. He took from a crate a bottle labelled SANSEGAL - Vin des différents pays de la Communaute Européene. This was the house wine normally served in carafes at the Hotel du Duc de Guise, and its name meant 'without equal'. Claude for one, who considered himself something of a wine expert, used to joke that the name was certainly apt.

William reappeared with the bottle of Sansegal and two plastic cups. He removed the cap of the bottle and served generous portions to Hugh and Miranda.

"Yes, this is lovely!" exclaimed Miranda.

"I can taste the similarity," said Hugh. "But why has it got a plastic cap on the bottle?"

"The French are doing this more and more with their highest quality wines. It doesn't spoil the taste. You see, corks can go rotten in time. And bits sometimes break off and get into the wine."

"Of course. The clever French. And what's all this on the label? Something about the European Community?"

"That just means that the wine has been made from specially selected grapes as approved by all the countries in the Common Market."

"Right. We must get some of this! How much is it a bottle?"

William reflected. A litre bottle of *Sanségal* retailed for about six francs, plus a small deposit on the bottle. "Twenty-five francs a bottle," he said.

"What an incredible bargain!" said Hugh. "And how does it come - I mean, do you have to buy it by the bottle?"

"No. They have boxes of six bottles."

"Let's take four boxes. That'll come to ... six hundred francs. Here, get it for me and take it out to the coach!" Hugh opened his wallet and took out three 200-franc notes, which he handed to William.

Miranda and Hugh drifted back to the rest of the party, where the last of the sparkling wine was being drained. William saw the manager of the cellars, paid him about a quarter of the money Bartlett-Nicholson had given him, and made four journeys out to the coach with the boxes.

The party which returned to the coach were mostly in high spirits. With the exception of the Tjeongs, they had all drunk at least a glass of wine each. Atkinson, from the look of him, had drunk considerably more. As they headed back to the hotel, William decided it was time to tell them his ghost story.

"If you've been to the Château in Blois," William began, "you will have heard of the Duke of Guise."

"Yes!" piped up little Miss Crosbie. "He was lieutenant-general of France and head of the League..."

William cut her short. "Well, the Duke of Guise was foully murdered in the Château in 1588." There were excited screams from the two Charlton girls. "As you must have realised," he continued, "the hotel where we are staying is called the Hotel du Duc de Guise."

"Ooh! Go on!" screamed Rebecca Charlton.

"Four hundred years ago, the very building where we are staying was the home of the Duke of Guise. There was even a secret passage linking the hotel and the château, so that the Duke could go and see the King without being noticed."

"Anyway, ever since the murder of the Duke of Guise, they say that his ghost still haunts his old room in the hotel. It's now room number 31. Every

Tuesday night, so they say, the ghost of the Duke appears in his old room."

There were 'oohs!' and 'aahs' from the Charlton and Tjeong children, and laughs from most of the coachload. Only Jonathan Atkinson remained strangely silent.

"Anyway, this ghost apparently never does any harm to women. But if a man should happen to see it, it means that something very bad will happen to him within a week!"

"You shouldn't tell stories like that!" said Claude, as he and William walked back to the hotel after dropping off the passengers.

"They love it really," said William.

At dinner that evening, William again could not resist giving the waitresses a hand. He was rather pleased when Atkinson ordered a whole carafe of house red for himself.

"Now, about this wine, William," said Hugh Bartlett-Nicholson. "Did you say yesterday that the hotel still had another bottle of 1968 Bordeaux?"

"Yes. They've got just one bottle left. Do you want it tonight?"

"Well, I thought I'd buy it to take away with us. I mean, it's very rare. We might not find another one."

That was certainly true, thought William. He had brought the bottle back down from his bedroom and concealed it under his table-cloth. "I'm afraid it will cost more. You see, the hotel can charge special prices if you drink wine on the premises. But, if you buy it to take away, you have to pay an extra tax."

"How much will that be?"

"The wine will come to seven hundred and fifty francs" said William.

"That's very expensive!" retorted Hugh.

"But darling, think about it!" urged Miranda. "It could be our last chance. We might never get another one!"

"You're right," said Hugh. He withdrew the money from his wallet and gave it to William. William came back a few minutes later with the bottle, urging Hugh to keep it hidden until after the meal.

"I will. Scout's Honour!" said Hugh.

After the group had finished eating, William succeeded again in doctoring Ian Bailey-Filmer's coffee.

The Orbit clients went to bed fairly early. Tomorrow they would be moving off again. William enjoyed a pastis in the bar with Claude before going up to his room. He set his alarm for 2 a.m.

****

Waking up suddenly, William wondered whether it was really worth it. Dressing up in a white sheet and pretending to be a ghost never fooled anyone. However, he remembered how pale and shaken Atkinson had appeared after being stuck in the lift for ten minutes. The young man was obviously a bundle of nerves. And he had noticed Atkinson drinking rather heavily since then, both at the wine-tasting and during dinner.

William pulled the top sheet off his bed, folded it across his shoulders, and crept downstairs to the deserted Reception Desk. Behind the desk he found a duplicate key to Room 31. He tiptoed back up to the third floor. Oh, bother! He had been seen! Two figures with a torch were walking along the corridor. He looked more closely... It was Rebecca and Josephine Charlton.

"What are you two doing up at this time?" whispered William.

"We wanted to see the ghost!"

"I'm sorry, but there's a problem - the ghost isn't coming tonight."

"Oh!" exclaimed Josephine.

"But listen you two! I want you to do something for me. You mustn't tell anyone else about it! And if you do this for me, I'll give you a bar of chocolate each!"

"What is it?" asked Rebecca.

"You see," said William, "you know and I know that the ghost isn't coming tonight, but Mr Atkinson in Room 31 is going to be terribly disappointed if he doesn't see the ghost, so I'm going to dress up and pretend to be the ghost. I want you two to come into Mr Atkinson's room with me, and make weird spooky noises as I talk to him. You can also shine your torch into his eyes so he can't see me very clearly."

"Won't poor Mr Atkinson be scared?" asked Josephine.

"That's the whole point. He's expecting to be scared. If he's not scared he might write a horrid letter to Orbit Tours saying the ghost wasn't scary enough. You've got to be as scary as you can!"

"All right. We promise to be scary!"

William put the sheet over his head and silently inserted the key in the lock. The door to Room 31 opened noiselessly. Followed closely by the two girls, William crept up to the sleeping figure in the bed. Motioning to the girls to get down behind the bed, William reached for Atkinson and began shaking him.

"And what are you doing in MY bed?" Jonathan Atkinson awoke to hear a ghostly white figure addressing him. Bright lights were flying around the room, settling sometimes on his eyes, so he could see nothing clearly. He remembered the courier talking about the ghost, but surely that was just a silly story. There weren't really such things as ghosts. Could it be a dream? He pinched himself and discovered it wasn't. Perhaps he'd just had too much red wine with his dinner. The figure spoke again in a terrifying unearthly voice:

"From the other world I have been following your movements, Mr Atkinson. I know you have done evil things. You must repent and change your ways." The speech was followed by some spine-chilling ghostly whines and wails: there must be a whole host of spirits out there.

"Who are you?" yelled Atkinson. But already the spectre was sinking away through the door and back into the pitch darkness of the night.

"Thank you very much. You were fantastic!" William congratulated the girls after they had all crept back to the fourth floor landing. The girls' room was almost opposite William's. He went into his room, took two bars of the delicious local Poulain chocolate from his morning shopping session, and handed them to the girls. It was a cheap price to pay for a masterpiece.

Jonathan Atkinson was now sitting bolt upright in bed, with the light on. He didn't think he would be able to get to sleep again that night. Just above him, on the fourth floor, William slid back into bed and was asleep almost immediately.

Chapter Nine

Audio-Visual French

On Wednesday morning the Orbit coach left the city of Blois and made its way along the long, slow, N152 trunk road that follows the north bank of the Loire. William enjoyed this road: although the scenery could not be described as spectacular, it was most pleasant, and he made stops along the way so that the passengers could get off and take photographs of the castles at Chaumont and Amboise across the river.

Jonathan Atkinson had been the very last person down to breakfast that morning. His face had been as white as the sheet from William's bed, and there were dark rings under his eyes. He had drunk a couple of cups of the Hotel du Duc de Guise's strong coffee before boarding the coach. Now he was lying across the rear seat snatching forty winks, set apart from all of the other passengers.

Claude took the coach through Tours, across the great divide of the Loire and south to Chinon. Here they had a coffee-stop and William showed the group the ruined castle, the largest in the Loire Valley. Miss Crosbie enthused about its historical associations, about Richard the Lionheart and Joan of Arc, and Mr Maxwell swept the ramparts with his camcorder. From Chinon they continued south to the amazing fortified town of Richelieu, named after the great Cardinal who founded it in the seventeenth century. William gave his passengers time to stroll along the tree-lined streets, and to admire the noble proportions of the buildings in what had been planned as a metropolis but had never become much more than a village.

The next place on their itinerary was Poitiers, but here William avoided the crowded city centre and directed Claude to an out-of-town shopping centre in the suburbs. Medium-sized French provincial towns tended to close completely between twelve and two o'clock, but here his passengers could buy a good meal, change money at the bank and browse in the hypermarket.

Miss Crosbie was not too keen on William's choice of stopping place:

"But I hate these big modern places! Why can't we stop in the town centre?"

William told her that in the town centre everything would be shut, and reminded her of the difficulties they had encountered in Chartres when they hadn't been able to park in the centre.

"Oh, yes - you're so right, of course! At least here I'll be able to find my way back to the coach!"

After Miss Crosbie had wandered off, William and Claude locked the coach and headed for the cafeteria. Apart from the places where he asked the passengers to wait for him so he could take them on a guided tour, William generally didn't see where they headed to, as he normally stayed with the coach until he had helped Miss Crosbie out. By that time, the younger passengers were often out of sight. He was conscious, however, that the Chestfield people were sticking together more and more. Steve Vicks seemed subdued since the loss of his ghetto-blaster, almost as if part of the man himself was missing. Mike Turner, the former J.C.R. captain, appeared to have taken on again the role of leader; William had noticed him walking ahead of the others and ordering the drinks in a restaurant or street cafe. He thought back to Chestfield days: during his first two terms he'd actually quite liked Turner; only then, in his third term, Turner had been appointed captain of the J.C.R. William had hoped that he would have an ally in Turner as J.C.R. captain, but, instead, Turner had joined the side of the bullies and had never done anything to stop them tormenting him. He wondered whether any of the others would take over this leading role once he had got rid of Turner.

After lunch in the cafeteria, William went for a quick look around the hypermarket. He almost bumped into Miss Crosbie, who was carrying two well-filled plastic bags.

"Oh, William! I love this place! I've got all my presents for next Christmas already. Can we stop at another of these supermarkets, please? I just didn't have time to look around everywhere!"

William told Miss Crosbie he'd do his best. Returning to the coach shortly afterwards, he noticed that Claude was holding the boot open as most of his passengers deposited cardboard boxes or carrier bags in the luggage compartment. It had evidently been a popular stop.

From Poitiers to Neuville-sur-Charente the direct route is only one hundred kilometres across open country, about an hour and a half's drive. But Orbit's planners, who had designed the 'Scenic Delights of France' tour, did not believe in rushing things. The itinerary demanded a stop in Saintes, one of France's old Roman towns, and a visit to a brandy distillery in Cognac, before finally reaching the overnight hotel.

William gave a brief explanation about the Roman occupation of France over the microphone. He kept it brief, because he realised it would go right over the heads of the Murrays or the Tjeongs, whereas if he had tried to do a longer explanation, he would be sure to have it corrected by Miss Crosbie, or perhaps by Ian Bailey-Filmer. William remembered that Bailey-Filmer had done some research on Roman France at University - there was something about it in the *Alumni 1971-1980* book at Chestfield.

The coach pulled in just above the enormous scooped-out hollow of the Roman amphitheatre at Saintes. Rebecca and Josephine Charlton leaped off the coach and tore down the steps to the arena below, closely followed by Erwin and Abraham Tjeong. Some of the older members of the party were content to remain on top and look down.

"So what was this place?" Mrs Murray tapped William on the shoulder. "Some kinda baseball stadium?"

"I suppose you could put it like that. They would have had fights with wild beasts and gladiators. Perhaps even chariot races, you know, like Ben Hur."

"Gee. Yeah, I could just imagine Charlton Heston riding around this place. Come, honey, let's take a look!"

And Mr and Mrs Murray started negotiating the worn stone steps down to the arena, where the blood-curdling cries of the Charlton and Tjeong children could be heard in a mock battle.

Ian Bailey-Filmer did not bother to go down to the arena. He had never visited Saintes on any of his field trips during his Cambridge days, as the site had already been fully excavated and was well-documented. But sitting on the old stones, where the lizards were sunning themselves in the afternoon heat, he felt, for the first time on the tour, as if he were back on a summer vacation from Cambridge. He was at last beginning to enjoy the tour. What a pity, though, that the French had forgotten how to make coffee. The revolting liquid he had drunk after dinner last night had been no better than the night before. He hoped fervently that coffee in France, like the weather, got better as you travelled further south.

Mr Maxwell came rushing up to William:

"Do you know, this is the most fantastic place you've taken me to so far! Do you think you can do me a favour? I'd like you to take some film of me walking across the Roman arena! I'd love to show that to my kids in Australia - their dad being a gladiator! Look, I'll show you how it works."

William was handed the camcorder and given a step-by-step guide of how to use it. It was really quite straightforward. You got the subject in focus, zoomed in and squeezed the trigger. Mr Maxwell sprinted down the stone steps and then rushed to and fro across the arena, brandishing a pullover like a toreador with an imaginary bull.

"Did you get that all on film?" asked Mr Maxwell, back at the top of the steps.

"I think so," said William. Mr Maxwell showed him how to rewind the tape. By looking through the viewfinder you could review what you had just filmed on a small black-and-white monitor. It was so easy.

A short run south-east from Saintes took them to Cognac. Here, Claude and William parked the coach and left the group in the hands of an English-speaking guide who took them around the cellars of one of the famous brandy houses. The visit finished with a free glass of brandy for everyone. Spirits seemed very high when the group got back on the coach.

It was about three-quarters of an hour's drive from Cognac to the village of Neuville, on the upper reaches of the Charente where the fast-flowing and meandering stream had yet to become the stately fully-fledged river they had crossed in Saintes. The countryside around here was delightfully rural, thought William, although quite different from his own beloved Kent with its hedgerows and oast houses. Vast fields of sunflowers stretched on both sides of the narrow route départementale, and snatches of the song of cicadas could be heard as the coach passed by.

The Hotel Beau-Séjour stood right on the bank of the Charente, alongside a medieval stone bridge with several arches. Across the road from the hotel was a small Romanesque church with a statue of Our Lady in a niche above the door, and behind the church was Neuville's only other watering-place, the Bar de l'Hôtel de Ville, where William and Claude usually went for a pastis before dinner.

When they arrived, William asked his passengers to remain seated on the coach until he came back with the room keys. At some hotels, it always took a bit of time to distribute the keys, but here in Neuville William just had to make sure everything was alright.

Monsieur Mollet, the proprietor, was polishing some glasses in the bar when William came in. Like the Duc de Guise at Blois, this was another hotel run with a bare minimum of staff.

"The keys are here in ze basket. I have given you some rooms in ze annexe as you requested. Please, you do ze distribution and give me ze names later."

He was handed a small basket with the room keys. This was exactly what William wanted. He took out his copy of the Rooming List and first allocated the rooms in the main part of the hotel. These rooms had been modernised to a high standard and all boasted private bathrooms and television. He then turned to the Chestfield names.

William had one superstition in his job. When an hotel gave him the job of allocating the rooms - rather than mark the numbers down on their own copy of the Rooming List as they were supposed to do - he always picked Room 22 for himself, if there was one with that number. It dated back to the first hotel on his first tour, when that was the room number that he had been allocated. Nowadays he felt that, provided he spent at least one night of a tour in Room 22, the tour would go well. On this particular occasion he had a particular reason to wish to be accommodated in Room 22.

He was delighted to see the key to Room 22, with its heavy old-fashioned brass fob, among the keys in the basket. He hunted around and pulled out key number 23. Rooms 22 and 23 were side by side on the second floor of the annexe. Room 22 was a single, whilst Room 23, though no bigger than a single and normally allocated as such, had a double bed. Between the two rooms was a connecting door which could be opened if, for example, the rooms were allocated to a couple with a young child. William knew that the key which opened the connecting door was usually kept on the keyring of Room 23. William slipped it off the ring and slid it onto the ring of Room 22.

Before going back to the coach, William went up to the second floor of the annexe by the back stairs, which doubled as a fire escape, and checked Rooms 22 and 23. There was no furniture blocking the connecting door, and, when he tried unlocking it with the key, it opened smoothly and silently.

Returning to his group, William went down the coach handing out the keys. He didn't like to mention the word 'Annexe' to any group, knowing that to some people the very word suggested inferior accommodation. Instead he just explained that certain room numbers were in a different wing of the building, which was reached through the small door on the left rather than through the main entrance.

After depositing his luggage in Room 22, William lost no time in walking over to the Bar de l'Hôtel de Ville.

"Un pastis, s'il vous plaît!"

Milou's head bobbed up from behind the bar, and he rushed around and greeted William as if they had been old friends who had not seen each other for years. He bestowed William with enormous kisses on both cheeks in a style which William, until he had been in his early twenties, had always thought the expression 'French kissing' meant when he had come across it in books or magazines.

Milou poured William an enormous pastis and gave him an account of the last few weeks of his life.

"Is Valérie here?" asked William, when at last he had a chance to get a word in edgeways.

"Oui, bien sûr! I'll call her. Valérie! William from England is here to see you!"

There was the sound of feet on a wooden staircase and a very pretty girl appeared behind the bar. She came around and, like her father, bestowed two kisses upon William's cheeks. In her case, William returned the compliment.

Milou returned to his duties at the bar and left William chatting with Valérie. She was eighteen and her main ambition in life was to get married and have a family. Her fiancé was at present away doing his military service, and meanwhile Valérie helped out in her father's bar. She had straight fair hair, blue eyes, and a round face with a slightly vacant expression. She was wearing a T shirt emblazoned with the name of one of the lastest rock groups, and a pair of cut-off jeans. Her breasts were full and well-developed, and her bronze thighs were perhaps a little on the plump side, but still deliciously palatable. William found himself thinking back once again to Helena Rogers. How he preferred the mysterious English maiden to this charming but simple French girl.

William handed Valérie the little bag which had come all the way from Virgin Records in London's Oxford Street.

"Ah! You have remembered. Le dernier de Morrissey!" At this she threw her arms around William again and gave him another dose of kisses.

"Are you okay for this evening?" asked William.

"Mais oui! I think you are so funny, you English! I am quite excited about it! I cannot wait to …"

"Ssh!" said William. He could see Ian Bailey-Filmer approaching the bar. He didn't want anyone from the Chestfield group to overhear what he was planning for this evening. He switched the topic of conversation to the current Top 40 singles, and poured more water into his pastis.

Back at the hotel, Hugh and Miranda Bartlett-Nicholson, Steve Vicks and Mike Turner were sitting dejectedly in the lobby.

"It's disgusting!" shouted Miranda.

"No telly or anything," moaned Mike Turner. "Not even a bleeding bog!"

"How clever of the courier to rush off as soon as we got to this place!" added Steve Vicks. "I bet he realised there'd be a riot!"

"He's been so helpful up to now!" said Hugh. "I'm sure he'll be able to change the rooms for us if we asked him."

"It's not a question of the rooms. The whole stinking lousy hotel needs changing!"

At this point Mr and Mrs Murray came down from their room.

"Hallo there," said Steve Vicks to Mr Murray. "We were just talking about this bloody hotel. We think Orbit Tours ought to be prosecuted for putting us in a dump like this!"

"Oh, really?" Mr Murray seemed puzzled. "I don't know what you're on about. I've heard you guys whingeing since the start of the tour. You should start enjoying yourselves."

"I think our room here's as good as anything we've ever stayed in back in Texas," added Mrs Murray.

"Oh, come on! For one night it's hardly worth worrying about it. Let's go and get a drink!" Miranda led the others to the hotel bar.

Mr Eveleigh rested on his bed in Room 23 and surveyed the scene about him. For the first time since the start of the holiday he felt he really was in France. The room, with its battered old mahogany furniture, enormous pedestal washbasin with brass taps, stained bidet and pink floral wallpaper covering the ceiling as well as the walls, could have come straight out of the pages of Shortman's Audio-Visual French. It was exactly the sort of place where Monsieur Aubert might have stayed if away on a business trip. He went over to the washbasin and turned on the cold tap. There was a hammering sound followed by a loud belching noise, and a trickle of reddish-brown water. How pleased he was that they hadn't spoiled everywhere in France.

Like Mr Eveleigh, Nick Patterson was also delighted by the Hotel Beau-Séjour. Not so much because of its old-world charm or spartan facilities, but because of its location. After arriving at the hotel, he had simply dumped his luggage in his room and headed straight over to the old bridge with his sketch book. He now had the basis for a good sketch: he would complete it tomorrow morning. After walking back to the hotel, he had flung open his window and seen a whole field of sunflowers dancing in the setting sun. Sunflowers! He thought of Van Gogh, whose painting of these very flowers had been sold for a world record sum. Could he do the same as Van Gogh? Not having brought any secateurs with him on holiday, he took his nail scissors from his sponge bag and made his way down the back stairs towards the fields. After dinner he would find a vase or something to stand them in, and sketch by the light of his bedside lamp.

As William walked back to the hotel, he fancied he could hear the distant rumble of thunder. There was a glorious sunset to the west, but over in the east the storm clouds were gathering. As he entered the hotel he was greeted by Mr Maxwell.

"Say, there! I've been trying to make myself understood by that man in the hotel for twenty minutes, but I haven't succeeded. Can you help?"

"What's the problem?"

"It's my camcorder," explained Mr Maxwell, brandishing it. "The battery's run flat. It needs recharging, and I haven't got the right sort of adaptor to plug it in. I hoped the hotel manager might have one."

"Just leave it with me," said William. He took it up to Room 22 and searched for the travel adaptor he always carried with him. As he plugged it in, he examined the video-camera more closely.

Mr Maxwell's camcorder was one of those big ones which took full-size VHS cassettes, the same sort you get in a normal video recorder. An idea had been forming in William's mind since they'd been at the Roman amphitheatre that afternoon, but it was only now, with the video-camera in his room, that he thought about putting it into action.

William always carried two or three video tapes with him in his luggage. Most coaches were fitted with video players these days. Although Orbit disapproved of their use on normal coach journeys, there were those occasions, such as three-hour delays at Calais while waiting for the ferry, when a video was invaluable. He sorted through his luggage. He found two tapes carrying feature films, which he didn't really want to wipe out. Then he found a video from the Norwegian Tourist Board, which he had picked up from the World Travel Market a couple of years ago. It was about ten minutes long and consisted largely of arty film shots of fjords and mountains. William carried it with him because it helped to advertise another country which the passengers could visit with Orbit.

He took the Norwegian Tourist Board video out of its case, and cut off a small piece from his pocket roll of sticky tape to cover the little hole where the safety tab had been removed. He then ejected Mr Maxwell's tape from the camcorder and replaced it with the Norwegian one.

William put on a clean shirt and made his way down to the dining-room. The main restaurant at the Hotel Beau-Séjour was a long, low room overlooking the river. It was divided longitudinally by a row of potted palms and a tank of tropical fish, forming a section at the back where he would normally have sat with the driver. This evening, however, William intended that the back area should be used by the Chestfield group. It was very handy that each section of the dining room had its own independent access to the kitchen, so that the diners on one side of the partition would never know what the diners on the other side were eating. This was a great boon to drivers and couriers when they wanted to eat something better than the normal set three-course meal, but didn't want their clients to spot them living it up.

Just to make sure that the Chestfield group all sat on the right side of the partition, William wrote out some small cards with the names of all twenty-three passengers and placed them on the tables. These cards were supplied by Orbit for special occasions such as Welcome and Farewell dinners, but were in actual fact seldom used. After placing the nine cards on the Chestfield side of the partition, William laid out the remaining fourteen on the other side. The Tjeongs and the Charltons occupied a table for four each. William laid the cards for Mr Maxwell, Miss Crosbie and Mr and Mrs Murray on a third table. There was only one more table laid out: the hotel had not given William a separate table with Claude. William wrote 'Driver' and 'Courier' on two more cards and put them on the table together with cards marked 'Miss Mora' and 'Miss Garcia'.

"Have you finished all your preparations?"

William turned around. It was Monsieur Mollet.

"Monsieur Mollet," he began, "I would like to pay for everyone in the group to have half a carafe of local wine with their dinner. How much will that come to?"

Monsieur Mollet did a quick calculation: "For twenty-four persons, Monsieur, let us say… five hundred francs."

"Here, I'll pay you now." William handed over the note. He didn't wish to profit personally from all the money he'd got from the Bartlett-Nicholsons.

Monsieur Mollet put the pottery carafes on all the tables. William opened the door and ushered the group in. He explained about the dining-room arrangements, and there was quite a bit of fun as everyone looked for their place.

"Oh! Look! We're with you! How sweet!" exclaimed Lucia.

"Oh, les filles!" shrugged Claude, taking his seat between Maria and Lucia.

William had chosen his table carefully. Although the table with the Chestfield passengers was almost completely hidden from view by the potted palms, William was only just across the partition from them, and he could pick up snatches of their conversation.

"Funny us all turning up on this tour!" said Hugh Bartlett-Nicholson. "We've had such fun talking about old days!"

"Remember that little bloke we used to rag all the time?"

"Oh, yes, Steve, I remember." This was Mike Turner's voice. "Little Willy with his little willy ... remember the showers in the gym?"

"I wonder what he's doing now!" said Hugh Bartlett-Nicholson.

"I dunno. Probably in some dusty old library, researching into Outer Mongolian watering-cans or something like that." There was a general laugh from the table at Steve Vicks' remarks.

"Do you know," said Mike Turner, "some of those things we did to him were pretty nasty really, weren't they?"

Jonathan Atkinson, who had been listening to the conversation, didn't comment. Whatever they may have done to Little Willy in the past, it was nowhere near as nasty as the things which were happening in his life at the moment.

"Soup?" William turned around and saw an enormous pair of almost-black eyes smiling at him. The waiter had left the tureen on the table and Lucia was offering some to him.

"Yes please." Lucia ladled out the soup.

"You've got something on your mind!" said Maria. "Are you worried about anything?"

"Oh, no, not especially," said William. "It's just the job. I have to make sure everything goes smoothly. Even at the end of the day I still have paper-work to do. I can't relax until the tour is over!"

"Oh, poor William! I understand. But you must relax sometime! Will you come with us to the night-club when we get to Paris?"

William thought ahead to the Grenouille Bondissante. "Of course I will," he said.

Over on the other side of the partition, the Chestfield group were having trouble deciding what to do with their escargots. They had arrived complete with shells, smelling of garlic and butter.

"These are revolting!" exclaimed Jonathan Atkinson. "How on earth can we be expected to eat this rubbish?"

"They're actually quite a delicacy," said Miranda, taking one of the snails to her mouth and attempting to suck out the contents. A green liquid ran down and stained the front of her blouse.

"You're not eating these the right way!" Mr Eveleigh could have been telling some third-formers that they were not declining *avoir* correctly. "You're supposed to use this." He lifted up an implement which looked a bit like some kind of patent device for taking the top off an egg. He deftly grabbed one of the snails in its metal jaws, whereupon it slipped and fell into Ian Bailey-Filmer's glass of wine. The wine tipped over into Bailey-Filmer's lap.

"I say, terribly sorry, old boy!" said Mr Eveleigh.

****

"What do you think of the tour, then?" William asked Lucia.

"It is fantastic. We have seen so many beautiful things."

"And what do you think of the other people on the tour?"

"Very nice. I like the Americans. And the family from Indonesia".

"What about the young British people?"

"Oh, you mean the people travelling together? I liked Signor Rottoli, but he was Italian, he wasn't English. He was sophisticated. But these English boys," - Lucia waved a hand towards the partition - "they are not real men. I talk with them. They are just boys."

"You don't like them, then?" asked William.

"Not like you and Claude." Now it was Maria speaking. "You and Claude have the experience. You travel. We like you".

The *roti de porc* and *petits pois* arrived, and once again Lucia served them around the table.

Across the partition, Bailey-Filmer had just returned from his room in the annexe where he had changed his trousers. He got back to the table just as the second course arrived.

"What's this froggy muck?" asked Jonathan Atkinson.

"Froggy's the right word for it!" replied John Bridger. "We've got frogs' legs!"

"Now, Hugh, we must try these!" urged Miranda. She helped herself to a portion, and passed the serving dish to her husband.

"They're really quite up-market, you know!" said Hugh.

"I was reading about how they produce these things," said Steve Vicks. "Apparently the frogs all come from polluted swamps in India. They pay these little boys a pittance to catch the frogs. When they've caught them, they just rip off the back legs and throw the rest of the frog back into the swamp. Still alive!"

Miranda gulped and spat out a mouthful of grenouille. Hugh refilled his wine glass from the carafe and took a large draught.

The dessert, *Tarte de la Maison*, was served to everyone on both sides of the partition. As they were finishing it, Monsieur Mollet came up to William.

"Well, Monsieur. I trust everything was to your satisfaction."

"Yes, Monsieur Mollet. Everything is excellent."

"I hope your friends enjoyed zeir meal. Do you have any other special favours to ask?"

"Yes," said William. He pointed through the partition. "You see the thin man in the white shirt?"

"Ah oui, Monsieur. Ze man who just had to go and change his trousers! What of him?"

"When you serve the coffee, you must take him a coffee that is very weak, very milky, and it must have a pinch of salt and garlic in it."

"Salt and garlic! Ah, what you learn in le public school! God save the Queen! Vive les Anglais!"

William and Claude accompanied Lucia and Maria across to the Bar de l'Hôtel de Ville for a drink after dinner. Valérie winked at William from across the counter. Milou looked up at the sky.

"There will be a storm tonight. A big orage!" he said.

As the four of them walked back to the hotel, William noticed how the sky had darkened within the space of half an hour. The black clouds now looked threatening. The wind was also getting up. He said goodbye to Claude and the girls and disappeared through the door which led to the annexe.

William spent a couple of hours going through his paperwork. He stapled his receipts together, filled in his mileage chart with the number of kilometres travelled each day since the start of the tour, and completed a Details of

Passenger Detached ... form for Mario Rottoli. He also started filling in a Lost/Damaged Luggage Report about Steve Vicks' ghetto-blaster, but abandoned it. Steve Vicks would have to ask him for one if he wanted one.

He saw the chink of light go out around the door which communicated with Room 23. Mr Eveleigh had retired for the night. He'd better get everything ready.

First of all he checked Mr Maxwell's camcorder. The battery was sufficiently charged for it to record. He tried out filming the inside of the room. It appeared to work well even in conditions of very poor light.

Next William extracted from his suitcase a Polaroid camera. It was a very old, simple-to-use model of the push-and-shoot type. He turned on the flashgun to make sure it was working.

Then he reached for the phone by his bed and dialled the number of the Bar de l'Hôtel de Ville.

Mr Eveleigh was drifting in a state of suspended animation halfway between full consciousness and sleep. His enthusiasm for the Hotel Beau-Séjour was now somewhat on the wane. He hadn't much enjoyed his escargots and cuisses de grenouilles, and the company of those silly boys he'd taught at school was beginning to tire him. With the exception of Bailey-Filmer, they were juvenile, spoilt brats who probably hadn't done a day's work since leaving Chestfield.

There was banging in the distance and he heard rain beating on the window. He had felt the storm coming. He turned over in his bed. Suddenly he was aware that he was not alone.

"Salut!" The person who had crept un-noticed into the other side of his double bed was obviously female and well-endowed. Mr Eveleigh felt her large breasts against his chest as she tried to get on top of him. She unbuttoned his pyjama jacket and fiddled with the cord on his trousers. What could he do? It was the kind of situation for which he was just not prepared.

A stream of light fell on the bed. Someone must have opened the door, thought Mr Eveleigh. He'd noticed the locked door, and assumed it just led to a cupboard or another corridor. He felt the bedclothes being ripped off the bed above him. A bright light suddenly burst from the open door. Of course, it must be lightning, he thought.

William had a better view of the proceedings than he could have imagined. He had propped up Mr Maxwell's camcorder on the bedside table and was filming all the action in the light from his own room. He himself was out of sight behind the door. He'd gone into Mr Eveleigh's room just once, to take a photo with his Polaroid camera. He really needed another one, for good measure. He tiptoed into Room 23. Valérie now had Mr Eveleigh pinned virtually naked to the bed. She smiled at the camera as he pressed the button. Mr Eveleigh was aware of a second flash of lightning. In the stream of light he could make out the young girl's round face, her straight fair hair and her somewhat vacant expression. Hell, she didn't look more than seventeen!

"Qui êtes-vous?" he at last struggled to say.

"Je m'appelle Marie-France Aubert. Je travaille dans une épicerie."

Chapter Ten

One-Way Ticket To The Blues

AROUND the Hotel Beau-Séjour the storm had raged all night. By the morning, the rain had died down to a fine drizzle, and it was possible to venture outside again without being soaked to the skin. Nick Patterson, sheltering under an umbrella, took up his post near the old bridge in an endeavour to finish his sketch. He had worked hard into the night on his version of *Sunflowers*, but knew it wasn't really up to Van Gogh's.

Bryan Arthur Eveleigh woke with a start. He had spent a most unpleasant night. He could remember parts of the awful dream: the flashes of lightning, the girl in bed with him, and the shaft of light coming from the open door. He got up and pulled the curtains. The day looked grey and uninviting. Then he turned around and examined the door through which he thought the girl had come last night. It was locked, and it was impossible to tell what there was on the outside. He put his eye to the keyhole, but he could see nothing: the key was in the lock, on the other side.

As he turned back from the door he caught sight of himself in the mirror and recoiled with horror. There were red marks all over his face. Someone had been kissing him, and their lipstick had left red kisses on both cheeks, his neck and around his mouth. So the girl must have existed.

He would have to go to the bathroom, he decided. It was at the end of the corridor, and he hoped he wouldn't be spotted as he walked down there. He put on his dressing gown and sprinted down the passage. After a refreshing shower, he made his way back to his room. As soon as he opened the door he noticed it.

A letter was lying on the floor. It was in a plain white envelope, addressed to 'Monsieur B.A. Eveleigh'. Hurriedly he tore it open.

Out fell one of those instant photos. It wouldn't have done much for the careers of Patrick Lichfield or the Earl of Snowdon, but the subject matter was instantly identifiable. There was he, Bryan Arthur Eveleigh, B.A., in bed with a very young and very attractive girl. Both of them appeared to be stark naked.

Mr Eveleigh unfolded the letter. It was written in French on the type of lined paper sold in French stationery stores. As he read it, he sank back onto the bed:

'Dear Mr Eveleigh,

You should know better than to go seducing young girls at your age. I heard the indecent proposals you made to my daughter last night, and then I followed her to your room. My family are outraged. My daughter's reputation is ruined. We shall become the laughing-stock of the village.

I urge you to leave France at once. We know the itinerary of your tour. If you go on the coach I shall be following you.

The enclosed photo is one of two copies. Unless you leave Neuville immediately I shall send the other to the Headmaster of Chestfield School.

Yours, etc.

M. Aubert.'

He recoiled in horror once more. How could he possibly have seduced a teenage girl last night and then forgotten all about it? He must be getting old, or going mad. He couldn't even remember the last time he had seduced a woman of any age, come to think of it, though there had been Miss Philpott, the assistant Matron, back in 1965…

The name was staring up at him. Aubert. AUBERT. Where had he heard the name Aubert before? It was a good five minutes before the penny dropped. Shortman's Audio-Visual French course! But could there really be a M. Aubert in Neuville whose daughter he had seduced? And how come he also knew about Chestfield?

Chestfield? Of course! There were all those old pupils of his on this tour. Could the letter be from one of them? He read it again. The French was perfect. There was not a single spelling mistake, not a single accent out of place. The style was rather better, he thought, than the French he himself wrote. He was certain that none of the young men he had been having dinner with last night could possibly have written it. Even Bailey-Filmer, who had spent some time in France, made a lot of grammatical mistakes in spoken French; his written French would be nowhere near this good. No, the letter had either been written by a Frenchman or by someone who was virtually bilingual.

As he reflected on the letter, he decided he could not afford not to take the threat seriously. He couldn't carry on with the tour. Even if it had all been an elaborate hoax, he would still have the difficulty of explaining it to the old boys from Chestfield, who, for all he knew, may well have witnessed the events of last night. And if it did turn out to be one of them who had arranged it all, then he would just become a laughing-stock. The last four days of the tour would not be worth living.

He thought of Chestfield and his sister in their little cottage. He just wanted to get back as quickly as possible. He reached for the phone and dialled Reception. He told Monsieur Mollet that he was not feeling well, and had decided to return home. Could M. Mollet advise him of the best way to get back to England? Yes, he could. He could get the fast TGV train from Angoulême, twenty kilometres away, to Paris, from where he had a variety of options to return home.

Mr Eveleigh booked a taxi to Angoulême and started packing. When he made it back to Chestfield he would have to go and see the Headmaster. He somehow couldn't face the prospect of another term.

****

At breakfast, William heard from Monsieur Mollet the story of Mr Eveleigh's departure.

"He calls me at seven o'clock, he says he is not well, he asks me to call a taxi. Fifteen minutes later he is in a taxi for Angoulême!"

"Why did he want to go to Angoulême?" asked William.

"Ze TGV to Paris. From Paris he goes back to England."

So they had lost Mr Eveleigh for good. William smiled to himself about how his little scheme was going. Now the next part of the plan was to get Mike Turner onto his train.

At breakfast, William handed the video-camera back to its rightful owner. "All charged up now!" he said.

"I can't begin to thank you enough!" said Mr Maxwell.

When they all got back on the coach to start their journey to Beaune, it was still raining. Nick Patterson put away his sketch-book, folded his umbrella, and joined the others on the coach. Despite the weather, he thought, the drawing had still turned out quite well. He was already looking forward to trying some sketching in Burgundy.

William decided it was better to make an announcement to the group about the missing passenger. He took the microphone and told the group that Mr

Eveleigh had been feeling unwell and had decided to return to England. After William had delivered his speech, a cheer came up from near the back of the coach. He suspected it was from Jonathan Atkinson and John Bridger. "Don't forget that we are stopping in Mansle-la-Jolie!" William reminded Claude.

"Of course. For the man who goes on the choo-choo!"

William had passed through the village of Mansle-la-Jolie countless times before without even noticing the railway station. As they passed the village sign this Thursday morning, Claude reduced his speed while William kept his eyes peeled for a notice. There it was! A little brown sign with the outline of a steam locomotive and the words 'Chemin de Fer Touristique de la Charente'. They followed the sign down an 'Avenue de la Gare' bordered with pollarded plane trees, to reach a solid nineteenth-century building at the end. A hiss of steam greeted them as they pulled into the station forecourt. Mike Turner was already almost half-way off the coach before it had stopped. He was carrying two cameras, a tripod and a zoom lens in a long leather case.

"Listen, Mr Turner. Remember you're to wait for us at Montluçon station. The train's going to stop there at about 2 o'clock. And take something to drink - it's a long journey." William handed Mike Turner a screw-top bottle of fizzy lemonade from the fridge at the front of the coach.

"What time's the train leaving?" asked Mike Turner.

"You come along with me. I'll introduce you to the people who run the railway."

William walked around to the platform. The Mikado stood on the single track in all its glory. It was enormous. Its exterior was so festooned with tubes and pipes that William could only make the vaguest guess as to their functions. Already Mike Turner had his Nikon out and was taking his first photographs. Two figures in blue overalls emerged from the station building and greeted William.

"Salut!"

"Salut! Henri! Pierre!" William shook a pair of rather grubby right hands and introduced them to 'Monsieur Turner'. Henri wasted no time in showing a fellow enthusiast over his locomotive. William explained to Pierre that he hadn't really got time to stop, that the coach was waiting for him, and waved goodbye.

William had in fact asked if anyone else on the coach wanted to come down and see the steam train, but, probably because of the driving rain, they had preferred to remain on the coach. Only Mr Maxwell, with his newly-recharged camcorder, had ventured out into the wet to take a few shots of the engine.

"Just like the old ones we used to have on Vicrail! I remember when we had to change at Albury before they built the through line to Sydney. ALL CHANGE, ALBURY! The three most hated words in Australia!"

William hoped that Mike Turner wouldn't be changing at Albury. In fact, he rather hoped he wouldn't be changing anywhere.

The drive from Neuville to Beaune was the most varied on the tour. It passed through the porcelain town of Limoges, little Aubusson famous for its tapestries, and over the foothills of the Massif Central to Montluçon. From Montluçon the scenery was rather less special as the roads took you north-east to Moulins, and thence via Autun to Beaune in Burgundy. The brochure described it as 'a drive across the scenic heart of France', but it didn't look especially scenic today, with the rain still beating down outside and the windows steaming up. Claude seemed quite happy, anyway. William slipped a tape of gentle background music into the cassette player and let the passengers doze peacefully through Limoges.

William made his next stop at Aubusson. Here the passengers could see the magnificent collection of tapestries in the Town Hall, and even buy their own if they wished. But the prices of hand-made tapestries were rather high, even for the likes of the Bartlett-Nicholsons, thought William. Nevertheless Aubusson was a delightful place to stop: large enough to be interesting, small enough not to get lost in, and somewhere you could find something to do indoors if it was raining.

Claude left the coach on the main street. It would not cause a blockage there unless another coach came along in the opposite direction, and he didn't think one would. Just in case one did, he had gone to a nearby café for his morning coffee, from where he had a clear view of the coach. William joined him after having shown the passengers the way to the Town Hall. As they were finishing their coffees, Miss Crosbie came along.

"Excuse me, William, but I'm a bit worried about poor Mr Eveleigh. Do you know what was the matter with him? I was speaking to him when we stopped in Saintes yesterday afternoon, and he seemed perfectly well then."

"I'm sorry, Miss Crosbie, I don't. I think it must be some medical condition he's got, you know, one of those things that plays up from time to time."

"I know. That's one of the perils of old age. Take my advice. You stay young, my boy!"

William thought about staying young. All he could think of was a little blonde girl, who was really twenty-seven, wearing a London Transport T-shirt and a pair of black corduroy trousers and waving at him from the platform of a red London bus.

He would have to telex Helena again today. He would have to tell her about the departure of Mr Eveleigh. And also, with any luck, that of Mike Turner.

****

At Mansle-la-Jolie, Mike Turner had been taken on an extensive tour of the station and the depot. He had photographed the 141-R from every possible angle, and even had a short ride on the footplate up and down a siding. He had felt thirsty up there in the intense heat of the cab, so he had drunk the small bottle of lemonade William had given him. Then one of the Frenchmen had told him the train was about to leave, and they had shown him into a compartment of the solitary passenger carriage behind the 141-R.

The Frenchman had muttered something about Montluçon. It was important, he had said. Montluçon or Vierzon. Mike Turner's French was about as good as Henri Rigaud's English. Never mind. He was now going for one of the longest rides behind a steam locomotive he had ever been on, and it was running just for him!

Mike Turner was feeling unusually drowsy. Perhaps it had been the storm last night, although he'd thought he'd had quite a good sleep. Funny. He lay back on the comfortable seat cushions of the restored PLM 1st class carriage as the giant Mikado chuffed away towards Montluçon and Vierzon.

****

William made rather a late lunch stop in Montluçon. After yesterday, everyone had been begging him to stop at another out-of-town shopping centre, and luckily Claude had found one on the eastern outskirts. He and Claude ate together in the cafeteria, where they were joined by Maria and Lucia. Lucia asked Claude if the bad weather would continue.

"Mais non, ma chérie! We have le mauvais temps today, but not tomorrow! I saw the Météo on la télé last night. When we get to Paris you will have le soleil!"

A delighted Lucia turned to her friend and smiled. Behind them, William could hear Ian Bailey-Filmer talking to John Bridger...

"But, I tell you, it's only in the hotels that they don't seem to be able to make the coffee properly. In both the last two hotels every cup of coffee I had was revolting. And now, here, in a supermarket cafeteria, I buy a cheap cup of coffee, and it's not too bad at all. True, it's a bit on the strong side, and those little packs of sugar they supply are really a most inconvenient size. I mean, one of them's not enough for me, and two are too much …"

Bailey-Filmer drifted on. John Bridger couldn't understand what the man was ranting about. All the coffees he had drunk on the tour had tasted the same to him.

William left the cafeteria and headed for the nearest public phone. He dialled the number for the Hotel Royale in Beaune. He wasn't expecting any trouble here, but it always paid to phone ahead …

Monsieur Laville from the Hotel Royale regretted that he was three single rooms short. Some of the single Orbit passengers were going to have to share.

William did some quick mental arithmetic. Monsieur Laville had of course been working off a full Rooming List. He didn't know that Mr Eveleigh had gone home, and he was still expecting Mike Turner. With these two gone, they would only be one single room short. William pondered about which of the two remaining Chestfield passengers he would put in a twin room together.

After calling the hotel, William thought he had better phone the railway station in Montluçon. After all, there was just a remote chance that Mike Turner had got off the steam train there and was waiting for the coach to pick him up. But a quick call assured him that the steam train had passed through the station ten minutes earlier, that no passengers had got off, and that there was definitely no Englishman called Mr Turner waiting at the station at that moment.

He wondered how Mike Turner was getting on. Even after nearly ten years on the road, William still occasionally had difficulty getting to sleep in strange places, and he always carried a bottle of sleeping pills with him on tour. He knew that the dose he had put in Mike Turner's lemonade would do him no lasting harm, but he was fairly sure that it would make him sleep very soundly for quite a long time.

The afternoon was even wetter and more depressing than the morning. Most of the passengers gave up any attempt to look at the scenery through the misted-up coach windows, and many of them fell asleep. William tried to jolly them along a bit by putting on a Max Bygraves cassette, which had Mr and Mrs Charlton, the Tjeong family and Mr Maxwell all singing along, and stony silence from the Chestfield mob.

It was about an hour after they had left Montluçon that Steve Vicks walked up to the front of the coach and spoke to William:

"Excuse me, mate, but weren't we supposed to be picking up Mr Turner somewhere back there?"

"Mr Turner? Ah, yes, that was the original plan. But he got talking to the railway society people at the station, and I think he was going to try to arrange to go all the way to Vierzon. There's a big exhibition on there."

"Do you mean he might not be joining us again?"

"Well, I phoned the station at Montluçon from our lunch stop, and he definitely hadn't got off there."

"That's just like him, you know. Lives, breathes and thinks railways. That's what's broken up his marriage. He's an old mate of mine, you see."

"I see." Steve Vicks returned to his seat. So Mike Turner's marriage had not been a success either.

William tried to show them the Roman Gate of St Andrew from the coach as they drove through Autun, but no-one was in the mood for a walk in the rain, even Mr Maxwell having temporarily abandoned his video-camera on the empty seat beside him. That afternoon they made only one short unscheduled stop, when Claude pulled in for diesel at a small filling-station, and some of the hardier members of the party including the Tjeong and Charlton children went off briefly to stretch their legs.

With the poor weather and the lack of suitable sightseeing opportunities, they were going to reach Beaune ahead of schedule. William took them for a quick drive around the ramparts, to show them something of the old town centre, before proceeding to the Hotel Royale on the far side of the town near the motorway junction.

As they were driving around the old town, they stopped at traffic lights. On one side of the road was a modest night-club, with coloured lights outside and steps going down to a cellar. 'DISCO - CE SOIR!' was written up on a huge advertising board.

The Hotel Royale in Beaune was typical of its kind. A budget two-star chain catering for group business, Royale hotels are normally to be found on the outskirts of towns, near major road junctions or on industrial estates. The exterior of this unprepossessing concrete building was just a blank wall with narrow slits for windows, and on the roof, illuminated at night, was a large yellow plastic crown above the letters H R.

As he walked up to the Reception Desk, William was still wondering who he would get to share a twin room. In such cases, on any normal tour, he would have given up his own single room and shared with the driver. He knew

Claude would not have objected in this case, but he thought that it might be more fun to put a couple of the Chestfield characters in together! He looked at the Rooming List again. How about Bridger and Bailey-Filmer?

William allocated all the rooms from his list, and took two keys for Room 121, one for Bailey-Filmer and the other for Bridger. How about if he didn't even tell them they were sharing, but just let them find out? He went along the coach handing out keys to right and to left, telling his passengers about the time for dinner that evening and breakfast tomorrow. Bridger took his key and went up to the room. Bailey-Filmer, on the other hand, went directly to the bar and ordered a coffee, presumably trying to disprove his theory about French hotel coffee.

A few minutes later, Bridger was downstairs again. He was joined soon afterwards by Jonathan Atkinson. Both were well wrapped up in raincoats: Bridger's looked more like an army greatcoat. He spoke to William with an air of military authority:

"We're off to investigate that disco we saw advertised in town. We might look around for something to eat as well. Don't worry if we're not back for dinner!"

It was quite a walk back to the town centre, thought William, but John Bridger would be able to cope with it. As for Jonathan Atkinson, perhaps it was just as well that Bridger had taken him under his wing. He really didn't seem to have recovered from Tuesday night.

Ian Bailey-Filmer was still drinking his coffee. William seized the opportunity. Grabbing the key to Room 121 which John Bridger had just deposited on the Reception Desk, he ran up to the first floor. All the rooms in the Hotel Royale were identical. John Bridger, as William had expected, hadn't made much impression at all on Room 121. The bathroom appeared to be untouched, but the cover of one of the beds looked a little crumpled as if someone had sat on it. William smoothed it down. There was also the matter of Bridger's rucksack on the floor. William lifted it up and placed it behind a curtain in a little alcove designed for hanging clothes - to call it a built-in wardrobe would have been an exaggeration. With any luck, Bailey-Filmer would never notice it, and Bridger, if he came back to the room, might think that the chambermaid had tidied it away.

William now went up to his own room. Thinking of Pepper back at home, he reflected that he had never had the slightest desire to swing a cat, but he was sure that there would not be room to swing one in a Hotel Royale bedroom. There was no room at all for a normal size suitcase on the floor; if you put it between the bed and the chest-of-drawers, which was the logical place, you couldn't get the drawers open. In one corner of the room was a tiny bathroom, with w.c., shower and washbasin: screening off the shower from the rest of the bathroom was a shower curtain which was at least six inches narrower than the opening it was supposed to fill. Since the shower head invariably sent out jets of water at unpredictable angles, it was practically impossible to use the shower without getting the bathroom floor hopelessly wet. Perhaps that was why they gave you so many towels, thought William: he had at least four to himself. Like the ashtray, the tumblers in the bathroom and the complimentary bottle of shampoo, the towels were marked with the crowned H R emblem.

William put a call through to his parents. As a rule, he didn't like to make calls from hotels, as they tended to be more expensive, but when you were stuck in a Hotel Royale miles from the town centre there was no practical alternative.

It was his mother who answered.

"Hello dear! How are you?"

"Fine, thanks. Is Dad alright?"

"Wonderful. We've been shopping in Maidstone today."

"That's nice. Er - how's Pepper?"

"You think more of that cat than you do about us! She's on the armchair by the TV at the moment, purring like a kitten."

"Give her my love!"

"I will. When will you be back home?"

"Should be Sunday evening. I'm not sure what time I'll get in."

"Will you need a lift home from anywhere? We can always come to pick you up in the Vauxhall."

"I'm not sure yet. I'll call you if I do. Look, I've got to go now. Bye!"

"Goodbye, dear!"

William went down to dinner in the Royale Restaurant. Like the bedrooms, the portions of food were compact and unexciting. At least the dessert was better than usual - a chocolate mousse. He looked around at the table where the Chestfield mob was sitting. Only Bailey-Filmer, the Bartlett-Nicholsons, Steve Vicks and Nick Patterson were there. John Bridger and Jonathan Atkinson had evidently stayed in town.

The long rainy day had provoked a certain amount of lethargy among the group. Most of them went up to their rooms straight after dinner. William asked Monsieur Laville if he could send a telex. The proprietor assured him that would be no problem.

William sat behind the telex machine at the Hotel Royale. Like everything else in the chain of hotels, it was standardised, and identical to the one he had used a couple of weeks previously to contact Orbit from Paris.

He typed out his telex message:

'ATTN. H.R. PAX EVELEIGH X 1 LEFT TOUR THIS MORNING, FEELING ILL. MAKING OWN ARRANGEMENTS TO GET HOME. PAX TURNER X 1 LEFT TOUR BY TRAIN TO VIERZON. TOUR NOW 21 PAX. EVERYTHING GOING OK. THINKING OF YOU + LOOKING FORWARD TO SEEING YOU AGAIN. LOTS OF LOVE XXXXXXXXXXXXXXXXXXXXXXXX WILLIAM F443/07'

He pressed the button marked 'SEND' and Orbit's answerback appeared on the green vdu screen, followed by his message. It was too late now to erase all those kisses. William hoped he hadn't gone over the top.

He returned to his room and switched on the tiny portable colour television which was high on a bracket in one corner of the room. He watched the news without really taking it all in, and then got ready for bed.

Rather later, a taxi pulled up at the hotel with John Bridger and Jonathan Atkinson. The disco had been a bit of a washout, but they'd found a lively bar which served good beer, and they'd sat there chatting to some young Inter-Railers from England for a couple of hours.

Atkinson went up to his room on the third floor. Bridger took the key to 121 from the deserted Reception Desk, and sauntered up to the room. He closed the door behind him, pulled off his clothes and sank into the bed nearest the door. He didn't bother to turn on the light - he probably wouldn't have been able to find the switch anyway, the way he was feeling.

****

Mike Turner felt terrible. Was it too much wine last night, he wondered? Christ! It must be pretty potent stuff! He looked out of the carriage window. It was almost dark. The train had stopped moving and he was in some kind of marshalling yard.

Montluçon? Vierzon? He remembered vaguely that he had been supposed to get off at one of those stations. Surely it was the responsibility of the 'Chemin de Fer Touristique de la Charente' that he didn't miss his stop. He wondered where the coach would be now. He wasn't even quite sure what day it was.

He opened the carriage door. It was a long step down to the ground. He started walking in the half-light between the railway tracks. His head was burning and he was staggering from side to side. All around him were specimens of SNCF rolling stock which in any other circumstances he might have travelled miles to see, but now they had no meaning to him.

"Tiens! Regardez là-bas!" From their little look-out post on a gantry above the goods yard, one of the security guards had spotted a movement. They patrolled the yards every night. Usually the main problems were vandalism and the theft of goods from freight trains, but tomorrow there was going to be this big new exhibition at the station to mark the electrification of the line. All the local bigwigs were going to be there, the Préfet, plus the Minister of Transport and the President of the SNCF. They had to keep a look out for suspicious types. There were these people from Provence who were protesting about the construction of a new TGV line. You might get any kind of nutter coming along and ruining the show. In France, direct action so often meant just that - just think back to May 1968!

"Henri, I think he's drunk! Look at the way he's walking!"

"I think he's got a gun! You see that long metal thing he's carrying! And I think I can see a black object in his other hand…"

"Do you think he's a terrorist?"

"How do I know? Perhaps he wants to shoot the Transport Minister because the trains on his local line are always late!"

"Henri, this is no joking matter. This man could be dangerous. I say we call the CRS. The place is ringed with them."

"Very well." Henri picked up his phone and called the CRS.

A van filled with riot police arrived at the gate of the marshalling-yard with a squeal of brakes. At least ten armed riot police entered the compound and surrounded the lone figure on all sides.

"Drop your gun! You are surrounded!"

Mike Turner had a terrifying vision of men in uniform coming at him from all directions. He didn't attempt to struggle. As they carried him off to the armoured van he was stammering:

"L-L-Lucinda! C-come b-back to me! I promise I'll never have anything to do with r-railways again!"

Chapter Eleven

Gay Paree

ON Friday morning it was sunny again. The countryside of Burgundy looked refreshed by the rain, and the ripening grapes glistened on the vines. In Room 121 of the Hotel Royale Beaune, Ian Bailey-Filmer stretched, opened his eyes, got out of bed and drew the curtains. That was funny. There was someone else in the room with him. A bundle of clothes had been thrown onto the floor by the other bed. And, in the bed, there was a man. He recognised who it was at once.

John Bridger became aware of the sunlight and the movement in the room, and stirred into life. He opened his eyes and found himself staring directly into the face of Ian Bailey-Filmer.

"What the hell are you doing in my room?"

"I was about to ask you the same question. This is my room!"

"Nonsense! I came up here as soon as we got in last night. Look, there's my rucksack behind that curtain!"

"I can assure you that I was allocated this room."

John Bridger drew himself up to his full height. With his erect military bearing he towered over Bailey-Filmer.

"I remember you from Chestfield. I know you. I remember how you used to stare at us third-formers in the Junior Dorm. You got the key to my room deliberately, didn't you, you bloody poofter!"

"I can assure you that I didn't…"

"You're not Head of bloody House here, you know! You can bloody well clear out of my room this minute! Or else!"

Bridger waved a large fist in Bailey-Filmer's face. Bailey-Filmer went into the bathroom to get his sponge bag, then hurriedly packed his luggage and left the room, still wearing his pyjamas. He would have to get dressed in the public lavatories by the Reception Desk.

William thought he would be the first down to breakfast that morning, but he noticed that Bailey-Filmer had come down before him. He was unshaven, his hair was untidy, and his collar wasn't straight: it looked as if he had got dressed in a hurry. William wished that he could have been a fly on the wall of Room 121.

Breakfast at the Hotel Royale in Beaune was largely a self-help affair. The entire Orbit Tours group had been allocated a long school-dinner type table in a rear section of the restaurant reserved for coach parties, whereas individual clients could sit at small tables in the main restaurant and help themselves from a lavish buffet.

William reached for the thermos jug marked CAFE in the centre of the table, and poured some coffee into a large yellow mug marked H R. He then reached for the jug marked LAIT CHAUD and added some milk. The coffee was not especially tasty but at least it was warm and wet. He could see Bailey-Filmer pulling a face as he drank his at the far end of the table.

In front of William was a yellow paper serviette bearing a crown and the letters H R, a knife, a teaspoon and a large dessert spoon. He always wondered what the dessert spoon was for, since there was nothing on the Hotel Royale breakfast menu that could possibly be eaten with it. He went up to the buffet and helped himself to the food: a small pack of butter, a small pack of jam, and a hard roll and croissant from baskets marked with the dreaded sign: ONLY ONE PER PERSON. There was also a machine distributing orange squash, but William didn't bother with that: the orange squash at the Hotel Royale was made with about one part of orange concentrate to about 1,000,000 parts of water.

Despite the meagre breakfast, the passengers all seemed in high spirits as they came down. Perhaps it was the change in the weather; perhaps it was the thought of the wine-tasting in Beaune that lay ahead of them.

William walked outside to the coach. Claude had almost finished cleaning it. When they had got to the hotel yesterday, the blue and white paintwork had been streaked with grime. Now it was sparkling once again.

"Are you ready?"

"Yes. I've just got to do the windscreen."

"Right. I'll count the cases and tell the passengers to get on."

William ticked off names on the cases against his copy of the Rooming List, and settled up with Monsieur Laville for the telex and the porterage. They were away from the hotel by nine o'clock and soon reached the town centre.

Early morning was not the best time to visit a wine cellar, but the itinerary of 'Scenic Delights of France' did not allow for an afternoon visit. The group followed William in an untidy crocodile to the *Caves de la Côte d'Or*, where the proprietor ushered them down a steep flight of stone stairs and invited them to take their places around a large circular table.

No self-respecting Burgundy wine-grower is going to give away any of his best produce to visitors from coach parties who rarely buy more than a few bottles. What the *Caves de la Côte d'Or* did was to serve their coach groups three samples of what Claude always called 'junk wines'. The first was in fact quite a respectable junior burgundy, the second a lightly sparkling white of dubious origin, and the third a fortified wine made from the dregs in the bottom of the barrels with added sugar and alcohol, misleadingly called *Vin Doux Naturel*.

Around the table everyone sampled the three wines. Even the Tjeongs, whom William had not noticed touching a drop of alcohol since the start of the tour, each took a glass of *Vin Doux Naturel*, and Josephine and Rebecca Charlton were enjoying the sparkling white wine. Miss Crosbie came up to William and confessed she had drunk three glasses and was feeling 'quite tipsy'. William could not help noticing that the Chestfield passengers were knocking it back a bit as well.

"William, can I have your advice on this, please?" It was Hugh Bartlett-Nicholson, of course. He was holding up an empty bottle of *Vin Doux Naturel*.

"Buy some if you like it," said William. He had already got the Bartlett-Nicholsons practically to fill the coach boot with cheap plonk: he didn't really want them to block up the aisle as well. Besides, the prices of all the wines in the *Caves de la Côte d'Or* were prominently displayed: he would not be able to make anything here.

"But is it good?" Miranda Bartlett-Nicholson implored.

"Do you honestly think that I would take you anywhere that sells bad wine?" asked William.

"No, I suppose not. Hugh, darling! We'll have a dozen bottles!"

After the group had left the wine cellars, and Claude had loaded their purchases onto the coach, William gave them some free time to walk into the town centre and get a coffee. He took a group of them, including the Charlton family and Nick Patterson, to see the beautiful medieval hospital called the Hôtel Dieu.

"But why do they call it the Hôtel Dieu?" asked Josephine. "Doesn't that mean God's Hotel?"

"I suppose medicine in the Middle Ages must have been rather primitive," suggested her sister. "I mean, if you were unlucky enough to have to go to hospital, you would probably go to see God quite soon after being admitted."

William explained that in the Middle Ages most hospitals had been run by the church, and the patients had been looked after by monks and nuns.

"Do you mind if I stay here to do a sketch?" asked Nick Patterson.

"No, not at all," said William. "But you'll have to be quick. We leave in forty-five minutes."

Nick Patterson was the last person back in the coach. He was ten minutes late, and was greeted by a slow handclap from the other passengers. But it was worth it. The glorious clear light of the summer morning, with the sun shining on the coloured roof tiles. The Hôtel Dieu had been designed to be sketched. You couldn't do justice to a place like that in a mere three quarters of an hour.

William directed Claude onto the A6 motorway for Paris. Now that they were on their homeward journey speed became important. As they stopped at Beaune motorway junction to get the toll ticket, William glanced back towards the town. In the foreground he could see the Hotel Royale, an ugly concrete cube with the crown and the big yellow letters H R on its roof. H.R. thought William: now, that was funny. All this time he had been staying in hotels of the Royale chain, and it had never occurred to him before.

****

In Orbit Head Office in London, Mr Papadopoulos was pacing the room. He had been looking forward to Friday. With a bit of luck he could have gone off early and played a round of golf. But he might as well cancel that now.

"Are you really quite sure about this, Margot?"

"Yes. I must say I'd suspected it for some time, but I didn't have any proof until now."

"And how long do you reckon this has been going on for?"

"At least six months. I got Vicki from accounts to run the excursion figures for Danny Bourget's tours for the last three years through the computer. You take a look at this".

Margot handed Mr Papadopoulos a long sheet of computer print-out. Some columns on it had been marked with a yellow highlighter. They showed how many tickets Danny Bourget had sold to the Grenouille Bondissante over the last three years. Danny worked throughout the winter and summer with the popular weekend trips to Paris. The sheets showed that for two and a half years he had consistently sold between thirty-five and fifty excursions per trip. From February, however, the figures had suddenly slumped. His recent sales for the night club showed figures ranging from ten to twenty.

"You are right. You are not telling me he is for some reason not selling the excursion."

"No, Mr Papadopoulos. In fact, we're certain that he's still sending as many clients to the Grenouille Bondissante as ever. Do you remember that time when there was the power cut?"

"Yes." Mr Papadopoulos remembered. The lights had gone out halfway through the show, the remaining acts had had to be abandoned, and the customers had had to finish their dinner by candlelight. Some of them had written in to Orbit Tours for a refund.

"Well, according to Danny's sales returns, there should only have been twelve passengers on that excursion. But Marjorie in Customer Relations has a file on that tour. They've had thirty-six people so far write in and ask for a refund of the cost of the excursion."

"Did you check the ticket stubs?"

"Yes. They tallied with Danny's report. I think he's been taking extra passengers to the Grenouille Bondissante but not issuing them with tickets. Then he just pays the money over directly to the night club, and we get no commission."

"That's bad. That's very bad."

Like all coach tour operators, Orbit made a fair proportion of their revenue from sales of optional excursion. Danny Bourget was entitled to receive 75 francs for every passenger he took to the night club. The night club itself received 150 francs, so the remaining 75 francs went to Orbit. If Danny was selling the excursion for the normal price of 300 francs, paying the night club directly and pocketing the remaining 150 francs, he could be depriving Orbit of two hundred pounds revenue a week.

Action would have to be taken, Mr Papadopoulos decided.

"Are you doing anything this weekend?" he asked Margot.

"Well, as a matter of fact I am. My boyfriend's taking me to that new West End musical tomorrow evening. We've waited ages to get the tickets!"

"You won't be interested in going to Paris, then?"

"Not me, I'm afraid."

"Well, send Helena in. Perhaps she'd like to go to Paris."

"O.K." Margot closed the door behind her.

H.R. was sitting behind her desk tidying up her Day File. Here she kept copies of every letter, fax and telex she had sent or received in the past week. She looked for the twentieth time at the telex which she had found on the machine when she had come in that morning. Thinking of you and looking forward to seeing you again… Lots of Love… and twenty-two kisses! Why twenty-two? Perhaps he had just come to the end of the line on the telex machine. Or perhaps there was some secret message hidden there, something which he would tell her about one day.

"Helena! Mr P. wants to see you!" Margot passed behind her desk. Helena quickly closed the Day File.

"Alright. I'm coming!" She went in to see her boss.

"Helena, have you got anything planned for the weekend?"

"No, nothing special."

"How would you like to go to Paris?"

"Paris? Could I - really?"

"I think you better sit down, Helena." She sat down on the typist's chair across the desk from him. Mr Papadopoulos explained to her about Danny Bourget. He wanted her to visit the Grenouille Bondissante and check exactly how many people Danny took there.

"And there's something else I want you to do."

"Yes?"

"You remember Mr Atkinson on William's coach. I want you to make sure he doesn't - er - give us the slip, I think is the expression. I want you to travel back to England on Sunday on Tour F443."

"With William?" Helena could hardly believe her luck.

"Yes. I shall book you in at the Hotel Royale Paris-Sud for Saturday night. You can travel down tomorrow on the Costa Brava Express tour. It leaves from the West London coach station at 6 a.m. Ask the driver to drop you off in Paris. I'll have a word with old George."

Helena's heart was in her mouth as she returned to her desk. She had wanted to join an Orbit Tour for ages! And now here she was, off to Paris! She thought of the shimmering Setra coach on the Costa Brava run which would take her down to Paris, and of the green-liveried Paris buses with their four-figure fleet numbers. Tomorrow she might even have a ride on one! Then she thought of William. She hadn't wanted to tell Mr Papadopoulos that another two people had left the tour, but she still couldn't believe that William was associating with a gang of criminals. After all, people did leave coach tours for quite innocent reasons.

She thought again about how she felt about William. What if Mr Atkinson was William's best friend? She ought really to tell William that he was wanted by the police, so he could warn his friend. She had to be loyal to William. But there was also her loyalty to Mr P and Orbit Tours. No, she must think of that first. William wasn't to know that she knew anything about Mr Atkinson. She could express surprise as well as he could when the police arrested him as they passed back through Dover Eastern Docks.

****

William stopped for lunch at a big motorway service area near Auxerre. The service area had been constructed on a bridge going right across from one side of the motorway to the other. Chiefly concerned about losing Miss Crosbie, William reminded the party that there were exits on both sides, and that they must make sure to come back down on the right side.

After lunch, all of the passengers managed to find the coach without great difficulty, with the exception of John Bridger. William had noticed the big man hitting the bottle rather a lot at the wine cellars that morning, and presumably he had got even more tanked up at lunch time. William called for Claude to come with him, and the two of them crossed the covered bridge. In the car park on the other side, Bridger was staggering around as he sang:

"Show me the w-ay to go h-ome! Oh, it's you! Why have you moved the bleeding coach?"

"Come on, Squadron-Leader Bridger! Time to go home!"

And together they half-dragged, half-carried the thirteen stones of John Bridger up the steps, across the bridge and back down the steps on the other side.

"Where shall we put him?" asked William.

"I know," said Claude. "In the driver's rest bunk." Like most modern coaches, Claude's Mercedes had a small bunk where a driver could rest, if, for example, two were sharing the driving during a long overnight trip. On Claude's coach the access to the bunk was through a sliding door opposite the on-board wc. They manhandled John Bridger into the bunk, aided by Mr Maxwell and Mr Charlton, and pulled the sliding door shut. As they started off for Paris they could faintly hear him singing in the bunk.

The hundred and fifty kilometres from Auxerre to Paris were accomplished in two hours. William passed the time by telling the group about the excursion to the Grenouille Bondissante. He always had his reservations about selling this excursion; he felt personally that it did not represent particularly good value, and under normal circumstances he would not try to sell it to passengers whom he felt might complain about it afterwards. On some tours he avoided selling the excursion altogether, offering his customers instead the cheaper option of a ride on the Bateaux-Mouches followed by a drive through the illuminated streets of Paris.

But this time William was determined to sell the Grenouille Bondissante. He wanted every one of the Chestfield passengers to go. He started his sales pitch. He could have sold coal to Newcastle or snow to an Eskimo.

As he went through the coach, he took the money from his passengers and handed them the tickets for the excursion. It was amazing. Every one of the fourteen 'ordinary' passengers wanted to come. As for the Chestfield passengers, John Bridger was hardly in a state to be asked, but William sold tickets to all of the others except Steve Vicks.

"You still owe me for my bloody stereo!" he said. "I'm not going to hand over any money to you until you pay me for my stereo!"

William explained that he would have to claim on his insurance, and said that he would give him a claim form.

They arrived in the outskirts of Paris. The Hotel Royale Paris-Sud was located just outside the Boulevard Péripherique near the Porte d'Italie. On one side of the hotel, the cars on the busy ring road roared by twenty-four hours a day. On the other side, the rooms had a view of an overgrown cemetery, a supermarket and some dreary apartment blocks. It was not the best location for an hotel in Paris, but it was an economical solution to the tour operator wanting to place groups in the city. As Claude drew up in front of the hotel, William could see Dutch, Belgian and Italian coaches parked there.

"How I déteste this hotel!" Claude remarked to William, fortunately not loud enough for the passengers to hear. "Nowhere secure to park the coach. We always get vandalism. Videos stolen, wing mirrors stolen... When I park the coach tonight, I take out the video and the wing mirrors and I keep them with me in my room!"

William asked the passengers to remain on the coach while he got the keys. He had phoned the hotel from the motorway service station at lunch-time, and updated them with the changes to the Rooming List. The Hotel Royale Paris-Sud was well-organised if nothing else. A smiling receptionist handed him a box full of small yellow envelopes. Each envelope contained a room key and a map of Paris, and the room numbers were all written on the outside of the envelopes.

"There'a a telex for you," said the receptionist. She handed it to William. He unfolded the thin piece of paper and read:

ATTN. WILLIAM ORBIT TOUR MANAGER TOUR F443 / 07 RECD. YR TELEX CLEARLY. I AM COMING TO PARIS TOMORROW ARRIVING ABOUT MID-DAY ON COSTA BRAVA COACH. STAYING SAT NIGHT AT H ROYALE + TRAVELLING BACK ON YR COACH. I'M THINKING OF YOU TOO. CAN'T WAIT TO SEE YOU. I LOVE YOU XXXXXXXXXXXXXXXXXXXXXXX HELENA

William almost jumped for joy.

"Are you okay?" asked the receptionist.

"Yes, fine!" He asked about the porterage and the breakfast arrangements, and went back to the coach with the room keys.

No dinner was included for the two nights in Paris. The passengers could either buy their own meal in the Restaurant Royale or go out for dinner. William reminded his group of the departure time for their included city sightseeing tour tomorrow morning. He arranged to meet some of the passengers later so he could walk with them to the nearest Metro station. As the passengers got down from the coach, Claude yelled to William:

"What do we do about our friend Monsieur Bridger?"

"Let's have a look." They moved around to the bunk and slid open the door.

"Wakey-Wakey Monsieur Bridger! Nous sommes à Paris!"

There was a groan from the compartment, and gradually the long figure of Squadron-Leader Bridger eased itself out of the bunk. The two hours' rest seemed to have done him some good. William handed him the envelope with his room key, sold him a ticket for the Grenouille Bondissante, and showed him the way to the lift.

He then went to the phone box in the hotel foyer and called Mireille Darsac. She was not only Orbit's agent who booked all excursions in Paris, but was also a qualified local guide who took the Orbit passengers on their sightseeing tours.

"Salut Mireille! Ici Guillaume d'Orbit Tours!"

"Oh! Bonjour Guillaume! You are on Scenic Delights of France?"

"Yes. Will you be at the Hotel Royale at 9 a.m. for the city tour?"

"Oui. Nine o'clock is fine. And for tomorrow night? Do you have any people for the Grenouille?"

"Yes. Twenty."

"Twenty! That is magnifique! Well, I'll see you tomorrow!"

****

In Orbit House, Mr Papadopoulos sighed as he left his office. It was past six o'clock. Helena and Margot were long gone. So was his golf partner. Whereas he would often stay at the office until seven-thirty or later from Monday to Thursday, he did like leaving on time on Fridays.

He had just had an annoying call from a Spanish hotel which had not received its Rooming List. It was not his job to check Rooming Lists, but the hotelier had somehow been put through to him. He remembered that Helena had been helping out with Rooming Lists earlier on in the week. Perhaps she had sent one. He opened the pink folder on her desk marked DAY FILE.

The most recent of the papers in the file was on top. It was a telex which had been sent barely half an hour ago. What could this be about? He read the short message, blinked, and read it through again.

I'M THINKING OF YOU TOO. CAN'T WAIT TO SEE YOU. I LOVE YOU.

He chuckled with laughter. So that was why Helena had been so eager to go to Paris! Other people might write poetry or love letters, and Yuppies probably nowadays penned each other love faxes, but somehow a love telex was just what he might have expected from Helena Rogers.

****

William left the Hotel Royale that evening with Maria and Lucía, Mr Maxwell, the Charltons and the Murrays. He escorted them safely across several major thoroughfares to Porte d'Italie Metro station. There he bought a carnet of tickets and distributed them to the group. He took them on Line 7 to Châtelet, and then walked with them to the Pompidou Centre. They travelled to the top on the escalator and admired the view over the rooftops of Paris.

"Just as good as the Eiffel Tower!" said Mr Murray, scanning the horizon with his camcorder.

"And it's free!" added William.

William left his group at Beaubourg, confident that they would all be able to find their way back to the hotel. He meanwhile returned to the Metro and travelled to Pigalle. Ignoring the girls on the street corners, he turned down a small side street towards the Rue Fontaine.

The Grenouille Bondissante was some distance away from the more fashionable Parisian night-spots, lost in a half-land of sex-shops and shabby café-tabacs. Above the façade an enormous green neon frog was flashing on and off.

He went inside and saw Yvette and Igor at the bar, The show was not due to begin for an hour or more. Yvette was the singer who did cover versions of Edith Piaf numbers. She also occasionally invited members of the public onto the stage for a dance. Seen from the back row of the theatre, she had the grace and the elegance of a twenty-year-old, but when you saw her close to, under the harsh lights of the bar, you could see that the long black hair was a wig and that make-up was hiding the wrinkles and ravages of time. Yvette had been elected Miss Romorantin in 1963 and had headed off from her provincial backwater in the Loir-et-Cher to the City of Light. She had released a couple of unsuccessful singles in the early sixties, and appeared on a few forgotten magazine covers, and now lived out her existence at a second-rate back street night club. Yet the sparkle in her eyes was still as sharp as ever. Tomorrow night, William knew, when Yvette sang Piaf's *Milord*, every man in the audience would think she was singing just for him.

William gave Yvette the bottle of Gordon's Gin which he had carried carefully from the hotel in its duty-free carrier bag. He told her he would be bringing a group tomorrow night, and asked her if she could dance with a member of his party. He gave her the name and told her where they would be sitting. It would be a pleasure. She folded up the little piece of paper and stuffed it into her bodice.

Igor was delighted to see William. William gave him the box of two hundred Marlboro which had been in his luggage since the Dover - Calais ferry crossing. Igor was not at all bothered by William's suggestion that he should make a little alteration to his trick with the cigarette and the hundred-franc note. It all added to the fun, he said as he drank his whisky.

William left the smoke-filled bar of the Grenouille Bondissante and stepped out into the streets of Pigalle. The painted girls were still there. He had never been tempted by this idea of love for sale. Even in Amsterdam, where he had walked right through the red light district with his coach parties and seen literally hundreds of girls, he had never succumbed to temptation. And it wasn't just the fear of AIDS or V.D. or whatever. He thought it was quite simply the effect of seeing all this beauty wholesale. He had heard much the same thing from some of his tourists when he had accompanied parties to Italy. Many an art lover who could quite happily spend a lifetime admiring a handful of masterpieces ended up rushing out from the Uffizi or Pitti half-way through the guided tour, unable to take the surfeit of pleasures which should really be savoured one at a time.

He was soon back at Pigalle metro station. There was no direct line from here to the Porte d'Italie, and the quickest way was probably by Line 2 eastbound to Stalingrad and then Line 7. But the Paris metro cost the same no matter which way you travelled. William took Line 2 westbound to Charles de Gaulle-Etoile, and then changed to Line 6, the very old, largely above-ground line which sweeps across the southern half of Paris in a great semicircle, crossing the Seine and affording a view of the Eiffel Tower.

Sitting in the Metro, William suddenly remembered the telex. He'd folded it and stuffed it into his jacket pocket when he had taken the room keys out to the coach. He took it out and re-read it. Helena was coming to Paris tomorrow! He could hardly contain his excitement, but why was that excitement combined with the sort of strange feeling in the depth of the stomach, which he used to feel when his parents were driving him back to Chestfield? Could this be what being in love was like? And yet, he was thinking about the same girl, the same Helena whom he'd known at the office for years, and who had taken him on the bus rally - months ago, it felt like. He realised that he'd had nothing to eat since his quick snack on the autoroute at lunchtime. He didn't feel hungry now anyway.

William looked at the telex again. I'M THINKING OF YOU TOO. CAN'T WAIT TO SEE YOU. I LOVE YOU. He had never heard these words from any woman in his life. Would the real life Helena be as loving as the girl on the telex machine? He counted the kisses carefully. She had even made sure that there were twenty-two.

William thought he might as well abandon his scheme for revenge. After all, of the remaining passengers he'd already conned the Bartlett-Nicholsons into buying all that awful wine, he'd nearly poisoned Bailey-Filmer with several cups of atrocious coffee, Steve Vicks had lost his stereo and he'd scared Jonathan Atkinson half to death. Only John Bridger and Nick Patterson had escaped practically unscathed. He was quite in awe of Bridger: alone of the Chestfield old boys, he had kept in top physical condition: he wouldn't want to fight him! And as for Patterson, the quiet, artistic man looked as if he wouldn't harm a flea. He quite liked the man. What could he possibly do against him now?

That night, in his room in the Hotel Royale Paris-Sud, beneath the yellow blanket marked H R, William dreamed that he was down below in the lobby. Romantic violins were playing. The automatic glass doors slid open and Helena drifted in. She was wearing a long white gown and her big brown eyes shone as he lifted her up in his arms. William Simpson had found that he was all wrapped up in love.

Chapter 12

Package Deal

SATURDAY morning started with the obligatory city sightseeing tour of Paris. William was outside the hotel by the coach at 9 a.m. with twenty passengers. Only John Bridger and Claude were absent.

"I'll just go and look for Claude," said William to Mr Maxwell, who was expectantly flourishing his video-camera.

In the lobby William almost ran into Claude. His shirt was undone, his hair was unkempt and he had a day's growth of stubble on his chin.

"You're late!" William said. "The people are waiting by the coach. What's up - did you have a good time in the Quartier Latin last night?"

Claude just scowled and left the hotel. It was so unlike him to be either late or untidy. What had got into him? The last thing you needed at the end of a tour was a bolshie driver.

William went to the internal phone on the Reception Desk and dialled the number of John Bridger's room. The phone rang for thirty seconds, unanswered. Just as he was about to put the receiver down, he heard Bridger pick up the phone.

"Yes, what is it?"

"William here. We're just about to leave on the city sightseeing tour!"

"I don't want to go on the tour. I'll see you tonight for the trip to the night club!"

By the time William got back to the coach, the passengers were all seated, and his place in the courier's seat had been taken by an attractive dark lady of indeterminate age.

"Guillaume, mon cheri! Comment ça va?"

William was treated to the customary kisses on both cheeks, which earned him a chorus of "oohs!"and wolf-whistles from the passengers. He introduced

Mireille Darsac to the group, manoeuvred past her and took a seat near the back of the coach. For three hours or so he could sit back and let someone else do the work.

Mireille Darsac was sophisticated Parisian elegance at its best. When he had first known her, he had been surprised to see her appearing out of Metro stations in her designer outfits, clutching her Gucci handbag. Now he regarded her as a friend. He remembered that he had been instantly physically attracted to her the first time they had met, when he had been in his early twenties and she must have been about thirty-seven. Nine years later, she looked no different, except that the cut of her clothes and the smell of her perfume changed with the prevailing fashions.

William genuinely enjoyed Mireille Darsac's sightseeing tours. She managed to inject just the right amount of humour and just the right amount of historical content. William knew that she was in fact a great expert on French Gothic architecture who could have spent half a day showing a group around Notre Dame alone, but she was perfectly happy taking them around it in half an hour, which was all the time that could be allocated to the visit on such a tour.

William spent the morning getting on and off the coach with his group, following Mireille Darsac's red and white rolled-up umbrella as she took them around the sights, and allowing himself to be counted back onto the coach. He could tell that the passengers were happy. On any tour of France, Paris was the jewel in the crown.

As always, Mireille finished her tour near the Opera. This was a handy place to drop the passengers around lunchtime. They could return to the hotel on the coach later, if they wanted, but William knew that most of them would prefer to spend the afternoon in Paris and find their way back on the Metro. Nick Patterson had already told him that he intended to visit both the Louvre and the Musee D'Orsay that afternoon. William thought that was being a bit over-optimistic.

There was a particular self-service restaurant in the Boulevard des Capucines where Mireille always stopped. Up the stairs she went with William and Claude, while most of William's group followed. The coach passengers ate their lunch from the cafeteria on the first floor. Mireille led Claude and William up to the second floor, where the restaurant proprietors operated a waiter service purely for the benefit of drivers and couriers.

William paid Mireille for the guided tour and for the evening trip to the

Grenouille Bondissante. She stuffed the bundle of notes straight into her Gucci handbag. A mugger would have a field day with her, thought William. Claude was still looking forlorn and dejected. He hardly touched the plate of crudités which the waitress placed before him.

"Mais qu'est-ce-que tu as?" Mireille demanded at last. "All morning long you are silent and angry. You don't speak to me. And when that German car got into the wrong lane in the Champs-Elysées I really thought you were going to get out and kill the driver! What is it, Claude? Tell me!"

Claude remained silent for a few more minutes, and then took a sip of Perrier.

"It is ma femme. She says she is going to leave me!"

"But she's threatened that before," said William. "She knows you're really a caring husband. She always stays with you."

"Not this time. This time she means it."

"Why?"

"I should never have accepted this tour. Tomorrow it is my little girl Virginie's birthday. She will be five. She will have a big party with all her friends. And I shall not be there."

"But your wife knows you won't be there. You've got to take us back to London."

"Of course," said Claude, miserably. "I must take you back to London. I do not want to lose my job. But my wife, she thinks I can pack in my job just like that and come home!"

"She'll get over it!" said William. But he was not altogether convinced.

William looked anxiously at his watch. It was getting on for one o'clock. Helena would probably have arrived in Paris. That was a pity. He would have liked to have been at the hotel when she arrived.

"Come on, mon ami!" said Claude. "I am not supposed to leave the coach out there. We must be getting back to the hotel!"

On their way downstairs they collected Miss Crosbie and the Tjeong family, and William again took a seat towards the rear as they drove back to the Porte D'Italie. He felt really sorry for Claude. He just wished that he could do something to help him.

When they reached the hotel, William rushed to the Reception Desk.

"Excuse me, has a Mademoiselle Rogers from Orbit Tours arrived yet?"

"No. I have a reservation under that name. But she hasn't come yet. Can I give a message for her?"

"No. It's alright. I'll wait here."

William sank down in one of the yellow plastic-coated armchairs in the hotel lobby. He idly picked up a brochure listing all the hotels in the Royale chain. Yes, they certainly had France well-covered. He looked at the names of some of the places - Albi, Rodez, Mende, Privas... A draught of air came from the automatic sliding door. He put down the brochure. Here she was.

She was wearing her normal office garb of large floppy sweater and knee-length navy blue skirt, with the addition of an Orbit name-badge similar to his own. She had those hideous glasses on, her hair was tied back, and a blue and white Orbit bag was slung over her shoulder.

She strode quite purposefully towards the Reception Desk. There were definitely no violins playing.

William didn't know how he felt. Here was the most wonderful woman in the world who had just walked into the hotel, and yet he was disappointed. What had he really been expecting? At least that awful feeling in his stomach, which he had felt yesterday on the Metro, had vanished. He ran up to her.

"Hallo!"

"Hi there! I'm sorry I'm a bit later than I expected. We got caught up in some horrific traffic on the Peripherique."

"Don't worry. We've only just got back from the city sightseeing anyway."

"Mr Papadopoulos has asked me to go through some paperwork with the hotel. I think I'd better do that first." Did William detect a glint in her eyes as she said that? It was hard to tell, because of those wretched spectacles.

"I'll see you later then. Shall we say in about an hour?"

"That should be alright."

Helena Rogers disappeared through a glass door into some kind of office behind the Reception Desk. William was just about to go up to his room, when he heard a voice:

"Please, please, excuse me! Are you the Reiseleiter of Orbit Tours?"

He turned around and saw an amply-proportioned Teutonic girl with flowing blonde hair, full lips and a slightly vacant expression on her face. She reminded him of a larger version of Valérie from Neuville-sur-Charente. Who was she, he wondered. Probably the tour manager from a German group, asking if he had seen one of her missing suitcases.

"Yes, that's me. How can I help you?"

"You know not me. I am from Germany. From Bavaria," she emphasised. "My name is Angelika. You have my boyfriend on your bus."

This was news to William.

"He is called John Bridger. He tells me he books a tour to France, but he tells me not the name of the company. But I know of Orbit Tours, they use hotel I know in the Schwarzwald. So I telephone them in England and ask if they have passenger called Bridger. They tell me. And I come to Paris!"

"I think Squadron-Leader Bridger is in his room at the moment. Shall I call him?"

"Oh yes, that will be very nice."

William picked up the internal phone and dialled the number of Bridger's room for the second time that day. This time the phone was answered almost immediately. William said simply that he had a call for him, and handed the phone over to Angelika.

William moved away. It was rude to eavesdrop on other people's private phone calls. In any case, he might not have been able to understand much of the conversation. Judging by what he could hear of Angelika's heated exchanges, they were talking in a mixture of English and German.

The conversation ended with Angelika flinging down the receiver. She was sobbing.

"He says it is all over between us. It is the same thing he said to me at home. We are finished. And I have followed him all the way from the Black Forest."

William was touched. He would have put his arm around the girl's shoulder, but she was several inches taller than he was, especially with her stiletto heels.

"You need a drink," he said. He led her to one of the yellow armchairs and ordered a gin and tonic from the bar.

"Telephone for you, sir!" It was one of the receptionists talking to William. He picked up the phone. It was an internal call.

"Squadron-Leader Bridger here. I just want to tell you to keep that woman away from me. I have finished with her and do not want to see her again. Send her away!"

William went back to the red-eyed Angelika, who was crying into her gin and tonic. Any girl who followed her man for hundreds of miles across Europe had to be something special.

"I know he loves me really," sobbed Angelika. "We are together five years. Then they post him back to England. I want to come with him, to be his wife. He say no, it is all over…"

William's opinion of Bridger was even lower than it had been sixteen years previously. How could any man sleep for five years with this beautiful woman and then cast her aside like a broken toy?

"I must see him again," she wailed.

"Of course you must," said William. "Are you staying in this hotel?"

"No. I have booked into a cheap little place near the Gare de L'Est. I have my luggage there."

"I can tell you exactly where you will find John this evening," said William. He pulled out of his wallet one of the business cards from La Grenouille Bondissante.

"Oh, you are so kind!" exclaimed Angelika. She seized the card and ran out of the hotel.

William went up to his room briefly. He took off his jacket and tie and pulled on a sweatshirt. He was not going to be with the group again until they left for the night club that evening. He wondered what he would be doing that afternoon with Helena. How he was longing to be with her; the last twenty minutes or so before he was due to see her were passing so slowly!

William was waiting in the lobby when Helena came out of the lift. Clearly she had been up to her room as well. Gone were the glasses, the baggy sweater and the navy blue skirt. Her hair was loose and she was wearing cut-off jeans, sandals and a T-shirt showing a map of the London Underground, bearing the legend I'D BE LOST WITHOUT IT.

"Where shall we go?" she asked. Clearly he had to take the initiative this time around: at least he was on familiar ground.

"There's not much to do around here, but there is quite a good supermarket around the back of the hotel. I quite often go there to buy things to take home."

"Let's have a look there!" she said.

They walked together to the supermarket. William wanted to take Helena in his arms and kiss her, but he wasn't quite sure how she would react. She seemed to be worried about something, he thought.

In the supermarket, Helena paused in front of the Poulain chocolate.

"I love this stuff!" she said.

"Funny. So do I!" said William.

They bought a couple of packs of the chocolate and then sat on a bench outside, where William pulled a bar out of one pack and offered it to Helena. She broke off a small piece and passed it back to him. He put some in his mouth and let it melt. Here they were, sitting on a concrete outdoor bench in a shabby suburb of Paris, sharing chocolate like a couple of teenage sweethearts. What else could be more natural?

William looked into Helena's eyes; Helena looked into William's. They said nothing, but moved their faces closer together.

For their first attempt at a kiss, it was not too bad an effort.

"Helena!" exclaimed William.

"William!" exclaimed Helena.

"I've got so much I want to say to you, but I don't know how to say it!"

"There's such a lot I want to say to you, too!"

"What's the matter, Helena?"

"What?"

"Well, when we were walking to the supermarket just then, I was sure you had something on your mind."

Helena broke off another piece of chocolate.

"Oh, William, I do love you! I've never felt like this about anyone else in my life before! But I've been so worried about you!"

"Worried about me?"

"Yes. You've invited these friends of yours on this tour, and one of them gets arrested for smuggling, then two more leave and now your friend Mr Atkinson is wanted by the poli…" She broke off, suddenly realising what she was saying.

"Who is Atkinson wanted by?"

"The police. They're going to arrest him as soon as he gets back to the country. Mr Papadopoulos said I shouldn't tell you. I was to stay on the coach and make sure Atkinson didn't try to escape. And now I've told you I suppose you'll tell him so he can go off and buy an air ticket to South America or somewhere!"

Helena was almost in tears. William lifted her hand to his lips and kissed it gently. "I have absolutely no intention of doing so!" he said.

"So he isn't your best friend who you've known for years?"

"No. He never was a friend of mine. And I hadn't set eyes on him for over fifteen years before the start of the tour."

"But why did you invite him, then?"

"Helena, darling! I love you and I trust you, so I'll tell you. But you must promise not to tell anyone else!"

"I promise. Cross my heart and hope to die."

"Here, have some more chocolate!"

And, so, as Helena devoured the rest of the bar of Poulain, William told her about the bullying he had suffered at Chestfield, the letters he had sent out to his old enemies, about the tricks he had played on Mario Rottoli, Mr Eveleigh and Mike Turner, about the wine he had recommended to the Bartlett-Nicholsons, about Ian Bailey-Filmer's coffee, Steve Vicks' radio-cassette and Jonathan Atkinson's ghostly night. He told her about the annexe and the food at the Hotel Beau-Séjour, and about his failure to think of any specific punishment for Nick Patterson and John Bridger.

"But that's wonderful!" exclaimed Helena, kissing him full on the lips. "But you really must try to get your revenge on the other two! I mean, it would finish the tour nicely! I'll see if I can think of something."

"You mean you're not horrified?"

"Of course not! I was bullied terribly myself at school. I would love to get my hands on some of the girls I knew there! Only I'd be too shy and too scared to do anything about it."

"I can't imagine you being bullied at school."

"You won't believe how I was picked on!" said Helena. "I was a day-girl at an all-girls' boarding school from when I was seven to when I was eighteen! Just think! Eleven years in the same place!"

William could imagine. Five years at Chestfield had seemed an eternity.

"I still remember my first day at school. I was such an ugly little girl, you know, having to wear glasses, and I had one of those awful brace things on my teeth. And I remember this big girl coming up to me. She looked so beautiful, so grown-up. And she asked me what my name was, so I told her. And then she asked me what my father did, and I said he ran a butcher's shop."

"And what happened then?"

"She said 'We don't want tradesmen's daughters here' and pushed me down into the mud. And then all these other girls came along and started kicking my pencil case around and things…"

"But that's terrible!"

"Do you know, I can still remember that big girl's name. It was Miranda Morrison. She left soon afterwards. She went into the sixth form of some posh public school in Suffolk."

William was dumbstruck. "And what would you do, Helena darling, if you could see that girl again now?"

"Probably push her over in the dirt!" she said.

They got up off the bench and started walking back to the hotel. They stopped on the street corner to let a bus go by.

"I suppose you're going to tell me what sort of bus that is?" asked William.

"Certainly. It's one of the new ones. It's an R312. Paris isn't really a very interesting city for buses, actually. If I was going to France just to see buses, I'd go to Lyons. They've got more variety. They even still have some little old 1964 Vetras on Route 6 to the Croix-Rousse!"

"You're amazing!" said William, as he grabbed Helena around the waist and hugged her. "I must take you to Lyons sometime. I've been there on several tours. I know the city fairly well, though I can't say I ever paid much attention to the buses."

They walked back to the hotel hand in hand. All was quiet in the lobby. The Orbit passengers were either still in the city centre, or else were resting in their rooms before the long night ahead.

"Shall we have a drink?" asked William.

"That would be nice! Nothing alcoholic, thanks." William got two cokes from the bar and they sat down side by side in two of the yellow armchairs. Helena fingered the ashtray on the table in front of them.

"I love this hotel! Everything here's got my initials on it! I asked the manager if I could have some things to take back, and he said he'd make up a bag for me, with ashtrays and towels and things!"

This was more the relaxed, excitable Helena he had known at the bus rally. Yet William still had the impression something was troubling her.

"William," she started.

"Yes, darling!" (How he loved at last being able to call someone 'darling'. He hoped Pepper wouldn't be too jealous!)

"You know you asked me not to tell anyone else about the thing which you asked me not to tell anyone else about?"

"Yes."

"Well, there's something I want to tell you about, and I want you to promise me you won't tell anyone else about it either!"

"I promise." This was getting complicated, William thought.

And Helena went on to tell William of how they had discovered that Danny Bourget was cheating on his excursion sales, and of how she had been asked to spy on him at the Grenouille Bondissante.

"I really shouldn't be telling you about this," Helena finished.

"That's alright. Leave it to me. I'll see Danny at the Grenouille and just drop the hint that someone from Head Office might be coming, and tell him to make sure his excursion sales tonight are all in order. Danny's not to know you've told me."

"Oh, William, you're so clever! But I don't understand why someone like Danny should need to fiddle his excursion revenue.

"He's getting on," said William. "He doesn't think he's going to be working for Orbit for much longer. For years all the money he's earned has gone on the good life. Now he's suddenly realising that he ought to put a bit away for a rainy day. He knows that some day Orbit will tell him his face doesn't fit any more, and he'll be sitting on his own in his rented flat in between taking the annual Mothers' Union outing to Skegness and the occasional overnight trip to the Austrian Tyrol with some fly-by-night operator."

"But that's terrible!" Helena had never imagined the reality behind the glamour.

"He's only got himself to blame, really," said William. "All those motorway services meals, the alcohol and the cigarettes. And he doesn't know where to stop. He should have given up the job long ago, when he was still enjoying it. Now money's the only thing that's driving him along."

"And what about you, William?" He felt Helena's hand on his own. "Do you know when you ought to give it up?"

"Until a couple of weeks ago I didn't. Now I think I do."

They heard rowdy singing coming from the lobby. It sounded like John Bridger. He must have gone over to the supermarket and bought some lager, thought William. Trust him to get tanked up even before the evening had started! William thought of Angelika and the Grenouille Bondissante. Perhaps he would get his revenge after all.

"Should we be getting ready for this night club?" asked Helena.

William glanced at his watch. It was astonishing how quickly the time has passed on the concrete bench behind the supermarket.

"Yes, I think we should," he replied.

Hand in hand they crossed the foyer to the nearest lift and pressed the button. They had the lift to themselves. As it soared up to the sixth floor, William and Helena enjoyed their first moderately successful snog.

They parted outside the lift and headed off to their separate rooms at different ends of the sixth floor.

"See you soon," said William.

"You bet!" said Helena.

Chapter 13

The Bright Lights

WILLIAM heard a tap on his bedroom door and opened it. Nothing could quite have prepared him for what he saw. Helena Rogers was wearing a skimpy black party frock, the kind of thing one platonic lady friend of his at University had once described as her 'Tart's Dress'. He would never have imagined Helena owning such a garment. Perhaps she had borrowed it from Margot at the office - the two girls were much the same size. How Helena had managed to bring it over from London in that small shoulder bag without it getting crumpled beyond recognition was something of a miracle. At any rate, on Helena, it definitely couldn't be described as tarty. "You look absolutely stunning!"

"You're not so bad yourself."

"Are you ready?"

"Yes. Let's get the lift."

They repeated the same procedure descending in the lift as they had ascending, but broke off when a party of German tourists got in on the third floor. William noticed something jangling from Helena's neck, above those gorgeous small firm breasts. Of course, it must be her ship halfpenny.

William took Helena out to the coach. Claude was replacing the wing-mirrors, which he'd left off while the vehicle was standing unattended. He seemed as morose and dejected as he had in the morning, although his spirits seemed to rise when he saw Helena.

"Ca, c'est ta copine? Ah, je comprends maintenant!!"

William introduced Claude to Helena, and left them happily discussing the respective merits of the Mercedes 0303 and Volvo B10M while he went to the hotel lobby to round up the passengers. Everyone seemed to be making the most of the last evening of the tour as an occasion to dress up. The Charlton girls were in identical floral print dresses, the Tjeong children in jackets and ties, and Miranda Bartlett-Nicholson was wearing an amazing green creation which had obviously come from somewhere in the Rue Sainte-Dominique that very afternoon. Even John Bridger, no matter how rough he might be feeling, had his hair neatly brushed and was wearing a smart sports jacket.

"Come on, Tour F443! Time to go!" shouted William.

They trooped after him to the coach. William decided not to introduce Helena to anyone. Introducing a stranger as someone from the Head Office was asking for trouble: the hapless colleague was liable to be bombarded with all sorts of queries, from complaints about the food in such-and-such an hotel to questions about the taxi fare from the West London Coach Station to Kensal Green.

Helena settled inconspicuously in the back of the coach. Just ahead of her she could hear the Chestfield boys joking and swearing. She could recognise each of them from William's descriptions. And who was the woman with them? When Miranda Bartlett-Nicholson got up to retrieve something from the overhead rack, she had a good look at her. So this was that appalling girl who had ruined her first day at school twenty years ago!

William was never too serious when escorting groups to the night club. He knew that many of the passengers would already have had a few drinks before starting out, and, besides, they had been on a fully comprehensive tour with a qualified local guide that morning. So William's commentary on the way to the Grenouille Bondissante went along the following lines:

"You see that river down there? You don't want to go falling in that. If you did, you really would be IN SEINE!"

This was followed by general groans from the whole coach.

"And there's Notre Dame. If you walk up the bell tower you might be lucky enough to see Quasimodo. You may not recognise him, but I'm sure his name will ring a bell!"

More groans.

And at last they arrived at Place Pigalle. William asked everyone to keep together close behind him as they went down the small side street to the night club. He didn't want to lose anyone in this part of Paris. Behind him he could see Helena and Claude, who were bringing up the rear. He felt someone tug at his sleeve. It was Miss Crosbie.

"Excuse me, dear, but what are all those ladies doing hanging around in the doorways?"

"Oh, them?" asked William. "I don't know. I expect they're just waiting for their husbands to return from the office."

"That's sweet of them," said Miss Crosbie.

They went through the door underneath the flashing neon frog. William showed them to their tables. They were seated in threes and fours at the very best tables in the establishment, near the stage.

"This looks a bit poky," said Miranda Bartlett-Nicholson to her husband. "Not quite what I'd been expecting."

"Oh, please, dear. Let's see what the food and the show are like. I'm sure this is one of the top places in Paris. I mean, the Lido and the Moulin Rouge are old hat now."

A waiter brought some bottles of champagne to the tables, which went down very well. Even the Tjeongs and the two Charlton girls drank some, William noticed. Making sure everyone was seated, he took a seat at the end table where Helena and Claude were already sitting. Helena reached out for his hand under the table and grabbed it. William poured two glasses of champagne and said a toast:

"To us!"

They clinked the glasses together and drained them.

"Shall we go down to the disco?" asked Helena.

"We can always have a look. Are you coming, Claude?"

Claude just grunted something which William took to be in the negative.

William had told the Orbit passengers about the disco which was held in the basement of the Grenouille Bondissante, but few of the group had gone down. When Helena and he went downstairs to the disco, they could only see Josephine and Rebecca Charlton and Erwin and Abraham Tjeong, who were bopping along to Abba's *Dancing Queen*, and Miss Crosbie and Mr Murray, who were attempting to waltz to it.

"This seems pretty mild," said Helena.

"I know. Anyone can make fools of themselves down here. Are you any good at dancing?"

"Hopeless."

"Good. That makes two of us. May I have the pleasure of this dance?"

"Certainly, kind sir!"

He grabbed her around the waist and they pirouetted around the floor in peals of laughter. The next record was a slow one. William had usually scurried to the side of the floor whenever a slow record came on at a disco, but this time he clung closer and closer to Helena as they occupied the centre of the dance floor in glorious isolation.

When the record finished, William noticed that Maria and Lucia had joined them in the disco.

"Are you going to dance with us?" asked Maria.

"I'm very sorry. I'm already taken," said William.

He went back up to the night club proper with Helena. Another group, of some forty to fifty people, had come into the club while they had been in the disco. William and Helena went back to sit with Claude.

"William," said Claude.

"Yes."

"A friend of yours has just come in. Big fat bloke. Said his name is Danny. He told me to tell you he's gone to the bar."

"I'd better go and see him."

"Best of luck!" said Helena.

The bar at the Grenouille Bondissante was on a kind of gallery overlooking the stage, reached by an open metalwork spiral staircase from the main seating area. William ran upstairs and saw Danny immediately. The fat, bald man was sitting on his own at the bar, his cigarette burning on the ashtray beside him and his glass of Scotch in his hand. He looked so lonely. William just prayed to God that he wouldn't end up one day like Danny.

"William!" Danny beamed at him. "Thought I was going to be here all on my own this evening! Pull up a stool! Got to do something to pass the time during this stupid show!"

"Well, actually, Danny, I was thinking of watching the show this evening."

"What d'you want to do that for? You've seen it hundreds of times! And if you sit down there with the punters you'll only get them complaining to you all the time and asking you to fetch them more wine!"

"Danny, you've got to be serious. Someone from Head Office is coming to the Grenouille Bondissante tonight."

"Who? Mr P? SS Oberleutnant Margot?"

"No. Helena Rogers."

Danny laughed. "I've got nothing to worry about, then. I'm not afraid of the Bloomsbury Ice Maiden!"

William tried a different approach.

"Danny, we all know you cheat on the excursion sales here."

"Cheat? Creative accounting, I call it. Surely you're not going to begrudge an old codger like me making a few extra pennies?"

"Pennies, perhaps not. But this amounts to hundreds of pounds."

"About four thousand so far this year, actually."

"But why, Danny, why?"

"They make it so easy for you, don't they! I just declare about twelve or fifteen sales and tell the rest of the punters I've run out of tickets. I pay Mireille Darsac for the twelve or fifteen, and the others I pay in cash directly to the club."

"And you pocket the remaining money?"

"Of course, old boy!"

"Danny, how many passengers have you got here this evening? Officially, I mean."

"Let me see. Fourteen."

"There must be at least forty down there. Danny, listen to me!"

"What is it?"

"Danny, you've got to write out excursion tickets for all your other passengers. Then you've got to ring Mireille Darsac and tell her that you've had some new clients who have suddenly decided to come on the excursion. Danny, do it, please?"

"Come on, man. You wouldn't tell tales about me, would you?"

"Danny, you've got to realise what's good for you. I'm telling you this as a friend."

"The kind of friend who stabs you in the back," said Danny. But as William turned to go back downstairs he saw Danny taking the ticket receipt book out of his briefcase.

"Well, did you do it?" asked Helena, when William was back at the table.

"I don't think you're going to have any trouble from Danny Bourget on this tour," said William. Helena gave him an unobtrusive kiss on the cheek.

William looked around at the other tables. The hors d'oeuvres had yet to arrive, but the Orbit passengers were still happily drinking their champagne. One or two more had drifted down to the disco. He knew that when the champagne gave out, they would be served ordinary table wine. Remembering that he still had some of the Bartlett-Nicholson drinks fund left, he might as well buy a few extra bottles for the group.

A waiter was approaching the table.

"Monsieur," said William, pressing some banknotes into his hand, "please could you serve some more champagne to my group?"

"Mais bien sûr, Monsieur. But I was searching for you. There are some people outside. They say they know you."

Who could this be, thought William. He got up and followed the waiter to the door. Helena was just behind him.

In the half-light William could see a large shaggy face with a red beard. But of course! "Don!" he shouted.

"Do you know these people?" asked the waiter.

"But of course. They are good friends of Orbit Tours."

"Show them in!"

William went to the door and ushered in Don and Maddy. Maddy saw Helena and embraced her, and then Don lifted her up in exactly the same way he'd seen him do at Tenterden.

"How did the filming go?" asked Helena.

"Oh, fantastic!" said Maddy. "They put us in a little hotel in Villejuif. A bit out of the city centre, but it's close to the Metro and there's even a secure parking place for the bus."

"And the bus ran well?"

"Sweet as a baby."

"Let's go and sit down!" said William. He led them to the table where he had been sitting with Claude and Helena. He took the nearest champagne bottle and filled everyone's glasses.

"But how come you are in Paris?" Maddy asked Helena.

"My boss gave me some work to do," replied Helena, truthfully. "Here, this is our coach driver, Claude. Claude, these are Maddy and Don. They are bus people."

Claude said hello to them both without particular enthusiasm.

"He's a bit put out," William explained to Don. "He's got to drive us back to London tomorrow, but he'd rather be at home for his little girl's birthday."

Maddy, who spoke fluent French, started talking to Claude. At length she said:

"Mes amis, I think we have a solution."

"What do you mean?" asked William.

"Claude has to take you back to London, but he wants to go home. We have a bus which we have to take back to England tomorrow. Empty!"

"But it's not exactly a modern air-conditioned coach!"

"Do you think anyone's really going to care about a thing like that on the last day?" asked Don. "All they're going to be thinking about tomorrow is getting back on that ferry to England. My old girl will do them just fine. "

"I do believe you're right," said William, "I've just remembered that I've got four Indonesian clients who have been complaining all the tour that they haven't been on a proper English double-decker. They'd be delighted if we could go back on your bus!"

"That's all settled, then!" said Helena.

"There is still un grand problème," said Claude. "I have the official duty to take you back to London. If I abandon you in Paris I will get into trouble."

"Even if I write a letter on Orbit Tours headed paper for you to take back to your boss?" suggested Helena.

"They will ask why Orbit Tours changed the vehicle. Then they say that Claude has problems with the passengers. Then they take away my Mercedes and give me an old Saviem and I am doing le ramassage scolaire."

"Wait!" exclaimed William. I have an idea. "What if your coach was damaged, so you could not take us back to London? Then I would have to hire another one!"

"That is true. But I cannot vandalise my own coach!"

"But there's the windscreen. You've told me already that it will have to be replaced before the next tour."

"Yes. What of it?"

"If," William continued, "you were to break the windscreen a little more. You know, have a great big hole in it. You could not drive us back to England then!"

"Mon dieu!" said Claude. "You are right."

"It's easy," said Helena. "When we get back to the hotel, you get some heavy object and smash the windscreen. Then scatter things about the coach so it looks as if it's been broken into. When William comes down in the morning, you say the coach has been vandalised, and he phones Don and Maddy who come and pick the group up. Then you leave the coach in Paris to have the windscreen replaced, and get the train home."

"Mais c'est formidable! I do no real damage to the coach, I get home early and I see Virginie for her birthday party! Merci, mes amis!"

At this Claude refilled everyone's glasses with champagne, drank a toast to William, Helena, Don and Maddy, kissed Helena and Maddy on both cheeks and shook hands vigorously with Don.

They chatted amicably for some time. As in many French eating establishments, the kindest word one could have found to describe the service was 'leisurely'. At last a waitress appeared with bowls full of thick onion soup and croutons.

"Bon appétit!" said Claude.

"Same to you," said William. The last of the champagne bottles was now empty, so he filled his and Helena's glasses with some vin de table rouge. Funny. He could have sworn there had been another full champagne bottle there a few moments ago. He was feeling delightfully light-headed and just hoped that Claude hadn't been drinking as much as he and Helena had.

"Look there!" cried Helena, tugging at his sleeve. "It's that bitch Miranda Morrison! I'm out to get her this time!"

A few feet away from them, Miranda Bartlett-Nicholson was climbing up the spiral staircase to the bar.

"Helena, come back!" But it was too late. Up the stairs she tore. William raced after her, leaving Claude and a bemused Don and Maddy at the table.

William grabbed hold of Helena just at the top of the staircase. Miranda was at the bar. She appeared to be asking the barmaid to give her a clean glass.

"Really, Helena! What do you think you can achieve?"

"I want to get at that stuck-up bitch. You've had a go at your enemies! Now it's my turn!"

She had a point, thought William. But this was the wine talking.

Miranda Bartlett-Nicholson returned to the top of the staircase. The way down was blocked by Helena Rogers. William was just below her.

"Excuse me, can I get past, please?" asked Miranda.

"You didn't talk to me like that twenty years ago, did you, Miranda Morrison?" screamed Helena. William might have been concerned that the whole auditorium could have heard, but in fact the orchestra had just started their warming-up routine and were filling the night club with what sounded like the runner-up for the 1956 Eurovision Song Contest.

"What the hell do you mean? I've never seen you before in my life!" shouted Miranda. She had drunk about as much as Helena, William decided.

"You've seen me before, alright. Only I was a nobody to you then, just as I am now!" William fervently hoped that Helena wasn't going to try anything silly. She now had her fists clenched and was trying to push the girl back up the stairs. Miranda got the advantage, forced Helena over onto the narrower edge of the spiral, and grabbed her neck.

This was more than he could bear. "You let her go! I think we've all had too much to drink!" Miranda did so and ran downstairs, shouting "Silly cow!"

Helena fell into William's arms and he held her tight on the staircase.

"You're right! I shouldn't have gone for her!"

"Come back down and finish your soup!"

"I will. Oh - help!"

"What is it?"

"My halfpenny's missing?"

"Your what?"

"My ship halfpenny." Helena showed William the broken chain. "It must have fallen off when Miranda grabbed me."

"It must be here somewhere!" said William.

"No, this staircase is an open metal one. It could have fallen through."

William looked below. Directly underneath them was the table at which the Chestfield clients were seated for the show. He suddenly spotted the halfpenny.

"I can see it."

"Where?"

"It's fallen into John Bridger's soup. It's sitting on a crouton!"

They hurried downstairs. John Bridger was talking to Jonathan Atkinson across the table, and was dipping his spoon in the soup and raising it to his mouth without examining the contents. By the time William and Helena had his soup-bowl in their sights, it was too late. Crouton and halfpenny had disappeared into John Bridger's mouth.

"Christ! Are you alright?" said Atkinson. John Bridger had suddenly slumped off his chair and was clutching his throat. He was trying to speak. Not a sound was coming out.

"Is he breathing?" asked William. He no longer felt as if he had been drinking. He knew he might have to take charge of an emergency situation.

"Yes, he's breathing alright," said Hugh Bartlett-Nicholson. "But he's obviously in pain. And he doesn't seem to be able to speak." They could see the hapless Bridger mouthing words as he clutched at the edge of the table.

"I'll call an ambulance!" William rushed up the spiral staircase. There was a phone at the bar.

When he returned downstairs, Bridger had been laid flat on a bench, and was looking a bit more comfortable. But he still couldn't say anything.

"I read something in the paper once," said Helena, "about this girl in Australia who got a silver threepenny bit from her Christmas pudding stuck in her throat for ten years, and completely lost the power of speech."

"Look, are you an expert on this or something?" asked Nick Patterson, who had come over to take a closer look at Bridger. "We don't know what he's swallowed."

Sirens outside soon announced the arrival of the ambulance. Two ambulance-men, carrying breathing apparatus, came to collect John Bridger and place him on a stretcher.

"Do you know what is the matter with him?" one of them asked William.

"Yes. He has swallowed a coin."

"Oh! Is that all? What sort of coin? A silver dollar, perhaps?" He drew an imaginary circle in the air.

"No. An old English halfpenny. About the same size as a 2-franc piece."

"Oh! He will live."

As they prepared to move the stretcher out of the Grenouille Bondissante, a figure in a red dress suddenly breezed through the door. Her long wavy blonde hair was immaculate and she stood a good six inches taller than the doorman who had admitted her.

"But, my poor John! What has happened? Has there been an accident?"

"Angelika!" shouted William. "I'm afraid he has swallowed something. It's not dangerous, but he seems to have lost his voice. He is being taken to hospital."

"Then I shall go with him! He knows he can always count on his kleine Angelika in his time of need!"

Angelika kissed Bridger's face as the ambulancemen lifted up the stretcher. She then walked with them out to the ambulance. As William and Helena followed, she cried:

"No. You not need to come. I go to hospital with John. I have hotel number. I phone!"

And with that she climbed into the vehicle alongside the recumbent Bridger, pulled the red double doors shut, and with the din of the sirens they drove off into the night.

Helena and William returned to their table to find their Boeuf Bourgignonne had arrived and was already cold. William poured both of them another glass of red wine. They needed it now. Helena was fingering her broken chain.

"Perhaps I should have given the ambulancemen your address, so they could send you back your halfpenny," said William.

"No, it's alright," said Helena. "I don't think I'd want to wear it again after knowing where it had been."

The dessert duly made its appearance in the form of little wrapped slabs of vanilla ice-cream. William realised he hadn't been paying much attention to the non-Chestfield passengers, so he walked along to see how they were. All looked in quite high spirits.

"This tastes just like pre-war ice-cream!" said Miss Crosbie.

Not sure if this was meant to be a compliment or a criticism, William moved back to his seat. The lights suddenly dimmed and the orchestra struck up. A juggler appeared on stage, tossing coloured balls in the air. The show itself had begun.

As Danny Bourget had said, William had seen the show countless times before, but for Helena, Don and Maddy it was their first time. William found himself looking at it afresh as if through their eyes. Mr Papadopoulos was right. It wasn't too bad after all. Or perhaps it was just the effect of the wine.

William found himself clapping as loudly as anyone else when the juggler finished his act. Then the orchestra started playing the opening bars of Milord. Yvette came on from the wings, wearing a sequinned dress and a silver stole.

For the first time in the evening, William found himself looking into the eyes of a woman other than Helena. Yvette *was* Piaf, the little street girl offering companionship to the lonely English gentleman.

Regardez-moi, Milord. Vous ne m'avez jamais vu …
Mais vous pleurez, Milord. Ça j'aurais jamais cru!

At this point in the song, Yvette left the stage and walked towards the audience. The music stopped as she headed to the table where the Chestfield passengers were sitting. A spotlight picked out the face of Jonathan Atkinson.

"Allez, dansez Milord!" Yvette looped her stole around Atkinson's neck, dragged him out into the centre stage to the laughs and applause of the audience, and, as the music started up again, she whirled him around as the song reached its glorious finale.

Jonathan Atkinson stood dazed, dazzled and dizzy, with the spotlights shining on him for all to see, as Yvette planted an enormous kiss on his mouth. Why had he come on this tour, he asked himself. Being in prison might well have been preferable. Somehow he found the use of his feet and shuffled back towards the audience.

Yvette was followed in turn by a fire-eater, and by a very good impressionist whose impersonations of various leading French statesmen and pop stars were unfortunately mostly lost on the chiefly foreign audience. Then a large box decorated with sequinned stars and signs of the Zodiac was wheeled onto the stage. It was time for the great Igor.

The orchestra struck a chord as Igor produced a series of coloured handkerchiefs and two doves from a hat, made several objects of increasing size and unlikeliness materialise in the apparently empty box, and performed a few card tricks with an invited member of the audience. Then all the lights went dim. Igor lit up a cigarette. The orchestra launched into Money Makes the World Go Round.

William knew just what was going to happen. The audience saw Igor walk over to the table where Hugh and Miranda Bartlett-Nicholson, Ian Bailey-Filmer, Jonathan Atkinson and Nick Patterson were sitting.

"For my next trick," Igor started, "I require a five hundred franc note. Can anyone lend me one, please?"

"Come on, Hugh! You're the one with the money!" said Patterson.

Hugh opened a wallet which was considerably slimmer than it had been one week previously, and handed Igor the note. Igor returned to the stage, holding the note up for everyone to see, and then took out an enormous pair of scissors and cut it into small pieces.

There was a gasp from the audience. Igor placed the fragments in a handkerchief, folded it up and waved his magic wand over it, and then unfolded the handkerchief again. The audience were expecting him to produce a miraculously-restored note from the handkerchief. They were astonished when he shook the handkerchief out in front of them. There was absolutely nothing in it at all.

Igor next found a balloon and blew it up, tied the end up, and threw it into the air a few times. He then grabbed his huge scissors again and punctured the balloon with them. Out of the remains of the balloon, he produced something with a flourish. It was a cigarette.

Igor drew two long breaths on the cigarette, which was already burning, and then said to the audience:

"That's funny. This cigarette tastes very strange."

He started peeling off the paper from the outside of the cigarette. The audience looked on in silence. From where he was sitting, William could make out the expression on Bartlett-Nicholson's face.

"No wonder this cigarette tastes funny. Because this cigarette must be very expensive. For they make this cigarette with …"

There was a sudden roll of drums from the orchestra pit.

"A - five hundred franc note!" said Igor. But there was no note. Frantically he pulled apart the cigarette, tearing the white paper to shreds. But there was nothing inside except tobacco.

"Ladies and gentlemen, I am very sorry. There should be a five hundred franc note inside the cigarette. I do not understand it. The trick has not failed before."

The great Igor gave a bow, and started packing his box before heading off-stage to a huge round of applause.

The audience, William thought, had enjoyed the trick even more than usual. Perhaps he had shown Igor a whole new career direction. Only Hugh Bartlett-Nicholson didn't seem to see the funny side of things.

"What about my money?" he demanded.

"Dear, don't make a scene! Please, everyone's watching!"

William saw Hugh sit down again and drink some more wine.

Not long afterwards, the three Italian brothers had finished their acrobatic act, Yvette had reappeared on stage to sing the closing number, and the clients began to leave. William went around to the other tables and told everyone it was time to go.

"That was a super evening!" said Maddy. "What shall we do tomorrow?"

"Have you got the number of your hotel?"

Maddy produced from her handbag a leaflet from the hotel in Villejuif.

"Thanks. I'll give you a call when we're ready. I don't want you turning up first thing in the morning. It would look too suspicious."

Don gave Helena a final goodnight kiss, and off they went.

It was a slow and extremely straggling crocodile that William and Claude led back to the coach. Everyone must have at least a litre of wine in them, William thought. As the children and Claude certainly hadn't drunk anywhere near that much, some members of the group must be well and truly sozzled.

On the return journey to the hotel, William put on a singalong tape featuring songs from various European countries. There was a great amount of joining in from the coachload, most of it out of tune. Nobody was sitting on the four front seats. William abandoned the jump seat and sat on the front seat behind Claude, Helena coming up the aisle and sitting beside him. In the dark of the Paris night nobody could see them holding hands and kissing.

"I do love you!" Helena whispered in his ear.

"I love you too," said William. "But we've both drunk far too much!"

The coach arrived back at the hotel and Claude helped the passengers off. William took the microphone to remind everyone about the departure time for tomorrow, and sat down again beside Helena.

"I've been a very very naughty girl tonight!" said Miss Crosbie, as she went past him. She was holding hands with Mr Maxwell.

"Gee, that was swell. Yvette and Igor oughta come over to Hollywood and make a movie!" Mr Murray grinned as he and his wife got off the coach. William was pleased that the Texans seemed to have enjoyed their holiday.

At last everyone was off. William got up and walked down the coach. In the overhead racks were an assortment of raincoats, sweaters and cheap souvenirs left there by the passengers. He pulled them down and strewed them around the coach.

"Good thinking!" said Helena. Her speech was getting slurred. She started removing the contents of the ashtrays and scattering them on the seats and over the floor. As smoking was prohibited on Orbit tours, the ashtrays normally got stuffed with an assortment of rubbish.

Claude had found a heavy iron bar in a builder's skip behind the hotel. Approaching the front of the coach, he hurled it towards the laminated windscreen. It made a loud crash and left an opaque area about the size of a grapefruit. He pushed again with the bar in the same place. The inner layer of glass gave. He would have to bang away for another half-hour from both inside and outside the coach before the damage looked really convincing.

"Come on," said William to Helena, "Let's go to bed!" William was not sure if he had meant that to sound the way it had sounded.

"I'm taking this!" she said. In her hand she held out a full bottle of champagne. How could she have smuggled it out of the night club, wondered William.

They darted behind the deserted reception desk to get their room keys. In the small office behind them, they could see a flickering silver light.

"Oh, look! It's the in-house movie!" said Helena.

The office door was open. On a shelf was an ordinary domestic video-recorder, with a red light showing it to be operating. A monitor above it showed the soft porn movie that was playing.

"William, you know the video you were telling me about. The one with your old French teacher?"

"Yes."

"Why don't you bring it down and play it?"

"What, here? That video's being screened to every room in the hotel!"

"So, why not? I bet hardly anyone's watching it. And it might give your old schoolmates something else to think about, if any of them have turned the movie channel on."

William reflected as much as he was still capable of doing. He had been wondering what to do with the video. He couldn't have played it on the coach, not with the children there, and he hadn't had any opportunity to do a private screening just for the Chestfield passengers. So, why not? He walked to the lift.

Five minutes later he was back with the Norwegian Tourist Board video. Helena stopped the VCR and ejected the cassette. The flickering screen went blank. They inserted William's tape and pushed PLAY. At first they saw just the interior of a hotel bedroom.

"That's my room at the Hotel Beau-Séjour. I was trying out the camera," explained William.

Then there was a white flash and the picture briefly changed to a view of a train climbing a mountain pass between Bergen and Oslo. Then it was back to the Hotel Beau-Séjour. They saw the plump, elderly figure of Mr Eveleigh in bed, with Valérie jumping on top of him and ripping the bedclothes off. A flash of light lit up her round young face. She mouthed something silently as she looked towards the camera.

"That's super!" said Helena. "Are you going to post it to him?"

"I think he's been punished enough already."

The picture changed again to a steamer crossing a fjord. William ejected the tape and replaced the in-house movie. Arm in arm they crossed the lobby to the lift.

"Shall we go to bed… I mean… together?" asked William, in the lift.

"Oh, yes! Let's!" Helena threw her arms around him.

They half staggered, half danced from the lift to William's room. He pulled back the bedclothes and lifted Helena onto the bed. She sat up and removed her party dress. William, not to be outdone, took off his shirt and trousers.

He pulled her beautiful body towards him. They kissed again, Helena's tongue finding its way into undiscovered corners of his mouth and giving him an entirely new sensation.

"I think we ought to have more champagne!" said William, after he had at last extricated himself from her wonderful lips. He went into the bathroom and reappeared with two yellow plastic tumblers marked HR.

They drained their glasses and refilled them. William stroked Helena's shapely thighs. For such a small girl, her legs were long and well-proportioned, and her thighs were covered with lovely soft golden down.

He kissed her yet again. Then he reached behind her back and fumbled with the fastening of her bra. She came to his assistance and pulled it off. He cupped her small, firm breasts in his hands and kissed them.

And then they both fell asleep in each other's arms.

Chapter 14

The Last Farewell

WILLIAM was woken up by the telephone. It rang three times, then stopped. Of course, it was the morning wake-up call. He had booked it for the whole group at nine o'clock, to give anyone who had slept until then just enough time to get ready for the coach. Last night he had forgotten to set his own alarm and clock radio. Wearily he tried to collect his thoughts together. He had a dry feeling in the back of his throat, an ache in his head, and the memories of a gorgeous taste in his mouth.

He opened his eyes. Helena Rogers was lying half-across him, in a foetal position. She had an innocent smile on her lips. It was a shame to wake her, but it had to be done. He lifted her limp arm to his lips and gently kissed her hand.

"Good morning, darling!" he said.

"Good morning." He guessed that Helena must be feeling fairly strange as well. "L-last night," she continued.

"Yes?"

"Did we … m-make love?"

William paused to think. "No… Do you mind?"

Helena gave him the biggest kiss he'd ever had. "I'd better be getting back to my room," she said.

She pulled on her dress. William put on his shirt and trousers, hurriedly packed his bags and ran a comb through his hair. They crept out of the room together. The door to the room opposite opened at exactly the same time and Mr Maxwell came out.

"Well, hallo there! I can guess what you two have been up to! Don't worry, your secret's safe with me!"

Helena hurried down the corridor to her room. William went down to the dining room. He was a bit late for breakfast, but then there was nothing that special about a Royale breakfast anyway. He poured himself a quick drink from the flask marked CAFE and took it out with him to the lobby.

Most of the Orbit passengers were already waiting down there with their bags.

At that moment Claude came in through the glass sliding door. His face bore an expression of doom. The man must have been in amateur dramatics, William thought.

"My coach! It has been broken into during the night!"

"Oh no!" cried William, convincingly.

There were horrified gasps from the Orbit passengers as they followed Claude out to the coach.

The whole windscreen of Claude's magnificent Mercedes had been smashed in, only a few shards remaining around the edges. Window curtains blew in the wind. Inside, the front of the coach was littered with glass. The passengers' possessions from the overhead racks had been scattered about.

"This is an outrage!" shouted Mr Murray.

Claude got down from the driver's seat, brushing off a few pieces of glass. He held up three empty cassette cases.

"Look! They have stolen all my cassettes!" he wailed.

William told the passengers to keep calm, and to go into the coach to see if they could find anything they'd left on board. He said that the vandals hadn't got into the coach boot, so that any wine or other purchases which they had put there should still be there. Hugh Bartlett-Nicholson breathed an audible sigh of relief.

"How long will it take to repair the windscreen?" asked Mr Tjeong.

"About three days, I think," said William. "The coach will have to go to a Mercedes specialist. And even then they might not have one in stock. And today's Sunday. All the repair places will be closed."

All the passengers were standing around now, listening.

"Then how do you intend to get us back to London?" asked Mr Murray.

"I can arrange to hire another vehicle," said William.

"But will you be able to get one in time?" implored Nick Patterson. "I've been looking forward to going up to Montmartre before we leave Paris! Will we still have time to fit it in?"

"I should be able to get a replacement vehicle in about ten minutes," said William. There were smiles and sighs of relief from his audience. "Of course, at such short notice, I won't be able to get a luxury coach."

"Oh, heavens! We're not worried about that!" said Mr Charlton. "As long as it's got seats inside and four wheels, and can take us all back to England, I couldn't care less what it looks like!"

"Hear! Hear!" said Miss Crosbie.

William suggested to the passengers that they returned to the lobby and sat down. Someone organised a collection for Claude. The group were feeling sorry for him, and gave generously. Mr Maxwell handed William a bag filled with notes and coins, which he took out to the driver.

"Oh! Merci!" With his trained driver's eyes, Claude swiftly calculated the amount of money in the bag. He would have no worries now about geting home.

Helena emerged from the hotel and walked over to the coach.

"What are you going to do?" she asked.

"I will take the coach over to the garage in Paris of another coach company. There will be someone there this morning. Then at twelve-fifteen I get the train for Troyes. From Troyes, taxi to Châtillon. And at three o'clock I am with my little Virginie for her birthday party!"

"That's wonderful!" said William.

"And I have to thank you both." He shook William by the hand, embraced Helena and followed them back to the hotel where he said goodbye to the passengers. He then returned to the ravaged Mercedes 0303 and drove it carefully up the road past the hotel, and away.

William was now on the phone, calling Don and Maddy. They were ready to leave, and promised to be at the hotel in ten minutes.

William had just turned back from the Reception Desk when a voice rang out:

"Monsieur Simpson!"

He turned towards the desk. All through the tour he had been careful not to let anyone hear his surname, and now one of the girls on the Reception Desk had blurted it out. He took the phone she was holding out to him. It turned out to be another courier, Ingrid, who was in Nancy heading south on 'The Magnificent Swiss Alps'. One of her passengers had lost a Burberry raincoat, and they thought they might have left it at the big Péronne motorway service area between Calais and Paris. Could he have a look if he stopped there on the way back?

He made a note of the passenger's name in his diary. Another of the girls behind the Reception Desk was trying to attract his attention. It was another telephone call.

"Hello! William the Orbit Reiseleiter?"

"Yes. Angelika! How are you?"

"Everything is fine! They had to operate on my poor dear John, but he is O.K. I am staying beside him in the hospital. Tomorrow I take him with me to my mother's in Dinkelsbuhl where he will recover. We feed him up on Kalbsvogerl and Brathendle!"

William said goodbye to Angelika. Whether Bridger eventually finished up with her or not, he knew he didn't deserve her.

Over by the lift, Jonathan Atkinson was thinking. Simpson. William Simpson. The name somehow meant something to him. He thought back to the conversation during that awful dinner in Neuville-sur-Charente. Yes. Little Willy. He was sure his surname had been Simpson.

Could William, their firm but friendly tour manager, really be Little Willy? It might explain why so many Chestfield Old Boys should happen to be on the same tour at the same time. It might also explain the disappearances of Mario Rottoli, Mike Turner, Mr Eveleigh, and, now, John Bridger. He turned to Steve Vicks who was sitting next to him.

"I say, Steve. Did you hear the receptionist call our courier Mr Simpson?"

"What about it?"

"I was thinking about school. I'm sure Little Willy's surname was Simpson."

"You don't mean to tell me you think this bloke could be Little Willy?"

"Well, the idea had crossed my mind ..."

"Little Willy," Steve Vicks began, "was a twenty-four carat wimp. You'd never have got him standing up in front of a coachload of people and giving them orders over the microphone! I wouldn't have the nerve to do that myself. Have you ever tried karaoke? Hell, it takes guts."

"I suppose you're right."

"What's more," continued Vicks, "Little Willy must be about the same age as us now. That bloke doesn't look more than about twenty-five. And did you notice him with that blonde bird this morning, you know, standing by the coach? Do you think Little Willy could pull a bird like that?"

Atkinson was silent. Steve Vicks must be right, of course. It had been a foolish idea. Nonetheless, there was something very strange going on. When he'd got back from the night club last night he'd switched on the TV. There'd been some Swedish bird having it off with a truck driver on the home movie channel. Then, just as it was getting to the exciting bit, he'd suddenly seen someone who looked like Bummer Eveleigh in bed with a teenage girl. He'd been so amazed he'd gone and vomited in the bathroom. Mind you, he had drunk rather a lot last night …

A vehicle of some kind had pulled up in front of the hotel. The Orbit passengers headed for the door. They were greeted by an English double-decker bus of obvious antiquity, painted maroon and cream and bearing posters on both sides showing the Union Jack and the words BRITANNIA ENGLISH LANGUAGE SCHOOLS.

William and Helena were already out waiting to greet Don and Maddy when the bus arrived.

"She looks terrific!" said Helena.

"I'll have to tell the passengers to get their things loaded," said William. He gathered all the passengers around him and explained that their replacement vehicle had arrived.

"Oh! Great!" shouted Erwin and Abraham Tjeong simultaneously.

"I knew you'd do it!" said their father. He turned to his wife and said "William has got an English bus especially for us!"

The Charlton girls looked equally delighted, but not all the other passengers were quite as enthusiastic.

"Are you sure this old wreck is going to make it back to London?" asked Mr Murray.

"It's not an old wreck!" said Helena, with true feeling. "It's been down to Paris, so it ought to be able to go back up again."

Miranda Bartlett-Nicholson was eyeing the AEC Regent V distastefully. "We can't possibly travel on that! I'd rather get the train!"

Hugh put his hand on her shoulder. "You know perfectly well, my dear, that we'd never be able to carry all our wine on and off the train. Come on, it's only for a few hours!"

Before leaving, Claude had placed all the luggage and shopping from the boot of his coach on the pavement in front of the hotel. The passengers now had to do their best to stow it on the bus. The AEC Regent V, built for commuters and schoolchildren rather than overseas holidaymakers, did not have any conventional luggage lockers.

"Look!" said William. "There are only about twenty of us. I suggest we stack up all the luggage on the seats in the lower deck, and then you can all sit on the upper deck."

This seemed a good idea. The passengers made several journeys backwards and forwards with their possessions. William carried Miss Crosbie's supermarket carrier bags and placed them carefully on one of the seats. Looking out, he saw Hugh and Miranda Bartlett-Nicholson. He was carrying one of the big boxes of *Sanségal* and she had some other bottles in a plastic bag.

"Careful, dear! That handle's going!"

"What?"

It was too late. The handle of the plastic carrier broke and the contents fell to the ground. Amazingly only one bottle was broken. Pieces of green glass lay on the pavement in a pool of beetroot-coloured wine as Miranda salvaged the remaining bottles and wiped them clean with her handkerchief.

"It was the 1968 Bordeaux!" she screamed at Hugh.

They left for the centre of Paris only some twenty minutes later than scheduled. William sat at the front near Don, so that he could do the navigating. Helena and Maddy sat together on a seat just behind, that had been kept clear of luggage. The Orbit passengers were all upstairs. It felt strange to William being separated from them and not having the use of a microphone.

William turned to Helena.

"I suppose I ought to fill in a Change of Coach form for this!"

"Here, let me do it!" said Helena. He handed her a form from his briefcase and she filled it in. He wondered what the filing clerks would make of Orbit having hired a vehicle built in 1959, with non-reclining seats and seating capacity for 72 passengers, for a tour that was normally operated by modern 49-seater coaches with full air-conditioning.

Although it was bright outside, it was not the sort of day that required full air-conditioning. A gentle breeze was blowing through the streets of Paris. William guided the bus along the Boulevard de Magenta and then into the Boulevard de Rochechouart. They came to a halt just down the hill from the Church of the Sacre-Coeur, not far from where they had been last night at the Grenouille Bondissante.

William gave the passengers an hour and a half free time here. He had been talking with Don and Maddy, and was feeling reasonably happy about the AEC Regent V's ability to reach Calais in time for their booked ferry.

Nick Patterson grabbed his sketch book and headed straight up to the Place du Tertre. He ignored the queue for the funicular and ran up the wide stone staircase. He had to be quick if he was going to get a sketch of the place in

Paris that attracted the greatest numbers of artists. And here they all were, with their paint and easels, some of them selling pictures to passers-by. Nick Patterson perched on the corner of a low wall and started his sketch. He could see the cafes with their colourful awnings, the tourists sitting on the terraces and the great white dome of the Sacré Coeur. All that he had to do was commit it to paper.

Helena and William left the coach together after the passengers had gone. How lovely she looked today, William thought. She had that shapeless floppy sweater and the corduroy trousers on again, but her hair was loose and was flying in the wind. And now he knew how beautiful she really was. They raced to the funicular. William put two Metro tickets into the turnstile and they went through. The previous car had just left and they were in the front of the queue. Soon the cabin arrived, and they were soaring hand-in-hand over the rooftops of Paris to the upper station.

From the funicular station they ran up the steps to the church. Many tourists were milling around. Africans had set up shop in front of the church, selling carved elephants and reproductions of tribal masks, and a man was trying to sell plastic birds, which you operated by winding up an elastic band and then throwing them in the air so you could watch them flap their wings as they came down.

"Let's go in!" said Helena.

As they entered the church they became conscious of the smell of incense and the hushed responses of the congregation. A service was in progress. It was Sunday, after all, William remembered.

"Listen, it's the Lord's Prayer!" said Helena.

They knelt on the floor side by side as the voice of the priest urged the Lord to forgive their trespasses as we forgive those who trespass against us. Even in French the words were easily recognisable.

"Do you think that I've been terribly wicked?" William whispered to Helena. "After all, I didn't forgive those who trespassed against me."

"And look at me with Miranda Morrison last night!" said Helena." I think we should both say to God that we are dreadfully sorry."

And so they did.

As they left the church, William asked Helena if she thought God really was looking at them at this moment.

"Of course He is. I'm more convinced of that than I ever have been in my life!" And she kissed him again and again on the mouth.

"Excuse me, I do hate to disturb you two young people, but I wonder, William, if I could just have a word with you?"

How enfuriating that Miss Crosbie should choose just that moment to turn up!

"Yes, what is it?" William hoped he did not sound too irritated.

"It's just that none of the shops will take this hundred-franc note. I must have had it since my last holiday in France a few years ago. Look, here it is! Do you think you could get it changed for me?"

Miss Crosbie handed him the note. It was of a type had gone out of circulation several years before.

"Well, Miss Crosbie, the banks are closed on Sundays, but there's a Bureau de Change down the road. I'll see if they can change it."

"You're very kind. I must start making my way back down to the bus. It'll take me ages with all those steps."

"You can come with me on the Funicular," said Helena.

Miss Crosbie had certainly brought the curtain down on one of life's magic moments, thought William. He ran down the ornamental staircase and turned right into one of the little streets of souvenir shops which ran parallel to the Boulevard de Rochechouart.

He was right. The Bureau de Change was open on Sundays. The man behind the counter changed Miss Crosbie's hundred-franc note with no trouble at all.

William noticed some gold coins in a glass-fronted case behind the counter. There were sovereigns, French twenty-franc pieces and American Eagles. He asked how much they were. The man explained that they were sold at the current *cours* - the value of the weight of the gold, plus a commission. The prices were on the board under the list of all the foreign exchange rates.

William did a quick piece of mental arithmetic and checked the contents of his wallet.

Five minutes later, back at the bus, he handed Miss Crosbie a crisp new hundred-franc note.

"Oh, you've changed it for me? How nice of you! But no, I don't want it back. You can have it now. I mean, you've looked after me so well!"

Helena was back on the bus sitting with Maddy. William did a quick head count upstairs: nineteen passengers. As he came down the stairs a breathless Nick Patterson pushed past him.

"Everyone's on!" said William to Don. "Full speed ahead to Calais!"

The old bus coped surprisingly well on the autoroute, thought William. All the way north from Paris they received friendly flashes from the headlights of southbound motorists, and waves from the cars which overtook them on their way to Calais.

"Are we going to stop at the Péronne services?" William asked Don. He had suddenly remembered Ingrid's passenger's lost raincoat.

"Yes, we'd better. The old girl could do with some diesel. And I daresay your passengers could do with a drink or the loo."

That was true. There were no facilities available on Don and Maddy's bus.

As the AEC Regent V pulled into the motorway service area, there were gasps of admiration from French children and a number of interested sightseers came up to have a look at it. While Don filled up with diesel, Helena went off to get some drinks from the service station. William had given her a couple of hundred francs to buy a selection of hot and cold drinks for the passengers.

William meanwhile found a desk marked ACCEUIL. It was deserted. He rang a bell marked SERVICE. Nothing happened. He rang it again. A harassed-looking man in a white coat asked him what he wanted. He gave a description of the missing garment.

"Non, monsieur, I am sorry. Nothing of that description has been found."

Ingrid's passenger must have been mistaken, thought William, as he walked back towards the coach. He almost bumped into Jonathan Atkinson.

"Excuse me, but you know what you said at the start of the tour about Passport Control?"

"Yes." William had been worried he might want to talk about something else.

"You know you said that normally we just stay on the coach and go straight through?"

"Yes."

"Well, now we're on this old bus instead of our proper coach, do you think it's going to make any difference?"

"No, it should be exactly the same." (Exactly the same as what, William wondered. From what Helena had told him it sounded as if the police would be on to Atkinson even if he drove through Passport Control on a green-spotted purple fire engine.)

"That's alright, then." He turned and went back to the coach.

On the upper deck of the bus, Nick Patterson took advantage of the vehicle's lack of movement by adding some finishing touches to his last sketch. He signed and dated it, and then looked back with pride through the sketchbook. There were the old church and windmill at Bercy-en-Artois, the view across the Loire from the Château at Blois, the bridge at Neuville-sur-Charente, the sunflowers, and the Hôtel Dieu at Beaune. For the first time for ages he at last had a collection of sketches of which he was proud. They might even prove saleable. He would have to think about a title. Aspects of France in July? Sketches of French Life? No, something simple was best. How about Visions of France? He wrote the title neatly on the cover of the sketch book and put it on the seat beside him.

At that moment, Helena Rogers came up the stairs with a tray of drinks from the service station; soft drinks in their cans, and tea and coffee in polystyrene cups. She passed along the coach handing them out. By the time she had been around everyone, only a single cup of coffee remained.

She walked back to the stairs. At that moment, without any warning, the bus jerked forward. Don had assumed everyone was ready and pulled off. The polystyrene cup shot off Helena's tray, travelled several feet in mid-air, and fell directly and catastrophically onto *Visions of France*. Brown liquid squirted everywhere. Nick Patterson reached for the dripping sketchbook, but it had been soaked right through with strong French coffee. The sketches were beyond any hope of salvage.

"You should watch what you're doing, you bloody bitch!" snarled Patterson. Helena mouthed a quiet "Sorry" and scampered downstairs. Patterson's holiday was ruined. But even he could not think that what had just happened was anything more than an unfortunate accident.

Helena sat down beside William and told him about the incident.

"You mean it was just a pure accident!"

"Of course. I really wouldn't have wanted to destroy his sketches."

"It's funny how some things work out."

Don knew the way from Péronne to Calais. Maddy was taking a nap on the back seat of the lower deck. With no microphone and no drinks to serve, William and Helena had nothing to do but kiss and cuddle on the seat.

"It'll be strange going back to the office tomorrow. I've been with you and your group for just twenty-four hours and already I feel they're all part of my life."

"That's what it's like," said William. "You're given a group of people. It could be twenty-four, it could be forty-nine. They can come from any countries and any backgrounds. And you've got to get to know them, look after them and spend all your time with them. The only thing that matters is the tour. You can hardly remember anything that happened before the tour, and you haven't got time to think about what's going to happen after it. And then, suddenly, you're back in Calais or at the West London Coach Station. It's all over. You're never going to see any of these people again in your life. It's like dying a little."

Helena kissed William. "And all these years I've worked in the office and I've never realised what it's like! It must take a really special type of person to make a tour manager!"

William now kissed Helena. She was wonderful, he kept thinking, she was the best thing that had ever happened to him.

"And at the end of this tour," Helena was asking him, "are you going to die a little as well?"

"Right now," said William, I feel more alive than I have ever felt before!"

The big old double-decker took the motorway exit to the docks at Calais and made its stately way through the ranks of dull and ordinary modern coaches waiting for the ferry.

On board the ferry, William took care to explain carefully to Miss Crosbie where she could find the bus.

"Oh, but I won't lose this one. It's a proper bus!"

Little old Miss Crosbie scurried up the stairs to the passenger deck, followed by Mr Maxwell with his video camera.

"May as well get a shot of us leaving Calais!" he said.

Don and Maddy had special-rate tickets for dinner in the Commercial Drivers' Restaurant. They asked William and Helena if they wanted to join them.

"Oh, no thank you!" said Helena. "You go ahead. We'd rather slum it!"

And they did. William had lost count of the number of times he had been on the cross-Channel ferry, but normally he would spend most of the time in the restaurant with other couriers and drivers. With Helena now he rediscovered the magic of travel. They shopped at the Duty Free, had a drink at the bar and even watched a cartoon. And finally, not long before it was time to go back down to the bus, they went for a walk on deck. Standing on the bow, they looked ahead at the White Cliffs of Dover.

"We're home!" said Helena.

"Yes," said William.

"Do you know," said Helena, "that no matter where I travel I still like England best!"

"So do I," said William. And beneath the excited cries of the seagulls circling overhead, he took her in his arms again.

A metallic voice rang out from the loudspeaker above their heads. It was time for all passengers to rejoin their vehicles.

The immigration officer at Dover Eastern Docks eyed the old double-decker with interest. Don operated the sliding passenger door so that he could speak to William.

"Which company is this vehicle on hire to?"

"Orbit Tours," said William.

The official murmured something into a walkie-talkie, and then turned to William:

"Please can you ask all your passengers to get off the bus and walk through Passport Control, taking their hand baggage with them? They may leave heavy items of luggage in the bus."

He went back to the terminal building. William conveyed the message to the passengers, who came slowly down the stairs, off the vehicle and through the glass sliding doors, above which a large illuminated sign proclaimed, somewhat ironically, WELCOME TO DOVER.

The last passenger to remain on the coach was Jonathan Atkinson.

"You told me they never checked passports on the way back into the U.K!" he moaned at William.

"It does happen sometimes, especially when there are a lot of non-U.K. passport holders in the group."

"Well, do I have to get off? Can't I hide somewhere on the bus?"

"There's nowhere to hide. Besides, the Customs officials could still check it. You'd be in real trouble if they caught you."

Visibly anxious, Atkinson picked up his meagre luggage and made his way reluctantly towards Passport Control. All the same, he thought, he had nothing incriminating on him. All he was carrying was the bag of clothing and belongings he'd hurriedly packed in London a week ago, and the Duty-Frees he'd just bought on the ferry. Perhaps the courier was right: it could be just a routine check.

He joined the queue marked "E.C. Passport Holders Only" and waited his turn. Outside, Don and William moved the bus alongside the terminal building and got off to show their passports at the small window reserved for the use of coach crews. Helena and Maddy had gone through with the passengers.

Two uniformed police officers were waiting just after Passport Control.

"Mr Jonathan Atkinson?"

Atkinson turned around but could see no way out. In the distance he could only see the face of William, who was showing his passport to the official in the little cubicle at the side.

"Ill - I'll f...ing get you for this, Little Willy! You see if I d-don't!" he stammered.

But all the other passengers were now through Customs and waiting for the bus. No-one heard him as he was marched off to the waiting police car.

The journey to London proceeded uneventfully. Nobody commented on the disappearance of Atkinson. It was after all quite usual for some passengers to leave at Dover.

Darkness was falling as the AEC Regent V at last pulled into the West London Coach Station. A number of black cabs followed the bus and took up position by the terminal building, like vultures swooping on the corpse of a recently-deceased animal. Tour F443/07 was finally dead.

One by one William said goodbye to the passengers. Mr Maxwell gave him a £10 note and said he hoped that he and Helena would be very happy together. From Mr and Mrs Charlton he got £20 plus an assortment of kisses and hugs from Rebecca and Josephine. Mr Murray was enthusiastic in his praise:

"You're the best damn Tour Director I've ever travelled with!" he said, pressing a $100 bill into William's hand.

William received equal treatment from the Tjeongs.

"Thank you for everything," Mr Tjeong said, "and especially for arranging the English bus. My kids will never forget this journey as long as they live!"

William received kisses on the cheek from Miss Crosbie, Maria and Lucia, all of whom left by taxi for the same West End hotel. The next day, Maria and Lucia were due to start their Lakes and Mountains tour, while Miss Crosbie would make her own way home by train to Norfolk.

Apart from the gratuities, William also collected addresses. He now had invitations to stay in Australia, Indonesia, Texas, Paraguay, Costa Rica, Bristol and Norfolk. They would all be receiving cards from him at Christmas time.

Ian Bailey-Filmer, Steve Vicks and Nick Patterson left with the minimum of fuss, but the Bartlett-Nicholsons spent a good fifteen minutes loading all their wine into the waiting taxi. William got no tips from any of them.

When the last of them had left, Helena came up to William.

"Well, I'd better be getting home. Will I see you in the office tomorrow?"

"Yes, tomorrow!" William gave her a quick kiss on the mouth. She turned to go.

"Helena!" he cried.

"Yes, William!"

"I've got something for you. It's because you lost your halfpenny. Open it when you get home!"

He slipped a small brown paper envelope into her hand and kissed her again, on the cheek. She crossed the road to a bus-stop. The attraction between Helena and buses must be mutual, William decided. No sooner had she got to the stop when a bus magically appeared.

Once again, William found himself watching Helena disappear from view as she waved goodbye to him from a red London bus.

On the bus, Helena examined the envelope. It contained something small and heavy. She decided she would open it now. Excitedly she tore off the end of the envelope and emptied the contents into the palm of her hand. It was a gold sovereign.

"Where are you going now?" William asked Don and Maddy.

"Back home to Edenhurst," said Don.

"Would you be able to drop me off in North Malling, please?" asked William.

"Well," said Don, "I can't take you into the village because the old girl won't get under that low bridge by the station. But I could drop you off at the top of the road, by Station Approach. Would that do?"

"That would be fine," said William.

As Don drove back over Lambeth Bridge and out towards Kent, William sat with Maddy on one of the double seats just behind the driver's cab. They were all clear of the passengers' luggage now.

"William?" asked Maddy.

"Yes".

"Could I have a word with you?"

"Of course. What is it?"

"It's just that I've been talking a lot to Helena on the bus today. Talking about you. Do you know, all these years I've known her, and I've never heard her talk like this about any bloke before."

"Oh." William was worried. Of course he had noticed Helena sitting chatting to Maddy on their way up the autoroute. Had she confided to her friend something that she couldn't bear to tell him face to face? Had she decided that, after all, their relationship was a non-starter? Was she going to retreat to the safe haven of her Bloomsbury flat in its mid-Seventies time-warp?

"William, you two have really got a good thing going. You've got to promise me that you'll marry her!"

"Marry her? There's nothing in the world I want more! If she'll have me, of course I will!"

Maddy kissed him and said "You've only got to ask her. I know how she feels about you."

"You're sure I'm not being a bit premature?"

"I know Helena. Trust me. It'll be marriage or nothing. Don and I were just the same. Did Helena tell you how we got together?"

"No."

"We met on our third day at University. Don proposed to me three weeks later and drove me up to Gretna Green in a grotty old GPO van he used to have. And I've never regretted one moment of it!"

Ron and Maddy dropped William off, and he walked the last few hundred yards home. His luggage was slightly lighter than it had been at the start of the tour, but nonetheless he stopped to rest a few times on the way.

He could see that no lights were on in his parents' section of the house. They would be in bed by now. As he opened his own front door he felt something brush against his trouser leg. Pepper wasn't often out at night these days. He picked her up and carried her to his bedroom, depositing her lovingly on his bed.

William brought his luggage into the hallway, locked the door and prepared for bed. His head was swimming with the events of the last eight days. He knew that his life was never going to be the same again after Tour F443/07. Tomorrow everything would change. But right now all he needed was a good night's sleep.

Chapter 15

Finale

WILLIAM woke from an unusually dreamless night to find Pepper purring loudly at the foot of his bed. He rose and got ready for the office. After breakfast he opened the connecting door to let the cat into his parents' section of the house. His mother was there in the hall.

"How did the tour go, dear?"

"Very well, thanks."

"No problems of any kind?"

"Nothing serious."

"Well, it's funny, but since you phoned me I've heard the phone ring twice in your flat and I've gone in and answered it, and both times it was people wanting to speak to Orbit. The first caller sounded Italian. Rotty, or something like that, his name was. The other was a Mr Turner."

"And what did you tell them?"

"I gave them the number of Orbit's Head Office."

"Thanks. That was the best thing to do."

As usual, William spent the train journey dealing with his paperwork for the tour. By the time he arrived at Victoria it was all ready.

He got into the office around eleven-thirty. Helena was at her desk, evidently absorbed in her work. She looked up and smiled as he entered. She came over to him and whispered:

"Thank you ever so much for my wonderful present! It must have cost a fortune!"

"Only gold is good enough for my Golden Girl!" he whispered back. "Can we talk?"

"You'd better finish your stuff with Margot first. Then we can go out to lunch."

"Great!"

William sat in the chair opposite Margot's desk. She was not there at the moment. He neatly arranged all his forms into little piles and got his large duplicated expenses sheet ready.

"William," Margot appeared, holding a coffee. "Mr Papadopoulos wants to see you."

He walked towards Helena's desk. The door to Mr P's office was open, and Helena was now standing in the doorway. As he approached the door, he heard Mr Papadopoulos call out:

"William, would you mind coming in here, please. And Helena, you stay here too, please."

Helena sat in the swivel chair where she normally took dictation. William sank into the plush leather chair opposite Mr P's desk, which was normally reserved for visiting hoteliers and agents.

"William, I think I have to ask you for an explanation."

"I'm sorry, Mr Papadopoulos?" There had to be more to come.

"I offer you ten free places on a tour, for your friends, and I don't like what happens."

"What has happened, Mr Papadopoulos?" William heard himself saying.

"I don't know why you invited all these persons on my tour, but I think you should look at the reputation of the company. Your friend Mr Atkinson, he is big crook. The police arrest him at Dover. I ask Helena to make sure you don't help him escape."

"I didn't help him to escape," said William. "And, the police arrested him very discreetly. I don't believe any of the other passengers noticed."

"That is something," said Mr Papadopoulos, "but that is not all. We have a call from a Mr Rottoli. He says he was wrongly detained by the Customs people and you just abandoned him. He says he was lucky to escape and he walked miles to a station for a train home."

Helena looked as if she were trying to suppress a grin.

"And," continued Mr Papadopoulos, "then there is Mr Turner. He claims you offer him ride on a special train. But you do not pick him up from station. He is arrested for being a terrorist. Eventually the British Embassy rescue him and fly him home!"

So that was what happened to Turner, thought William.

"And this is not all. This morning one of our tele-sales staff receives an extremely abusive call from a Mrs Bartlett-Nicholson. She says our holidays are rubbish and says we must stop our computer sending her brochures. But when we check her details, we find she is not on our mailing list! She is one of your friends on 'Scenic Delights of France'. So please, William, tell me what is problem with your friends? What are you trying to do?"

"I think I'd better tell you," said William.

And, just as he had done to Helena on the bench behind the Paris supermarket, William went over the whole story. He also made a brief mention of the events on Saturday night in the 'Grenouille Bondissante', although he explained that the mishaps suffered by John Bridger and Nick Patterson had not been intended by him.

For a moment Mr Papadopoulos looked as if he were about to explode. His huge body was heaving to and fro. Then he erupted in the most enormous peal of laughter William had ever heard.

"William, this is fantastic! Holidays for your enemies! I can see us doing more of these. I like your ideas about the wine and coffee. I think we have a possibility for a new gastronomic holiday!"

"But who would want to buy holidays which they aren't going to like?" asked Helena.

"Parents send their children on them. Children send their parents. But also people go on them because they like complaining and they like being uncomfortable!"

"You're right," said William. Some people are only happy when they are complaining."

"We could send groups to the annexe of the Hotel Beau-Séjour," said Mr Papadopoulos.

"We could send them in an old bus with no reclining seats or air-conditioning," suggested William. Helena winked at him. He wasn't sure if the news of his 'replacement coach' had filtered through yet to Mr P.

"What about those old army camps on Salisbury Plain? We could rent one for the summer and put people there. Take them for military excercises, feed them awful food…"

"For that matter," said William, "perhaps we could use my old school during the summer holidays. Put everyone in dormitories, make them go to Latin Lessons, and put them in detention if they do anything wrong!"

"This is great," said Mr P.

"I think we should send people to some of the great British resorts in November when it's cold and everything is shut," added Helena. "Or, instead of 'Scenic Delights of France', we could have 'Scenic Horrors of France', with all the hotels near slag heaps or on grotty industrial estates!"

"That sounds like the Hotel Royale chain to me!" said William.

The managing director of the Hotel Royale chain happened to be a very good friend of Mr Papadopoulos, but William's little joke didn't bother him at the moment.

"William, I think you have been out on the road long enough. And things are changing in the industry. There is the Channel Tunnel, and, what do they call it, the super-information-highway. And then there's the ECU coming, the new single currency, and all those communist countries coming back into Europe. I need new people to bring Orbit into the twenty-first century. How would you like to come and work for me? As my new Product Developer?"

"Well... yes, please!" said William.

"Of course, I expect you'll want to carry on living in Kent, so I'll let you have flexible working hours. And I think it will be a good idea to send you out on the tours sometimes. And I think you're going to need someone to work with you." He turned towards Helena.

"Helena, you'd be happy to work with William, wouldn't you?" he asked.

"Yes, of course."

"Have we still got any of that sherry Mr García from the Hotel San Pedro brought us?"

"Yes, it's in the cupboard here." Helena indicated the cupboard.

"Get out the bottle and three glasses. I don't generally approve of drinking in the office, but this is a special occasion."

She got out the bottle and handed it to Mr Papadopoulos. He poured three generous glasses.

"Cheers!" he said. "And welcome to the firm!"

They drank a toast and put down the glasses. This opportunity should not be wasted, thought William. He got down on his knees before Helena.

"William, you feeling alright, my boy?" asked his boss.

"Helena," pleaded William, looking up at her, "will you marry me?"

Helena removed her glasses and lowered her head towards his.

"Oh, William! Yes! Yes! Yes! Of course I will!"

And, as William got to his feet they embraced beneath the poster of the Chapel Bridge. Mr Papadopoulos was fortunately spared from feeling embarrassed by Margot, who rushed in to say that an important supplier from Hungary was on the phone.

****

It was a glorious Saturday in late September, and the bells were swinging to and fro in the flint fifteenth-century tower of All Saints Church in Upper Nazeing. There really was an Indian Summer that year, and the Essex village was looking delightful.

Even the brash new filling station in the village centre looked picturesque, as an elderly Morris Minor pulled into the forecourt, and its even more elderly driver wound down her window to have a word with the attendant:

"Excuse me, I'm terribly sorry, but please could you tell me the way to All Saints Church? My poor dear father always said I was not to be trusted anywhere…"

Other wedding guests had arrived in Don and Maddy's bus, suitably decorated for the occasion. Mr Papadopoulos was there from Orbit, and Mr Maxwell, who had stayed on in Britain a little longer especially to attend the wedding, was recording the proceedings with his video-camera.

Since Helena had accepted his proposal, William had continued to escort 'Scenic Delights of France' every other week. Mr Papadopoulos wanted him to start in his new post in October, and in the meantime he did not want to lose a good tour manager.

William and Helena had seen a lot of each other since then, of course. William had spent much of his free time in London, and Helena hers in Kent. William had been to stay with her family in Essex, and she had stayed at the spare room in William's parents' house. They had not shared a bed together since Paris.

"Do you know," Helena had said to William as they had discussed their plans, "I think we were meant not to sleep together until we married."

William's only response had been to hold her tighter than ever before and to kiss her delicious lips. After all, he thought, when you have waited a lifetime for an experience, what difference is a few weeks going to make?

They had enjoyed picking the music for the wedding service. William had insisted on having *At the Name of Jesus*, which he said was his favourite hymn.

"And why exactly is it your favourite hymn?" Helena had asked.

"It was the last hymn in the last Chapel service on my last day at Chestfield!" William had replied.

"Well, I like it too. It's a nice bouncy sort of hymn to finish the service with."

"And what hymn would you like, Helena?" the Reverend Wilson had asked her. He was a cheerful-looking man in his late thirties.

Helena had looked embarrassed.

"Does it have to be a hymn? Could I choose a pop song?"

"Well, it all depends on which one. You'd be very surprised what we get asked for these days. *Everything I do, I do for you* has been very popular lately, and the other week a couple had Rod Stewart's *Sailing*. Mind you, I think I'd draw the line at Meatloaf's *Bat out of Hell*, or, come to think of it, Cliff Richard's *Bachelor Boy*! Who is it that you have in mind?"

"The Bay City Rollers."

"I hope it's not *Bye Bye Baby* or *Money Honey*!" The Reverend Wilson was proving to be something of a connoisseur.

"No. *Give a Little Love*."

"I've no objections to that."

"No? Really, you'd let me have that for our wedding?"

"I don't see why not. God is Love, is He not? I think it would be quite appropriate to have my congregation singing that they've got to give a little love, take a little love and be prepared to forsake a little love!"

"Oh, thank you!"

It had been all William could do to prevent Helena from throwing her arms around the vicar and kissing him.

And now the ceremony was under way. Helena was facing William, and had his right hand in hers, as she took him to be her husband.

"…To love, cherish and obey…"

William hadn't been quite so sure about the obey part, but Helena had insisted on it.

After the service, they assembled outside the porch for the obligatory photographs. Helena looked stunning in her virginal white. After some hesitation, she had asked Margot to be her bridesmaid, and Rebecca and Josephine Charlton had been delighted to come along from Bristol to be Maids of Honour.

After the photographs, there had been uproarious scenes when Helena tossed her bouquet into the crowd and it was caught by Margot.

The reception was held in a nearby hotel, with Don and Maddy again providing the transport. William gave his speech; his parents and Helena's made their contributions, as did the best man. It must be said that the best man's speech was one of the shortest on record, Claude Chasseur's English vocabulary being, after all, somewhat limited. And he had a job to do that evening.

At last it was possible for William and Helena to detach themselves from the guests, the drinks and the cake, and to run, showered with confetti, to the waiting limousine which took them and their best man away to Helena's parents' house, where they all changed into something a little more comfortable.

There was a short unscheduled stop on the way, when the bride asked the driver to stop the car outside a small corner shop. Begging some money from Claude, she had gone running into the shop in her bridal gown, to reappear a few moments later with an enormous bar of milk chocolate.

"I was feeling a bit peckish!" she explained to William.

Mr Papadopoulos had offered to arrange a honeymoon anywhere in Europe for them. William had asked Helena to choose the destination.

"Lyons! It's got to be Lyons!" she had said. And Mr Papadopoulos had arranged complimentary accommodation at the Hotel Royale Lyon-Est. Declining offers of air or rail tickets, William and Helena had chosen to hitch a ride there on Orbit's overnight coach to the Costa Brava.

The limousine dropped them off at the West London coach station, where a figure was waiting for them.

"Danny!" shouted William.

"So you've tied the knot and made it all legal?"

"That's right!"

"Well, I'll be taking you down to Lyons. Can't think why you want to go there. Hope you haven't been letting my driver get at the booze!"

"He'll be alright!" said Helena. At that moment, Claude was already unlocking his Mercedes 0303 for the waiting Orbit passengers.

"Do you know," said Danny, "I don't think I've ever really said thank you to you two for what happened in Paris. I do believe Mr P. was going to sack me. But when I got back, I just made a clean breast of it and offered to pay Orbit back the money."

William and Helena smiled at each other.

Danny managed to keep the rear row of seats on the coach free for them, as they travelled south in the night through France. The newly-weds received some curious glances from other passengers, as Danny had explained about their situation to everyone on the coach.

Early on the Sunday morning, Claude left the motorway at Lyons and dropped William and Helena at the Hotel Royale.

"Bonne Chance!" shouted Claude.

"Best of luck, you two!" Danny added. "You're both completely bonkers. You should get on well together!"

William and Helena checked into the hotel, deposited their luggage in the double-bedded room and had breakfast. They then went for a stroll to see what the city had to offer. They took the Metro to the city centre and attended morning Mass in the Cathedral of St Jean. Next, William took Helena to the big stamp market on the Place Bellecour. Here was somewhere he had always wanted to visit. They strolled among the stalls until Helena found a packet of stamps all showing buses.

"I say, these are super! I wonder how many different ones with buses there are. It'll be exciting to build up a collection of these."

William couldn't resist kissing Helena full on the lips right in the middle of the Place Bellecour. But then, Lyons seemed to be a city for lovers. Out in the streets, on the buses or on the Metro, everywhere they went there were couples necking in the light of day.

"It used to depress me when I saw couples snogging like that in public," Helena said to William.

"Same here. I thought one day I'd like to go out with a machine-gun and shoot the lot of them!"

"And look at us now!"

They strolled together along the tree-lined banks of the Rhône and enjoyed a delicious meal in an excellent restaurant just off the Place des Terreaux. In the afternoon they travelled on the funicular up to Fourvière, where they saw the Roman Theatres and the famous Basilica. William was reminded here of the Church of the Sacré Coeur in Paris.

Afternoon was turning to evening as they took the rack-railway up to the Croix-Rousse hill. They left the station and crossed the road to the bus-stop. There, William took Helena in his arms and kissed her once more.

"It's coming!" shouted Helena excitedly.

Almost noiselessly, the trolleybus scurried around the corner and came to a halt at the stop, its white-painted trolley poles reminding William of the ears of a terrified rabbit. The bus bore a dignified red and white livery enhanced by artistic scrolls and flourishes. The names of the places on its route were shown in elaborate lettering below the windows.

The folding doors opened with a 'whoosh' and they got on. William cancelled their tickets in the stamping machine, and they headed for the bench